PENGUIN BOOKS

BRIEF LIVES

Anita Brookner was born in London in 1928 and, apart from three postgraduate years in Paris, has lived there all her life. She trained as an art historian and taught at the Courtauld Institute of Art until 1988, when she abandoned her title of Reader in the History of Art at the University of London for the anonymity of a small flat in Chelsea and the cultivation of certain fictional characters who may one day appear in future novels.

ANITA BROOKNER

BRIEF LIVES

PENGUIN BOOKS

PENGUIN BOOKS

Published by the Penguin Group
Penguin Books Ltd, 27 Wrights Lane, London w8 5tz, England
Viking Penguin, a division of Penguin Books USA Inc.
375 Hudson Street, New York, New York 10014, USA
Penguin Books Australia Ltd, Ringwood, Victoria, Australia
Penguin Books Canada Ltd, 2801 John Street, Markham, Ontario, Canada l3r 1b4
Penguin Books (NZ) Ltd, 182–190 Wairau Road, Auckland 10, New Zealand

Penguin Books Ltd, Registered Offices: Harmondsworth, Middlesex, England

First published by Jonathan Cape 1990
Published in Penguin Books 1991
1 3 5 7 9 10 8 6 4 2

Printed in England by Clays Ltd, St Ives plc

I

Julia died. I read it in *The Times* this morning. There was quite a substantial obituary, but what immediately fixed my attention was the photograph, one of those studio portraits of the late 1930s or early 1940s, all huge semi-transparent eyes, flat hair, and dark lipstick. I never liked her, nor did she like me; strange, then, how we managed to keep up a sort of friendship for so long. Had our husbands not been partners I doubt whether we should ever have exchanged more than a few words, or seen each other on more than a few formal occasions, although we were, for quite some time, in the same line of work. As things turned out we were in fairly close contact and even spent a couple of holidays together, after the war. I can see us now, strolling along Riviera esplanades in white pleated skirts, our husbands chatting behind us. It must be years since I was last in Nice; it holds no pleasant memories for me. Julia was older than me by nearly eleven years, although she never looked it, and had become very arthritic while still in her fifties. Arthritis is a disorder I associate with her particular aquiline beauty, as if there is too little flesh to protect the bones. After Charlie died nobody saw much of her: she stayed at home, in that spacious but chilly flat of hers in Onslow Square, where I visited her sometimes, perhaps not as often as I should have done. She was never pleased to see me: why should she be? In the end I tried to stay away, unsuccessfully, as I did most things. I telephoned her from time to time, out of a dragging sense of duty, and also out of something more complicated, more timorous than pity – grief, perhaps. I realize now that I had not seen her for at least five years. That was why the photograph gave me such a shock.

She had been quite famous in her youth, when presumably the photograph was taken. She had won a reputation as a *diseuse* and appeared regularly in intimate revues until these things went out of style. People were amused that so obvious an aristocrat should condescend to entertain the public in this manner. That element of condescension in her performances commanded respect, but not in every quarter: when she tried to entertain women in factories in the war years her manner was found to be too snobbish for popular taste. She looked anachronistic in her long dresses, with the chiffon handkerchief tied to the little finger of her left hand: this was an affectation of hers, but it did not go down well when the fashion was for sausage curls shoved under a turban and overalls that tied round the waist. Although she had had a number of lovers, some of them prestigious, others quite shady, Julia never achieved the sort of informality that would have put her on a par with other women and invited the confidences that amused her so much when they came her way. Latterly she was tended by a devoted and rather sickly-looking woman called Maureen who had originally come to interview her for the local paper. Julia never said no to an interview: interviews were her natural mode of communication. There was plenty of room in the flat: no problem there. And Maureen was undoubtedly useful with the shopping and general maintenance of the household. Otherwise, I think I should have called more often. As it was I saw quite a lot of her. In the end Julia gave up doing anything for herself and treated Maureen as a slave. She treated most people like that.

She was not a very nice woman, but then neither am I. We were able to get along because we had a few things in common, principally our husbands, while they were alive, and our experience in the profession, although I always deferred to her on that score. She expected a certain amount of deference. And then we were both good at summing people up: we warmed into life when discussing acquaintances, and she was an excellent mimic. Basically, I found her alarming and she found me boring, yet in our heyday, when we were both married and healthy, it was natural for us to telephone each other two or three times a week. Such conversations as we had were almost entirely inconsequential and in time became more rare. Neither wanted to hear about the other's aches and pains, and widowhood does not exactly increase the number of things one has to talk about. Julia was a stickler for amusement, although she had absolutely no sense of humour: she wanted to be amused all the time. Her category of amusing topics was mainly marital or sexual, who was having an affair with whom, who was divorcing, and why – that sort of thing. She could usually say something scurrilous about all the parties involved, this being her idea of amusement. I found such talk distasteful, which was why she found me boring. Most people to her were an audience, and out of a sense of *noblesse oblige* she would deign to entertain them, but then they were under an equal obligation to entertain her. She would say, 'Let's have a discussion,' when what she meant was, 'Let's have an argument,' for she was restless most of the time. And she liked danger, which was why I found her alarming. Although I had known her for so long I was a little afraid of her, never at ease in her company. And in the end there was every reason why I should feel this way.

Julia was very beautiful, but she was devoid of softness. Her beauty was of a dry immaculate kind, the kind that never deteriorates. She was strikingly tall and slim, and always remained so. Her feet were so narrow that she had always had to have her shoes made. Over the pale blue eyes the eyelids were heavy, and capable of conveying multiple innuendoes, of an unvaryingly derogatory nature. Those eyelids featured prominently in her performances and were the focus of every caricature. I believe – I have reason to believe – that she was far from sensual by nature, yet she had a number of hard sexy mannerisms: the eyelids, of course, and the bad language that fell constantly from her chiselled lips. I always felt that somewhere in the remote fastness of her being, a long way behind the eyelids, and the ringed hand clutching a glass of whisky, she was a girl, but a girl of a rather lost variety, dreaming, unawakened, incurious, almost pure. Two clues to this: her animation in the presence of her mother (both of them drinking whisky, yet laughing together like schoolgirls) coupled with her devotion to her brother, who had let himself down in various ways, 'poor darling', and who was working as a car salesman; and her habit of placing her underclothes on a chair in her bedroom and covering them with a square of silk reserved for this purpose. Where had such an archaic habit come from? It was common to my mother's generation, but it has rarely survived to the present day, when women treat their bathrooms as their dressing-rooms, and in any event do not leave their clothes lying around.

But then Julia was a strikingly old-fashioned woman. Even at the height of her fame, in the late 40s and early 50s, she appeared to me mature, worldly wise, even perverse, although by today's standards she was still quite young. She dressed like a middle-aged woman, in beautiful severe clothes by Lelong and Patou. She made her comeback, most successfully, in a white dress and turban by Mme Grès. Such elegance inspired respect in those shabby days before the country was on its feet again: one only saw well-dressed women on the stage, which was why so many people went to the theatre. Yet she appeared out of date even to the faithful, the lonely men out of the war, the young hairdressers. That was part of her attraction: she incarnated a style which had vanished. In fact Julia was always out of date. She blamed everyone but herself, yet the only time I ever felt pain on her behalf was when I saw those beautiful eyelids lowered and knew – in a flash – that what she felt was not disdain, as she thought, but incomprehension. The next moment she would be sweeping one into her bedroom, flinging open her many wardrobes and demanding to be told what to wear. She had already made up her mind on this point, and she was never wrong, but she liked to deplore one's own lack of taste in hazarding what she perceived to be a laughable suggestion. This exchange, which was frequently repeated, was one of a

4

number of rituals by which she reinforced her ascendancy. She was famous for it, as she was famous for most things. 'Oh, Julia,' her friends would laugh. 'Why not go mad for once and make a mistake?' But she never did. She never ever did.

She was Margaret Julia Wilberforce, and she always referred to herself as Wilberforce, although to her mother she was Meg. On stage, of course, she was simply Julia. Yet it meant almost as much to her to be a Wilberforce as to be Julia, and I was given to understand that to be a Wilberforce was to have access to a certain magnificence. This was never made explicit. The only reason she regretted not having children was that there was no one to carry on the name, for the unfortunate brother was unlikely to marry, being given to all the excesses except those pertaining to love and responsibility. The magnificence of the Wilberforces, now reduced to that of Julia herself, resided in those great-grandfathers, grandfathers, and uncles in the army, together with the cherished memory of her father, also in the army, whose photograph, in a silver frame, had pride of place both in the drawing-room and on the table by Julia's bed. This honour was awarded to neither of her two husbands, Simon Hodges, always referred to as Hodge, and Charlie Morton. When Julia's father was mentioned, both she and her mother would have tears in their eyes, after which, shakily, they would pour themselves more whisky. Hodge, whom I never met, had also been in the army but had otherwise proved unsatisfactory, and had been fairly summarily divorced. 'We were too young,' Julia would say, with a rueful self-indulgent smile: somehow one gathered that the interlude – for it had been an interlude rather than a true marriage – had meant very little to her.

Charlie was different. 'Charlie is my prop and mainstay,' Julia would say, and it was neither less nor more than the truth. Soft-voiced, soft-footed, bulky, vague, and charming, Charlie was the ideal husband for a woman like Julia, though, not being a Wilberforce, he remained somewhat marginal when in the presence of Julia and her mother. I suspected him of maintaining the mother, in her service flat somewhere off Sloane Avenue: he certainly kept the entire household supplied in Onslow Square, for if ever Julia went to a shop, which was rarely, it was to produce a hopelessly shattered clock to be mended ('But you must! It was Granny's! Promise me that you'll try') or, very occasionally, to visit the hairdresser if her regular man, who came to her at home, was on holiday. She insisted that her wants were immaterial, so it was Charlie who telephoned Harrods or Selfridges with a quite substantial order, or, his jacket off, cooked Julia an omelette in the evening. She lived on omelettes and whisky, maintaining that she liked neither, and appeared none the worse for it.

I was indignant that she should make Charlie wait on her, but he accepted it as a natural obligation. I think he was always conscious of having married a great beauty, of having taken her out of the running, as it were, and therefore had in a sense to enter her service. She treated him as her suitor, was all reminiscence of how he had waited for her at the stage door, had sent flowers night after night, and had finally written a letter, to be delivered to her dressing-room, saying, 'You are the woman of my life. There will be no other.' This was recalled several times in my hearing. I thought it overdone, beneath the dignity of a man like Charlie, who was, after all, a reasonably eminent and certainly fashionable solicitor, with offices in Hanover Square, where my own husband, Owen Langdon, was a junior partner. Yet he would acquiesce uncomplainingly in Julia's little performances, as if he were conscious of being somehow not quite up to the mark, would sometimes pad round unobtrusively with a duster, although a Mrs Wheeler was supposed to clean thoroughly every morning. He was a nice-looking man, tall, broad, perhaps a little plump, with warm brown eyes and a cheerful expression, always ready to break into a smile. Occasionally his face would take on a faraway look, as if he might welcome a change of subject, but he was too good-hearted ever to feel irritation, and it was more natural, even pleasant, for him to smile and to concur than to strike out on his own. It occurred to me to wonder whether he were lonely, or whether he felt the burden of not being a Wilberforce. I never believed that Julia had much of an inner life. She was quite extraordinarily self-sufficient and therefore had a natural authority. She depended on no one, not even Charlie, for all that he was her prop and mainstay. Her brain, I sometimes thought, was perhaps sharper than his, and he was a very intelligent man, certainly more subtle than his wife. They were a handsome couple. He always stood a little behind her, throwing her into relief. It was only fitting that his greying hair should show off her own dark auburn bob. Artfully wrought, and a subject of intense discussion with Bobby, her hairdresser, her short sleek dark pageboy (also old-fashioned, now that I come to think of it) remained a fixed feature of her appearance until the end of her life.

Charlie was a darling. When he died Julia remained in control, was undoubtedly desolate, yet never shed the sort of tears that the memory of her father summoned up. She remained dry-eyed, but she must have suffered, or at least registered the heaviness of the blow, for she rarely went out after that. She hardly needed to, for Maureen had moved in by then, but it struck me as odd. Julia was not infirm, although she was very stiff, and she was only in her sixties. It was simply that she felt more in control in Onslow Square than she would have done in the street, where she would have been just another widow.

We rallied round. I was called on to do quite a bit for her in those days, although what I did never quite met with her approval. 'Never mind,' she would say. 'My standards are probably too high.' Maureen, and Julia's former dresser, Pearl Chesney, would laugh sympathetically, for they were nearly always in attendance, together, incredibly, with her mother, now aged eighty-four. It looked as if Julia would also be long-lived: she was protected from the manifold stresses of this life by her reclusiveness and her own steely resolve. I can see her now, sitting in her acid yellow and white drawing-room in Onslow Square, whisky in hand. Through all her various ages she appeared to me unchanged, slender, fine, sardonic, hieratic, heartless. 'I hear Nigel's run off again,' she would say. 'Well, you can hardly blame him. That wife of his . . . Did you ever meet such a boring woman?' She was never on the side of the woman in such a situation. I felt there was something almost

7

masculine in her solidarity with men who behaved badly. One had to be very tough to qualify with Julia, or even to gain her attention. That was why she had so little time for me, although fate had bound us together in a way that my nature could hardly tolerate or withstand.

I would come into that drawing-room, with flowers, or some little trifle – one always brought an offering – which she would take from me with a gesture of palpitating gratitude, and then pause to consider. 'Oh,' she would say, on a note of dwindling enthusiasm, pretending to examine it or them more closely. 'Oh. How charming.' She would mark a pause, and then the eyelids would fall to half-mast, at which anyone in attendance – her manicurist, Maureen, Pearl Chesney, Mrs Wilberforce – would burst into delighted laughter. 'Quite charming,' she would go on, losing interest. 'Put them there, would you? I'll see to them later.' Any flowers I brought her, and I brought her many, always ended up on a side table, sometimes to be put, much later, into a vase, sometimes to stay there until they ended up in the wastepaper basket.

It was all a long time ago. She was nearly eighty when she died, and I am getting on for seventy. She never came to terms with age: in a sense she never had to, for she never lost her power. For myself things have been different. I was always hapless, timid. Yet age has dealt with me kindly so far. I keep well, and although I have put on a little weight my figure is still quite trim. I make the most of my appearance, follow the fashions, abide by my mother's rule: brown in the autumn, navy in the spring. One or two people still remember me from the time when I sang on the wireless. I was Fay Dodworth, quite a favourite in those early days. I did the lighter sort of ballad, the serious spot on various comedy shows, before they all became too sophisticated. I had a pretty voice. Some said I was a pretty girl, although standards were lower then: one could be admired for such things as wavy hair or high cheekbones or a small waist or even a straight back. I was not sorry when it all came to an end; I never had the temperament for a performer. But I made a little comeback when I read the serial on 'Woman's Hour':

my voice was still musical, and my diction had always been good. That brought me quite a few letters from people who had listened to me in the early days. I felt quite bucked. Nothing of note has happened since then, but I keep busy, and cheerful. I have been complimented on my high standards. I do try to keep them up.

Of course, I know the truth of how I really look, at night, with my hair down. I watched, almost objectively, the emergence of the asexual body, the body that must be treated with care, until it finally takes over, at the end. As my figure lost its definition, became subject to greater gravity, I knew that love was gone for ever. But it is the same for everyone, I told myself; everyone is bound by the law of change. One evening, I remember, I looked in puzzlement at my long hair, from which nearly all the colour had gone, and felt the softness at my waist. I wept then, briefly. But I slept that night as usual, and in the morning I woke and thought how foolish I had been. I am always light-hearted in the mornings. The late afternoon is my bad time, when the light goes. I get nervous then, and long for someone to come. At those times I feel fatally like my mother, waiting in the dusk for me to wave to her as I approached the house. But after a while I get up and make a cup of coffee and switch on for the news. There is absolutely no point in giving way to melancholy. There is always another day, or so I like to think.

'Arcady' was my song. 'Arcady, Arcady is always young.' I sang it at the end of the programme, sometimes as an encore. Such a pretty song. And I sang 'Only Make-Believe', and 'You Are My Heart's Delight', and 'I'll Be Loving You Always'. Beautiful songs, all of them. Sometimes the words come back to me, even now, but I try not to think about the melodies, which, since I have grown older, strike me as unbearably sad, plaintive, modest, wistful, redolent of everyday disappointments, even tragedies. I try not to brood, although I suppose I have as much to brood over as anyone else. So much gone. So much lost. But then I rally again, somehow or other. I have been lucky, really: nothing drove me off balance, which

9

is so important if one at least tries to keep one's dignity. On the whole my life has been very easy, very pleasant. I was a pretty girl, I married well . . . It all seems a long time ago. But what most women want I once had. I try to remember that.

2

My father, Jimmy Dodworth, was a cinema manager, in the days when cinema managers stood in the foyer every evening in dinner jackets, dress shirts and bow ties. We lived in Camberwell, in one of those narrow Georgian houses now sought after by the sons and daughters of merchant bankers. We thought the house was just an ordinary house, rather dark, with too many stairs, and not much of a garden. My mother, who was highly strung and tired easily, disliked it: she dreamed of a modern flat, in a suburb like Ealing or Golders Green, with a fitted kitchen and central heating. I loved the house, which was the only one I had ever known. I played quite happily, as a child, on the landings or in my small bedroom, bounced a ball against the wall in the garden, which also contained a coal shed and an outhouse. There was an elderberry tree at the end, where the garden overlooked a narrow alley which ran out into the main road, and I would take my chair and sit underneath the tree, pretending I was in the country. I had no notion of what the country was like, for I rather think we never took a holiday: Father made a point of being on duty, as he called it, and Mother was a nervous traveller. Although restless and over-imaginative, it suited her to stay at home, to leave the house only when necessary, to do her shopping or to see a film. The cinema satisfied her cravings for a better life, revealing to her a world of possibilities, of luxury and extravagance, in which all one needed was a pair of dancing feet, a pretty face, or a singing voice which would captivate the man of one's dreams and secure one's heart's desire. My mother believed in these things, and I did too.

Our lives were shaped by the cinema, both in a physical and a moral sense. The appeal of the cinema in those days was its classlessness. The heroine was, more often than not, a plucky orphan, at most a modest dancer on a chorus line, or a shop-girl with blonde curls and a gift for repartee. The convention was that the hero should be of more elevated rank, that he should be astonished, beguiled, and finally swept off his feet by this spirited little nobody, who nevertheless was always impeccably turned out, spruce and provocative in her puffed sleeves and her silk stockings, as very few real working girls had the energy or the resources to be in those hard times. In virtually every Hollywood comedy there would be a villainous comic chorus of snobs, with cigarette holders and archaic hats – usually the hero's mother and a discarded fiancée or two – all of whom would be vanquished by the heroine's pertness and the hero's sincerity. There would, inevitably, be an offer of marriage, for they were very moral tales. A girl won through by charm, or personality, not by influence, while if the hero ever had any base idea of seduction he was soon reformed by the virtue demonstrated by the object of his fascination – it was never, ever, passion – until such time as the knot was tied, to the accompaniment of a full-blown song and dance extravaganza.

Those innocent films of the late 30s and early 40s influenced the outlook and the behaviour of a generation or two of young men and women. Girls with no experience whatever learned to be provocative, and boys, with even less experience, to be dashing. In reality they were fledglings, playing at desire, and finding the game delightful, arguably more delightful than the real thing, which they learned about much later, sometimes with bitterness, sometimes for life – for divorce was thought to be a disgrace, something not even to be contemplated – and without any sign of singing or dancing. Women with small children always appeared to me to be middle-aged when I was a child, while the cinema was the world of eternal youth. I learned, when I grew older, that eternal youth is too precious a delusion ever to be relinquished: it has to find a place somewhere, be enshrined in a myth, an ideal, even a fantasy. In those days before the war we lived a dream of innocence that the war years did not entirely shatter, even when we had seen sights which should never be seen by anyone, man or woman. It seems to me now, looking back, that one's chances of happiness pertained only to youth, that one avoided adulthood for as long as possible. Adulthood came abruptly with marriage, and middle age with children. People rarely seemed to be as happy as they had hoped to be, before they grew up.

I dare say it is all different now. The young people I meet, the daughters and sons of friends, seem incredibly experienced, although their faces are still tender. Studying these sons and daughters, all hard work and practical endeavour, all high standards and high achievement, and thinking back to my own young days I see myself, when I was their age, as totally unawakened, and not only unawakened but protected. I had no conception of worldliness other than what I saw on the screen or read about in Mother's library books. Worldliness was quite simply for other people. Except that in the cinema one could gain one's heart's desire (without losing one's head, of course) simply by possessing a pair of dancing feet or a pretty singing voice. Mother's ambition for me was born in those early days, and although I should have been happier sitting under the elderberry tree, dreaming, or bouncing a ball against the side of the house, I was made to learn the piano, to take dancing lessons, and, when, to my mother's disappointment, I revealed myself to be lacking in the sort of petulance and spirit then thought necessary in a dancer, to learn to sing, under the direction of Mme Mojeska, who was a real Polish lady, of some distinction, living on a small pension of mysterious origin and the fees of a few stolid little English girls, and probably the greatest stroke of luck I ever had in my young life. She taught me to sing, and not only to sing but to breathe and to hold myself properly: I

13

learned to walk tall and to strengthen my chest and diaphragm, which is probably why I kept my figure for so long.

In addition to being a cinema manager, my father was a Freemason and a poker player, which I thought enormously sophisticated of him. Throughout my childhood my father was a hero to me: did he not wear evening dress? I see now that he was an easy-going sort of man, indulgent, cheery, probably undistinguished. He had a sort of *bonhomie* that I have always appreciated in a man, an ability to put himself and others at ease, to impart a feeling of goodwill and whole-heartedness. Amiability: too few men possess the gift. I realize now that this amiability compensated for a certain weakness of character, and then I remind myself that even his weaknesses were amiable. No women in his life except my mother; only cards, and a certain amount of drink. Mother grew agitated when she saw him sitting in his shirt sleeves and braces, a glass of beer to hand, the dinner jacket discarded until the following evening. She always had more ambition than he had, more desire, I should now say, although it was a desire that was never satisfied. Father was too amiable to feel desire: what he wanted was an easy life, without challenges or impossible dreams, and with a certain provision of popularity and entertainment. Standing in the foyer, greeting patrons with a dignified and welcoming smile, he was a far more impressive figure than the man who later sat in his shirt sleeves and braces, wiping the froth of the beer from his brown moustache. Mother would hiss at him to put his jacket back on: he would simply pour himself another glass of beer. Sometimes Mother would leave the room in a huff; sometimes there would be tears as she saw the prospect of the modern flat in Finchley or Acton receding, saw herself condemned to pressing her husband's evening trousers at the ironing board in the dark scullery for the rest of her life. And no lift, no jazzy carpet, no landscaped forecourt to compensate her for her labours. She grew haggard even in my lifetime as a child. But always dutiful, always obedient, a good wife. This was all the more remarkable since they were not very well matched. My mother should have had a chance at a more glamorous existence, not the harassed timid routines she repeated in our house. She was a fine looking woman, with great dark eyes, but she lost her looks too soon, when she was still young, although I never thought of her as young. She was simply my mother, who needed my protection when she went to the cinema, in case anyone should grow bold enough to speak to her; she was the woman who scolded my father, whose side, of course, I took; the woman who walked me to my singing lessons and waited for me so that she could walk me home after them. Something in her was appeased by those lessons. She seemed softer, quieter, as we strolled back, through the modest streets, looking at the modest shops. 'Stop a minute, Fay,' she would say. 'I'll just get one of those brown loaves for Father. He does so enjoy fresh bread.' I loved her all the more at those times.

I wanted my parents to love each other, as I dare say all children do, but really I loved my father best. I wanted him to go out and enjoy himself, even when Mother raised objections. The Freemasons were just about all right, although she felt nothing but contempt for the mysteries men got up to among themselves. I think she felt that men had no business to exclude or ignore women. But the Freemasons did good work, supported hospitals and schools, which in part satisfied her sense of propriety. What she could not stand were the all-night card games, which was why they never took place in our house. My father had a number of cronies who were keen poker players, and on a Saturday night he would change his evening clothes for a pair of grey flannels, a clean shirt, and a pullover, kiss my mother goodnight and go to the pub, where, because one of his partners was the publican, and because the publican's wife was an easy-going sort of woman, he would join up with Harry and Joe and Paddy in a back room and stay there after hours, playing poker and drinking beer, until about three o'clock in the morning. On Sundays he rarely got up before noon. But he was a careful man, and I never saw him neglected or shabby, and he was always good-humoured. He loved my mother without ever understanding her, while I was the pride of his life. And whatever Mother had against his card-playing friends it was through the good offices of one of them, Harry, a small-time theatrical agent, that I got my first engagement. But this is to look into the future, and to the times that were beginning to be more grown-up, when what I like to remember is the golden days when we were a family, and, despite everything, loved each other so much.

I grew up thinking that the world could be won with a pair of dancing feet or a pretty singing voice, and that all one had to do was to keep one's white collars fresh and one's hair regularly shampooed. And so it proved for me. But that came later; later too came information of a more unwelcome kind. What I remember, and what influenced me for so long, was the ritual that was enacted on Sunday afternoons in that narrow house, which now, I suppose, belongs to someone far wealthier than my parents ever dreamed of being. On Sundays, in the dying afternoon, we were at peace. Mother would have changed into one of her nice dresses – she was always well-dressed – and Father would fold up his newspaper and lay it aside with a sigh of contentment. 'My girls,' he would say. 'My two beauties.' Mother would briefly smile, her irritations forgotten. When I went to Paris on my honeymoon I saw that Mother was one of nature's Frenchwomen, restless and active, with high social aspirations and a sense of style, both available and potential, and not much given to relaxation. But on Sunday afternoons we seemed to blend into one another, to form one dreaming unit, while the light faded outside and the fire shifted in the grate. I would sit on a stool at Father's feet: Mother would be knitting. Or we would be reading, the simple honest stories which Mother brought home from Boots Lending Library and which were for us a source of endless pleasure, an integral part of Sunday, with nothing harsh or disturbing to tell us, and always a happy ending. Few people nowadays would be content with such diversions, yet that interval before it got too dark to read seemed to me – still seems to me – magical. I could not recreate it now, no matter how hard I tried, and part of the desolation of my last days will stem from the knowledge that I have never managed to replace it with anything of equal weight. But I was never destined for a happy ending, although I was so very happy at the beginning. I still wonder how this came about, although I am now in full possession of the facts.

They wanted me to be happy, to be admired, to be a success. And I suppose they wanted me to be married, although they hoped that this would be in the far distant future. They never spoke of grandchildren: I was enough for them. And they were so good to me. There was no fuss when I moved out, into the little flat in Foubert's Place which I shared with a girl I met when I was working with the orchestra. We broadcast in the mornings at eleven o'clock: Millie was the mezzo and I was the lyric soprano, and we sang on alternate programmes. I've kept in touch with her, although we see each other only rarely; she lives in the country now, a widow like myself. She comes to town to do her Christmas shopping and we meet for lunch. She is much heavier now, but still sweet-natured, still smiling. She was a lovely girl, older and more experienced than I was, and very kind. The kindness of Millie prolonged my innocence for even longer than was natural, I suppose, although it seemed natural to me. She was out nearly every night, and I was happy to wake her the following morning with a cup of tea. Mother was pleased for me: she felt that her ambitions had been fulfilled when she had a daughter living in the West End, sharing a flat as bachelor girls were supposed to do, and being busy and bonny and hopeful. She never missed one of our programmes. And Father would forgo his Sunday morning rest to bring over some of the good china that Mother never used and some new pots and pans. Which was silly, when I come to think of it, because I always went home on Sunday afternoons and could have brought them back myself. But really he wanted to see how we were living and whether we were keeping the flat clean and tidy. Mother came too, but not on the same day. This was an enormous adventure for her; she hated to go out. She would bring a cake and I would make tea for her, and afterwards I would show her the shops in Regent Street and walk her to the bus stop. 'Wait a bit, Fay,' she would say. 'Is there a shop where I could buy something for Father? A little loaf, perhaps?'

My father collapsed in the foyer of his cinema one night in early December. An ambulance was called, although it was quite obvious that he was dead: it was unthinkable that he should be found on the premises. Mother had him brought home, and the following day I was sent for. I remember standing at the window, looking out at the black skeletal trees, and wondering how such sadness was to be borne. My grief was literally painful to me: I could hardly breathe. I have had other sorrows since then, and maybe the virtue of growing older is that one is more stoical; one accepts the burden of life, knowing that the alternative is simply death, non-existence, non-feeling. And it is inherent in the organism to want to endure for as long as possible, even for ever, so that one becomes willing to take on all the mishaps, all the tragedies, if they are the price to be paid. But I only learned this much later, and even now I have to learn the lesson every day. At that time, looking out of the window at the bare frightening leafless trees, I simply wondered if life could ever be the same again. And it never was; time had passed over it, and change was now the rule.

I laugh at people who tell me, now, that life will never be the same: perhaps I am too cheerful with the widows I meet. And, as I say, I have had other sorrows since then. But life never was the same after that. I was young; I recovered. Mother never did. Immediately after the funeral she lost the will to live. She had been intermittently furious with my father for as long as I could remember, but now that his chair was empty her agitation disappeared, and she sat for hours, unwilling to move, her eyes full of fear. Even with me she was fearful. Her only brave reaction was to send me back to the flat and to Millie, although I wanted to stay with her. 'You're no good to me here,' she said. 'I'll manage. There's not much to do. And I'm not going to let you ruin your life for me. I'll manage,' she repeated. 'He's with me all the time, Fay. I feel him near me. You go, dear. My place is here. Not yours.' I thought that magnificent of her, but I left only because

I felt myself to be excluded, knowing nothing then of the nature of married love. I left, and took a taxi back to Foubert's Place, where Millie was waiting for me with hot tea. She was such a good friend to me, and Mother had been so impressive, so dignified, that I felt very lucky and was soon myself again. So I think now. But then it was different, in the long dark days of that winter. There was a place in my heart that could never be filled, and I felt the pain of it for many years, years in which I enjoyed an apparently happy and successful existence, years in which, gradually, my heart died, until at last it was brought to life again.

3

Lavinia Langdon, the woman who was to become my mother-in-law, instructed me to address her as Vinnie at our first meeting, which took place in her flat in Swan Court, Chelsea Manor Street, on an unnaturally hot spring day in late April. I remember being dazzled by the many cut glass mirrors and decanters in her tiny over-furnished sitting-room, but not too dazzled to notice a fine bloom of dust. Vinnie herself had something of the same glitter and dustiness. She was a small, very thin woman with a blatantly made-up face; lustreless dark curls were confined under one of those little spotted veils which were so fashionable in the 50s, and lipstick seeped from her pursed mouth to the deep, bitterly indented lines at the corners. The eyes were fine, dark and haunted, set in a landscape of blue shadow and ornamented with quill-like lashes. She was wearing a pink tweed suit which looked as if it had been made for a child; even so it seemed too big for her, but the effect was deliberate, for it showed off her slim and astonishingly girlish legs, of which she was obviously proud, for she habitually crossed and uncrossed them, and made as if to pull down the skirt with a freckled hand loaded with rings.

It was four o'clock in the afternoon and she was drinking gin. She looked as if she had taken up residence in her dark blue button-backed chair for the evening, although I was to learn that she was rarely in, but, rather like my father, went out to play cards – in her case bridge – in one or other of the Swan Court flats, which seemed an ideal haven for widowers and divorcees of a gin-drinking and bridge-playing kind. Their games could, and did, go on uninterrupted by any domestic obligations, for there was a restaurant on the ground floor, and I believe one could even have food sent up, as if one were in an hotel. This suited Vinnie, who was incompetent on many levels. Her daily routine was to get up at about ten-thirty, smoke the first cigarette of the day, take a bath and dress, and then apply the heavy make-up, without which she looked like a seamed and battered twelve-year-old. She would eat lunch in the restaurant, take a short walk to buy gin and cigarettes, and then settle down in her sitting-room with a drink to await the daily visit of her son, whom she worshipped and indulged, as did every woman with whom he came into contact. After he had gone she would make a few telephone calls, heave herself from her chair, apply a new layer of powder, and take the lift to another flat for an evening of bridge.

This seemed to satisfy her perfectly. Her life, though restricted, had the merit of being self-contained, and apart from her painful love for her son she had no passions that could not be satisfied. If there were no food in the flat she did not eat. If she were extremely hungry, as I suppose she must have been from time to time, she simply turned up at the door of one of her bridge-playing friends – deeply enthusiastic elderly men, women as distracted as she was herself – and plaintively demanded a cup of coffee. When I got to know her better I realized that she could eat for two days at a time. She was an opportunistic feeder, putting away amazing quantities of whatever happened to be around and then lapsing vaguely into her gin and cigarette routine until another meal happened to come her way. After I married Owen I got into the habit of taking food round to her flat, but she regarded this as insulting and left it in the fridge to go bad. She preferred to drop into our house, poke around in the kitchen, and demolish two very large slices of apple tart if it happened to be on the table, swinging her tiny legs all the while and making up her face immediately afterwards. The adjusting of her curls under the spotted veil signified the end of the day's ingestion of nourishment and the beginning of the evening's entertainment.

At that first meeting she manifested a friendliness which facilitated conversation but did not entirely warm the atmosphere. She was not a disarming woman, although she was an accessible one; she gave the impression that she knew all about men, having discussed them at length with any number of women, but the tight mouth and the lonely eyes told another story. I later learned that she came from a family of runaway husbands: her own father had defaulted, before her husband, Henry Langdon, got himself mixed up with another woman, was forced to abandon his legal practice, and moved to southern Spain, where he still lived with his mistress, being neither sadder nor wiser for the experience. Mr Langdon was only mentioned swingeingly and with disgust, although Vinnie lived quite comfortably on the alimony he paid her, and had insisted that he abandon all claims to the marital home in Gertrude Street, where Owen now lived, Vinnie having thankfully decamped to Swan Court and the eternal bridge game that was to be her only occupation. All this I learned much later. What impressed me straight away was the hunger with which she looked at her son, so much so that she paid me little attention, thinking, perhaps rightly, that I was one of many and would soon be discarded. Since she was clever enough to realize that Owen might be irritated and embarrassed by the intensity of her love she disguised it with a number of flirtatious routines. When she left the room she would pause in the doorway, kick one leg back behind her, and, with a radiant smile, say, 'Don't let them start without me. I'm just going to change.' Five minutes later the lavatory would flush and she would be back, rubbing cream into her hands and twisting her rings back the right way.

I was intimidated by her at that first meeting, for I did not see how she could be anyone's mother. She was unlike any mother I had known, my own mother being shy and self-effacing, and Mrs Savage, Millie's mother, who came down from Manchester from time to time, being a charming highly coloured woman, with her daughter's lovely smile, who would give us tips on how to make ourselves attractive to men, how to brighten our hair, where to wear scent, and so on. All of this we knew, of course, but we thought it generous of her to try to enter our world in this way. Moreover, Mrs Savage had a certain claim on our attention, for she made no secret of the fact that she was still deeply in love with Millie's father, and several times we sent her home with new lipsticks, or eye shadow that we had decided was the wrong colour, or, once, a pair of high-heeled sandals that I had bought and found uncomfortable. Mrs Savage had the good manners of the good-hearted. 'Kind wishes to Mother,' she said to me, after her first visit to the flat, and, later, never failed to send her her love, although they had only met once. 'I'll ring Isabel when I get home and tell her you're all right,' she would say, for by that time my mother would hardly leave her house. This was the centre of my unhappiness, but I tried to hide it, for I realized that it made the young men who took me out impatient. I would see her at the weekends and sometimes in the week as well, although my heart grew heavy as I reached the house. 'Belle', I called her now, as my father had done, but she looked at me as if I had committed a solecism, and turned away.

Through all the restrictions and the worry that my mother's condition imposed on me my love for her grew, as, I think, did hers for me. This love was not a pleasure to either of us; it was, if anything, a burden. My mother felt it harnessed her to this world, which she tried so hard to ignore and which she was ready to leave, while to me it was the magnet that drew me unwillingly home, back to that narrow house and my mother's almost noiseless footfall, and the cup of tea that she silently put before me, as if appeasing a stranger in some primitive ritual. She had grown thin and frail; when I took her in my arms I could feel her heart beating under her cardigan. I took to staying with her until she had got into bed, and then sitting with her while she drank the hot milk and honey that I brought her. She would relax and smile at me then, briefly reverting to the mother I had always known, and I would lay my cheek on her hand in relief and gratitude. 'You go, dear,' she would say, with something of a return to her old manner. 'Mind you take a taxi, now.' Five minutes later, looking for a taxi in the dark and empty street, I would be harassed and burdened once again.

Therefore I did not think I need take Vinnie seriously, for she conformed to no idea of motherhood that I had ever entertained. Evidently she felt the same about me: I was not the sort of girl to wrest her son away from her, although a more enlightened mother might have noticed that he was in urgent need of being rescued. Handsome, spoilt, and apparently well-off, he had been one of the youngest Battle of Britain pilots, and the experience had made him so avid for excitement, yet at the same time so devoid of any motivation of his own, that he had had trouble settling down, had taken a long holiday from work after the war, and, only at the insistence of his father's brother, had finished his interrupted law studies and eventually joined the firm in Hanover Square. Had I been more experienced I should have seen in him the makings of a rather brutal success; the word tycoon was not yet common in those days but now that I have survived him I realize that that was what he would have become had he lived into late middle age. There was a cynicism there that I could never understand. His mother, with her anxious eyes and fashionable legs, her gin and her dazzling dusty mirrors, understood it far too well. All I knew, at our first meeting, was that the hot sun brought out the smell of her scent, *Arpège*, with something older and more hidden underneath, and drove prisms of light from the mirrors into my eyes, giving me a migraine headache, the first one I had ever had. The idea that she might become my mother-in-law did not occur to me for a single second. While as far as Vinnie was concerned I was so far removed from what she considered to be suitable that I was dismissed out of hand.

And yet, with all this unsuitability being demonstrated, there was anxiety in the air. Both Vinnie and I knew that Owen's emotions were in a tangled state and that he was both susceptible and on his guard, likely, in fact, to make a reckless judgment and a wrong decision, or, worse, no decision at all, and become old, sitting with his mother in her little flat, drinking gin, for want of anything better to do. For Owen had been married, briefly, before, to the beautiful Hermione, who had left him for an American colonel with whom she had been having an affair about which Owen had known nothing. She had walked out of the house in Gertrude Street, on which she had lavished so much of Owen's money (or rather Owen's father's money) and was currently in Orlando, Florida, still with the colonel, who was now something substantial in marinas. Hermione Langdon, as she was then, possessed suitability in abundance: she was striking, 'amusing', and had advanced ideas on interior decoration. When I first visited Owen's house I had felt my eyes watering: she had done out the rooms in dark harsh colours, indigo, sage green, and the brooding red of claret. There was a large chandelier in each of the two rooms on the first floor, which opened out into each other. Everything was spotless, excessive, and chilly. Owen's bed, which seemed to me twice the normal size, had a white satin coverlet with sculptured edges to match the white satin padded and buttoned bedhead. I did not see how any woman other than Hermione could sleep in such a bed; maybe that had been her intention. In any event, when I saw that bed I realized that Owen was not – could not be – for me.

Vinnie, after offering me gin, when I was badly in need of a cup of tea and an aspirin, asked me what I did. I told her that I sang, to which she replied, 'Oh, how clever of you. All you girls do something these days. I never did. I was married practically from the cradle.' Then she realized that she had uttered the word 'married', looked frightened, and changed the subject.

She feared that Owen would marry me, or the next girl he brought home, or the one after that. But I knew that he had no such intention, and, although I was hopelessly in love with him, I was almost reconciled to being forgotten once he had got tired of me. We had met at a party, to which I had not wanted to go. Millie dragged me there, and I felt tired and bad-tempered. Neither of us knew our host – a journalist

– well, and we were intimidated by his flat, which seemed full of noisy, excitable and superior people. My first sight of Owen was prophetic: he was talking to a girl who had her back to the wall; he had one hand extended behind her, so that she was imprisoned by this arm beside her head. I registered a sort of antagonism at the same time as I caught my breath, for I had never seen such a beautiful man. He was tall and exceptionally graceful; his hair was longer than average, and he had a restless fatigued expression, which I later came to identify as boredom. So strong was my reaction, which was almost one of fear, that I turned to leave, for this was a contest I had no desire to enter. I knew that I was too placid, too simple for such a man, and that even if I won his attention I should not be able to hold it. 'Oh, don't go,' he said, releasing the girl inside his arm. 'We haven't met yet.'

He later told me that he fell in love with me then, and although I believed him I never felt confident that he loved me as a man should love a woman he intends to marry. But perhaps it was exactly intention rather than volition on his part that brought us together. He was bored with his mother's anxiety, bored with finding different girls to sleep with, bored with his life, bored with the restless existential boredom that plagued him when things were not going well. I represented an easy way out of both his boredom and his entanglements. I was straightforward, transparent, unlikely to present him with problems or complications, was traditional enough to lavish care on his home, horrible though I thought it, and a good enough daughter to my own mother to spare some thought for his. Yet all this he did not know until later. My own feeling is that he had no desire to marry me on that first evening, although he always gallantly emphasized that this was the case. I was a pretty girl then, and he had probably marked me down as one of his future conquests. It was only after we had met a few more times, and he was impressed by the obvious quality of my devotion, that marriage came into the equation.

Whatever I had in the way of character or attainments never counted as much with Owen as the pleasure I could give him in the way of dressing well, looking good, and providing an agreeable atmosphere for his guests. That was my attraction for him: I was nice to look at and my eyes were empty of calculation. But although I knew, on that first occasion, that my dress was becoming, and although I felt the colour rising to my cheeks as he stared at me, what I felt was uncertainty, an uncertainty which was to accompany me throughout my married life. For a question mark hung over my status. There was nothing grand about me, as there had been about Hermione, and it was clear – to everyone – that of the two of us I was likely to love the more. Owen's boredom meant that he had a limited attention span: he always needed new people to break what he experienced as the monotony of the old. Whereas, to me, falling in love was a lifelong commitment, and the prospect of marriage a solemn undertaking. And I think that at that stage in my life I too was feeling a little restless; I considered that I was no longer a novice either in age or in experience. I had gone as far as I was likely to go in my career, for here too new faces and new voices were called for and were constantly being discovered, and the novelty was beginning to wear off. I realize now that I was tired, simply tired. The flat in Foubert's Place struck me as too small, and much as I loved Millie, I did not really think that women were meant to live eternally together, like schoolgirls in a dormitory. I wanted to be looked after; I wanted babies. This all sounds very commonplace, and I dare say it is. Looking back I see that all women are programmed in this way and are hardly aware of it. I was aware of it only because I never intended to be anything but married. Therefore becoming Owen's lover as I did was a particularly dark and hazardous enterprise for me, making the idea of marriage one of overpowering importance, although in cooler moments I could see that the whole thing was inappropriate.

It embarrasses me now to look back on my passion for Owen. Probably all love affairs, when they are over, evoke a very slight reaction of impatience, distaste. What I felt then could not be captured in words, certainly not at this distance. I grew distracted, jumpy, absent-minded, but I sang better than

27

ever. The only shadow on my happiness, when Owen finally asked me to marry him, was the stipulation that I should give up my work. 'You do see, don't you, darling?' he said. 'It really wouldn't do. Besides, I want my wife to stay at home.' I was won over, of course.

Millie, on the contrary, was not. And neither was my mother, when she met Owen at Foubert's Place. That was a little cowardice of mine. I knew that Owen would be shocked if I were to take him to Camberwell Grove, where my mother sat in dark rooms all day, and the only sound was the dripping of the tap in the stone sink in the scullery. Evidently she felt the same, which was good of her – but she was always good. I sent a car for her, and although she was pretty silent throughout the afternoon she did not appear to be frightened or dismayed, as I had feared. She did not like him, that was clear, but she was such a reticent woman that only I knew this. Owen was charming to her. Superficially all went well. I got on with Vinnie; Owen got on with Mother. But we all met together exceedingly rarely. There was no love among the four of us, only passion between Owen and myself, which we tried to impose on the others. They shrank back from this, sensing its promiscuity, its impropriety. After our marriage I visited my mother and Owen visited his. The only times I saw Vinnie were when someone gave her a lift to Gertrude Street and she ate whatever she could find in the kitchen. I continued to spend a day with Mother once a week.

I wore blue, with a matching pill box hat and a short blue veil for my wedding, which took place at Caxton Hall at the end of a beautiful spring, with the promise of a beautiful summer. I had known Owen for a year, which I thought was the equivalent of a lifetime. Mrs Savage had taken Mother out and made her buy a new dress, grey silk with white spots, very pretty. Millie was in pink, and not at her best. Her face was troubled. 'Are you sure?' she had said to me while I was dressing. 'He's not the sort to settle down, you know.' But I thought that he might, and did not much care if I was wrong. I shall never forget how he appeared to me on my wedding day, impossibly handsome,

28

too good for me. I thought that I had been granted my heart's desire, and was almost frightened. Now I realize that I had been frightened almost from the beginning, frightened of losing him, frightened of boring him, frightened of my own feelings, even of his. Since knowing Owen a certain degree of fear was so natural to me that I no longer even noticed it.

4

Owen was away a lot on business. The senior partners in the firm of solicitors for which he worked entrusted him with those clients who wanted to acquire property abroad and did not understand – or even wish to understand – the laws pertaining to the places in which they intended to have a second home. Monaco and southern Spain seemed to be the favourites: few English people had as yet invaded the Dordogne. Switzerland was for the super-rich, and Owen hoped to extend this market. He used to fly to Spain or the south of France on an average of once every two or three weeks, leaving me with a list of things to do in his absence. Since he had to entertain clients, or be entertained by them, his wardrobe, which was extensive, had to be kept in good repair, and he liked me to be at home so that his secretary could telephone me with the latest news of his movements. Sometimes I relied on her to tell me which flight he was catching, for he rang the office at the end of every afternoon and myself only first thing in the morning, before he went off for the day.

I accepted this routine without demur. I felt no indignation that he should give priority to the office; I doubt if many wives did in those days, or at least the sort of wife who came from my background, which I began to perceive was a little too simple for a man like Owen. He was used to complexity, trickiness, ambivalence; he would rather, I thought, be intrigued by a woman than disarmed by her. He hated those moments of unavoidable truth-telling which occasionally passed between us. I really think that he hated desire. He wanted a wife who would cause him no anguish, yet at the same time he wanted to hold her at arm's length. He never seemed to sense the incompatibility of these two needs, the one for trust, the other for distance, even for a sort of formality, and I soon learned not to draw his attention to what was, to me, faintly alarming, his abrupt cancellation of intimacy as soon as the occasion for that intimacy had passed. My fault was precisely this, that I would seek to prolong our moments of closeness when I could see that he was already restless with the wish to do something else. My mistake was to lie in his arms moist-eyed with tenderness and gratitude, when the correct stance would have been a certain detachment, an irony, as if to imply that he would have to love me to a much higher standard to convince me that I had to take him seriously. I should have found such a tactic odious, but now I see that it is sometimes necessary to meet withdrawal with withdrawal, dismissal with dismissal. I did not know this then, and because of what has happened since I remain unconvinced of it even now, but I see that if a woman has it in mind to bring a man to heel she may have to play a part which runs counter to her own instincts, unless her instincts are those of an aggressor, which mine certainly were not.

Contrary to Millie's prognostications Owen did settle down, but in a way that surprised me. From being bored by, or at least indifferent to, his profession he became keenly ambitious. Mixing as he did with people who were wealthy, some of them shamelessly so, he began to have aspirations himself: the reluctant young man that he had once been was fascinated by the open-handedness, even the coarseness, of some of his clients. Men did not yet wear a chestful of gold medallions, but they were beginning to acquire them. The medallions, I later learned, were not for decoration but for hard currency in a tight spot. It was not the swimming-pools and the girlfriends that attracted Owen, not the luncheon parties on terraces that went on for a whole afternoon and to which itinerant film actresses were invited – it was none of these things. It was, rather, a kind of thoughtless enthusiasm and well-being, an absence of reflection combined with a keen appetite for profit and speculation, effects without causes, as if all of life could be contained in the sort of conversation that would take place between two men, stripped to the waist, smoking cigars after lunch in the Mediterranean sun, champagne glass to hand. My husband, who had always struck me as complicated, and whose complexities I had promised myself to study and to understand, now yearned to be simple, with the sort of simplicity that only the very rich can command. Straight deals mixed with fabulous entertainment, the one indistinguishable from the other: that was what Owen liked. I met some of his clients, for it fell to my lot to entertain them when they were in London, although Owen in fact preferred to meet them on their own home ground. I could see why: the house in Gertrude Street, commodious as it was, was not really fashionable, as it was soon to become, and those terrible brooding colours of Hermione's were far from welcoming. Even in summer the house was dark, and my cold salmon, on which I had spent the entire afternoon arranging cucumber slices in the form of scales, seemed chilly even in June, while the pale wine, in Hermione's engraved glasses, seared my mouth. The guests – Owen's guests – ate well but absent-mindedly, smoked between courses, and after greeting me ignored me completely. They had not become rich by being charming to unimportant people like myself.

I was a stranger to the guests in my house, the Harrisons, the Smiths, Sir Victor and Lady Eberlin, the Sandford-Roches, and they were eternally strangers to me. It was not yet seemly to be rich, and the girth and laughter of the men, and the deep brown faces and long red nails of the women made me feel a little uncomfortable. I did not know how these people spent their time, nor did I see how I could ever spend time with them. I resented their hold over my husband, and I suspected that they made him presents of money that the partners knew nothing about. He was their man of business and therefore a licensed hanger-on; he was to be there when they needed him and could be telephoned in the middle of the night if necessary. When I suggested, mildly, as a respectful wife should, that some of these people were perhaps not very nice, Owen laughed at me and said I was a prig. 'You don't think I take them seriously, do you? But they're not so bad when you get to know them. Old Jack's a very amusing character. And Molly's quite a sweet girl really. You got on all right with Molly, didn't you?' Old Jack was one of the first property tycoons, and Molly, his third wife, was his junior by twenty-six years. When Owen had brought them to the house for the first time she had struck me as rather drunk, and I had taken her upstairs to tidy up, at her own request. Once in my bedroom she had become tearful, and told me that her life was not as easy as it looked. Downstairs again she placed a loaded hand on Jack's thigh, squeezed it, and said, 'She has the most darling bed.' She made it sound like a cot. 'Take a look at it before you leave. Jack loves beds,' she told us, with a trouperish but still tearful smile. 'All kinds. All the time.' Jack, to his credit, remained impassive throughout this announcement. I did not think that Molly was in for a very long run.

Although these people were strangers to me, and although Owen's appreciation of them appeared misplaced, what really frightened me was the fact that his work had become the centre of his affectivity. His entire emotional life seemed to consist of an enthusiasm for people, for places, even for activities far removed from the home I had tried to make for him, far, too, from my own settled expectations. In this he was ahead of his time. Having lived so much longer than he was able to do I now see young men, and young women too, whose working lives represent and contain all their aspirations, their desires, almost. Nowadays I read that in New York work has replaced love as the highest priority. I also read that the women who make what they call a commitment to their careers are likely to confess to being lonely and desolate and to lament the shortage of men. Given this fact, of course, men in the same position are not likely to lament the shortage of women, but they will tend to treat them differently. Owen's behaviour towards me became

33

perfunctory, as I suppose it always does when a man's work is more important than his wife's peace of mind. Orders would be given for the week's entertaining, telephone calls would be made and received all the time, when we were eating, frequently when we were in bed, and love became purely functional. The strangest thing was that this kept him perfectly happy. The house ran smoothly, I offered no objection to his way of life, I was docile and malleable still, but best of all, from his point of view, there was no longer any real intimacy between us. Intimacy, I see now, was what he feared the most; intimacy made him uneasy, as if he had forfeited or lost part of himself in the process, as if it had made him vulnerable to criticism, to attack. I had seen his face after I had once, in the early days, prevailed on him to love me; it was fretful, pained, resentful. All this I saw in one terrible moment, as he turned away from me. He sat on the edge of the bed, naked, his clasped hands hanging between his knees. Poor Tom's a-cold, I thought. I was so frightened then that I vowed I would keep my distance. For that was what he wanted, and I still loved him enough to try to please him.

Vinnie would turn up from time to time, and say, 'And how's that naughty boy of mine?' She almost never asked me the same question. I remember on one occasion I had put a careful casserole of chicken and peppers on the kitchen table to cool and she began to dip into it with a teaspoon. The teaspoon was supposed to indicate that she was not really interested in eating it, but had merely come into the kitchen to keep me company, since that was where I inexplicably chose to spend my time. I remember reacting rather sharply. 'Please, Vinnie! That casserole is for this evening!' She looked surprised and annoyed; I had never scolded her before. 'I was only tasting it,' she protested. 'But you keep using the spoon,' I said. 'And it's got your lipstick on it.' I felt the tears of exasperation and hopelessness rising to my eyes, took the spoon, and dropped it in the sink. She immediately lit a cigarette, and said, 'Bad time of the month, is it? I used to be the same. Just find me an ashtray, would you?' I quickly put the lemon mousse away in case it got a flake of ash on it. I wanted her to go away; I wanted to cry my eyes out. When I took my head out of the fridge I caught sight of the face she was putting to rights with the aid of a mirror and a lipstick-stained handkerchief which she kept in her bag for the purpose of adjusting the contours of her mouth. This disgusting habit repelled me, but now I caught sight of her eyes, those uncensored eyes which were always lonelier than the rest of her face. 'I'm sorry, Vinnie,' I said. 'Let me make you some coffee. Is someone coming to collect you?' She smiled frostily. 'As you may have noticed, I'm on my own today. Just get me a taxi, would you?' There was usually a taxi on the corner, but it meant my going out into the street. I switched off the oven, reflecting that in doing so I had probably ruined the batch of coconut *tuiles* that I had intended to accompany the mousse, went out into the street without removing my apron, in time to see a taxi driving off. 'There's going to be a slight delay,' I said, back in the kitchen. 'You'd better have that coffee after all.' I was aware of the need to appease her, but she had decided to take the incident seriously. 'Perhaps you would be kind enough to telephone Godfrey Burton for me,' she said. This was a neighbour of hers in Swan Court, much in demand as a squire to various ladies, whose colours he was then obliged to fly. 'I'm sure he would not mind bringing the car round,' she said with awful majesty. She was, of course, perfectly capable of catching a bus, but liked to boast that she had never been on a bus in her life.

When Godfrey Burton turned up I had to offer him coffee, to which he assented enthusiastically. 'Tell Owen to telephone me, would you?' were her distant words to me as she left on Godfrey's arm. I had no doubt that complaints were to be made. This did not bother me unduly – it had, after all, been a squalid little incident – but the fact that Vinnie hated me, had probably always hated me, hurt me suddenly. It was as if she had bequeathed to her son the same propensity, a decision to dispense with emotions once they had served their purpose. She had been pleasant enough until I had shown real exasperation over the spoilt casserole, and what she had, quite rightly,

35

intuited as some kind of watershed. The exasperation had been so real, so charged, that it was an unmistakable emotional fact. This was distasteful to her, as was any emotion, and so she decided to punish me for it. And in that moment I began to wonder if Owen would eventually do the same.

It should have been clear to me then that there was a great deal wrong with my marriage, but these things only become clear in retrospect. And it was a matter of pride to me not to believe that anything was wrong, or that I was not entirely happy. On the surface Owen was an excellent husband, more handsome than ever, bronzed from frequent Mediterranean business trips, successful, hardworking, and extremely popular. To look at him, to be in his company, one would have thought that he was a man in love with life. But in fact he was only in love with a certain sort of life – a tycoon's life – and it was a life in which I was cast for quite a minor role. I began to feel like the poor girl I had once been, before I started earning my own money. Now I no longer had that resource, and although Owen gave me a handsome housekeeping allowance we entertained so much, and he insisted on such elaborate meals, that there was little left over at the end of the week. I longed to go up to town and take Millie to lunch and out shopping for the afternoon, but in fact I did not want to meet her penetrating eye. And I was aware that my own clothes, for which allowance was also made in the budget, were far more expensive than hers could ever be, although I thought they looked too old for me and longed to buy something cheap and pretty. So the sad thing was that I occasionally made excuses when she telephoned me or I telephoned her – I was always theoretically preparing for a dinner party – and when she asked me, as she always did, what I was going to wear, and I said, 'My green silk,' she would say, with surprise in her voice, 'I don't know that, do I? I don't know half your clothes now. Do let's get together soon. I'll come over and bring a cake, and we'll have a really good talk.' 'Lovely,' I would say, but when we met there was a tiny constraint between us. 'Are you happy?' she would say. 'That's all that counts.' 'Of course,' I would reply. But there was too much heartiness, too much airiness, too much flippancy in my attitude for Millie's taste. She knew otherwise, and she was never wrong. She knew before I did.

I would escape from the house, which I hated, and take long walks, but Gertrude Street, which is a handsome street, filled with handsome houses, merely feeds into other streets exactly like itself. It is also treeless and sees practically no traffic since it is closed at one end by a long low building the purpose of which I never discovered. Every time I left the house my spirits, already low, would be further lowered by the emptiness and the silence, and I would hurry round the corner to the place where the buses stopped to change drivers and look longingly at the small café with the steamy windows where the crews went for their tea. In memory I see those walks of mine as eternally overcast, under a white sky. The meagre light and the occasional whine of a car on its way to somewhere more interesting oppressed me almost as much as the house had done, and after a half-hearted excursion to the shops to buy something that was not really needed I would hear my footsteps ringing out as I turned back into Gertrude Street. Those eternal winter afternoons, when Owen was away in the sun, stretched before me in an endless progression; there was something implacable about their changelessness, and about my own despair. I had always been so lighthearted, but now I seemed to sigh a lot, and even to feel unwell. The headaches, announced so dramatically that first day in Vinnie's flat, had become a regular feature of my life, and I had frequently to sit at my own dinner table unobtrusively pushing food about my plate and smiling at Jack or Molly or their equivalent with a pulse beating behind my eyes and a feeling of nausea in my throat.

When Mother, whom I still visited regularly, asked me if I were happy I replied instantly and warmly that of course I was. She knew the truth of the matter, as did Millie. But I did not. That was another strange thing. As far as I was concerned I still loved my husband, and I think, even at this distance, that I really did. Owen never failed me, in his limited fashion, but

37

his requirements were too formal, too impersonal, to satisfy my hopes. He wanted me to remain the devoted and humble girl that I had been when he first married me, and in my heart I was. But I was older now, old enough to be tired, and while I had been getting older and more tired (I who had never been tired before) the world seemed to be getting younger. We were told that we had never had it so good, and the greater part of the nation seemed to think that this was the simple truth. But I noticed that the new frenetic music had put an end to the pretty songs which I used to sing and which only old people now seemed to remember. I suppose I had always sung for a staid and settled population, modest people for whom listening to the wireless was treat enough at the end of a working day, or housewives and mothers at home. They were songs of love and longing, all kept in decorous perspective and proportion. I did not understand the shouting and enthusiasm of the new music or its lack of charm. I had no piano in Gertrude Street, and when I tried a few scales unaccompanied I noticed how my voice had darkened. The voice deepens as one gets older. The change was infinitesimal to anyone who was not trained, but I knew, as I sang those scales, that my singing days were over. 'Arcady,' I sang fearfully, in the cruel indigo room. 'Arcady, Arcady is always young.' My voice cracked very slightly on the high note, and I blushed, a deep suffusing blush that ebbed away slowly, leaving me quite weak.

Owen had been abroad a great deal recently and there was some feeling in Hanover Square that he should put in more time at the office. His reaction to this was to tell me that he was inviting the senior partners to dinner, with their wives. This meant three separate dinner parties, for it would look too obvious if they were all to be invited together. His uncle Bernard and Lady Frances were no problem, nor was there any difficulty with George and Claire Gascoigne, who were elderly. But on the day that we were expecting Charlie and Julia Morton – famous Julia – in the evening, I had a head-ache and was unusually low-spirited. My fingers were clumsy as I laid the table and I should have given anything to be able to go to bed. In fact I did lie down for half an hour and fell asleep, which annoyed Owen, who woke me when he came up to dress. 'For God's sake,' he said. 'I'm not asking you to do anything difficult. You don't even have to go out. Just put a good face on it, that's all I ask.' He added, 'And you'd better see the doctor tomorrow, if you really feel rotten. You don't suppose . . . ?' 'No,' I said, for I had never become pregnant and now I knew I never should. Some part of me must have resisted being taken over even further, and although I did not grieve too much then I do now. Growing old is so meaningless when there are no young people to watch.

I got out of bed, had my bath, and dressed. My head was throbbing, but I thought it might be all right if I did not eat: the smell of the roast veal, as I opened the oven, made me turn away, momentarily faint. Owen was on edge, and it looked as if the evening could not be anything but an outright failure. The Mortons had never been to us before because Julia was still on the stage and did not go out in the evening, at least not to any house connected with her husband's business, which she deplored, as if he conducted it only out of some weird caprice, when he could have been spending more time at home with her. But the changing fashions had evidently reached Julia and she roundly condemned the tide of popular taste which was turning against her and the particular impression she conveyed. From her first entrance into our drawing-room that evening, in ravishing black silk, with a black silk turban, it was evident that she had thrown herself body and soul into the character of a simple suburban wife. 'My darlings!' she announced, sweeping a black chiffon handkerchief from her bag and draping it round her neck, 'I want you to treat me as one of yourselves. Forget about Julia. Julia is no more. Let the people have what they want. If they want ruffians there are plenty to go round. My day is done.' She put her hand to her throat and I swear there were tears in her eyes. Charlie, who must have brought unobtrusiveness to a fine art, removed the black chiffon scarf and put it in his pocket. 'What's the matter?' she said. 'Isn't that the sort of thing middle-class housewives wear? For I suppose

39

we are all middle-class now,' she added, and the eyelids came down. 'What about the ruffians?' said Owen, laughing. The eyelids were slowly and suggestively lifted. 'I dare say they are available if one knows where to look for them.'

I was laughing now and the evening looked less dubious than it had done. Although she had very little to say to me ('Oh, do show me what you are cooking. I am so interested') she appreciated Owen wonderfully. He was, after all, a handsome and attentive host. The dinner was as good as I could have hoped, although I could manage very little of it. Charlie and Julia ate heartily, and in Julia's case with enormous pantomimes of appreciation. As I cleared the table and went to get the coffee Charlie held the door open for me, and said, very quietly, 'All right, my dear?' I nodded, touched, and felt a little warmth creep into my half-numb face.

That was the beginning of our friendship, 'for we are not going to let you go now,' said Julia, who was obviously fretting at the loss of her public. She was fifty, a difficult age for letting go, still young enough to have ambitions and desires but with fewer opportunities of satisfying either. Owen was delighted with the evening, and Charlie gave the impression of being happy whenever his wife was happy. I decided that he must be exceptionally good-natured to act as her foil in the way that he did: there was something so gallant in that, I thought, as I thankfully prepared for bed. I took off my make-up without even looking at my face, which was an indication of the tiredness I felt. But even as I slipped into that wonderful half-dream that announces sleep I realized that my headache had quite gone.

5

Julia was a dedicated woman. She was dedicated principally to herself, but that did not seem to lessen her charm, which was powerful if capricious. I know now that inside every one of us there is another self, wistful, wary, uncertain, but also cruel and subversive, a stranger who can respond to any suggestion, any impulse, whether wise or unwise, though it is usually the latter. In Julia's case this other self seemed to be absent: she was the same, from her polished outward appearance to her ironic inner heart. I never knew a woman so little given to self-doubt or self-questioning. If she thought a thing she said it, and if she wanted to do something she did it. She was impervious to remorse, for in her eyes her desires were always justified. I sensed in her a will as hard as her heart, although she was kind in an absent-minded fashion. But if her kindness was absent-minded it was nevertheless designed to serve her purpose. After flattering attention to oneself she would signify the end of this particular phase of the conversation by asking one, negligently, to perform some small but onerous service. 'You're so clever with food,' she once said to me. 'What should I get for Charlie's dinner tonight? What was that delicious vegetable thing I had at your house?'

'That was *ratatouille*, Julia. It's very simple, but it takes a little time. I'd bring you some if I had some made.'

'Too sweet of you, but you must remember I'm a housewife

now. Come along, Wilberforce! Pencil and paper. Can you see my pencil anywhere? Over there, perhaps, under the *Tatler*.'

She adjusted a pair of spectacles which hung on a chain round her neck.

'Now! What do I need?'

'You need tomatoes, aubergines, courgettes . . . '

The glasses were removed.

'Don't go on. I haven't got any of those things. And I couldn't possibly carry them, with my poor hands.'

She flexed her narrow chalky hands, which were beginning to get stiff.

'The next time you buy these things, Fay, could you possibly get a few for me? Then you can come and show me how to cook them.'

'I suppose it would be simpler if I gave you some of my own, when I next make it.'

'Yes, that might be best. What a lovely idea!'

The subject was closed.

'But what about Charlie's dinner?' I said.

'Oh, he can have an omelette. It's what he usually has. Now I've never been able to like eggs. Funny, isn't it? I find them incredibly boring. Eggs and avocados. Whereas I can eat all kinds of shellfish and sleep like a baby afterwards. I remember a very grand dinner party in New York once: our ambassador was there. The first course was prawns and avocados. So silly. Why ruin prawns? I ate mine and gave the avocado to the ambassador. My hostess was furious, but she was a very tiresome woman. What were we saying?'

I could see that with Julia one's natural position was one of subservience, and I was no exception to this rule. I got into the habit of going round to visit her, since this was encouraged by both Owen and Charlie, for different reasons. Charlie was worried that she might feel lonely without the theatre to go to, and Owen was keen to please Charlie. I liked Julia well enough in those days, although I thought her selfish and outrageous, and no substitute for Millie. But Millie had married and gone to live near Oxford, and I felt the need of a female companion. My own

42

state of mind was unstable. Mother, on my recent visits, had seemed to me so much more frail, so removed from my life and the world I had come to inhabit, though not comfortably, far from that. Fortunately I was able to secure the services of a neighbour, Mrs Barber, Joan Barber, who had a small child at school and was glad to go into Mother every day and sit with her. That way, at least I knew that she was not alone, although my heart ached for her and I could hardly wait for the opportunity to see her to come round. As always, I felt for her a mixture of love and pain, and I only hoped that as she drifted away from me she felt easier in her mind than I did.

But there was another cause for concern. I had found, in Owen's sock drawer, several bundles of twenty-pound notes, which were evidently not destined for the household budget, and I was frightened. I assumed that this money was some kind of payment for services of a private nature, an investment, if you looked at the matter in an indulgent frame of mind, on the part of his clients, who would then have access to him for whatever purposes were under discussion. I knew that he was declaring this money neither to the Inland Revenue nor to the partners, and I was alarmed, so alarmed that I closed the drawer with a blush and never asked Owen where the money had come from. He was noticeably more short-tempered these days, as if his conscience, so much more malleable than I had ever suspected, was making him very slightly uneasy. Communication between us was reserved to whatever had to be said, which was convenient, for we had few evenings on our own. Owen was rarely at home; when he was not abroad he was dining with clients in London restaurants, which he found easier than entertaining in Gertrude Street. Thus my role in our marriage was reduced even further. When we got to bed it was to sleep, for which I now had an enormous desire. I got into the habit of taking a nap in the afternoons, and even then I slept deeply. When I awoke it was with a familiar feeling of oppression, and I was anxious to get out of the house. On some days I was happy to go round to Julia, who never seemed to worry about anything and whose preoccupations were confined entirely to herself. When I did not go round she would telephone.

'Now look here!' This was her usual greeting. 'It's no good my sitting here and your sitting there. Why don't you come round? I was thinking I might go through some of my clothes. I'll never wear any of them again.'

'Oh, nonsense, Julia.'

'No, I mean it. They ought to go to the Red Cross.' She pronounced it 'Crorss'. 'You could help me; I'm sure you're clever about these things. And you're out and about so much more than I am, you could tell me what's in and what's out. Not that I ever went by that. But then I always had dressmakers to tell me. And I suppose I ought to cut down now that I'm no longer earning.'

She would sigh, and I knew the sigh to be genuine. So I went. At the end of the afternoon there would be piles of dresses all over the drawing-room. As far as I know Maureen put them all back again: at any rate the same process was repeated several times. The Red Cross, so frequently invoked, never got anything out of it.

It is always hard for a woman who has been well known to drop out of sight. In a very real sense she loses significance. This had happened in my own case, although my own case was modest compared to Julia's. I suppose this is why so many women are ambivalent about marriage these days: they are reluctant to give up the independence for which they have worked so hard and which they occasionally feel as a burden. They are not being frivolous: they fear that genuine loss of significance. It is all the harder for them if they have had to postpone their own desires, for these desires dwindle and are experienced as pain. Julia's case was less harsh, of course, for she already had Charlie, the perfect partner for a woman with a famous presence, and the least self-serving of men. But the higher the achievement the greater the regret. And although I thought that Julia exaggerated her own fame – she never, for example, acknowledged anybody else's – there was no doubt that she had achieved an enormous visibility. Julia was iconic, featured in *Vogue*, known for her amazing elegance as well as her rather *louche* performances. Her appearance in a restaurant turned heads and subdued conversations. She had the fearlessness of the true aristocrat: her announced intention of becoming middle-class was in fact a jeer at those who already were. Being of more modest condition myself I kept quiet, another little cowardice of mine, but with Julia one had to protect oneself as best one could. She was genuinely devoid of shame. Or of humility. Yet I could see that it pained her to sit at home in Onslow Square, with such a reduced audience. It pained her, but she was resolute. Nowadays she rarely went out.

It pained me too. I felt that we were in a similar situation. I missed my singing days, now long gone, and even looked back wistfully to the time when the boys in the orchestra were so kind to me. And sometimes it was an effort to maintain my appearance. Julia was invaluable on that score. Always immaculate, she kept me up to the mark. She would gaze at me quite impersonally. 'Shorter hair,' she would pronounce. 'And you need a manicure. And you might ask whoever does it if she could come round and do mine. Tell her the morning is my best time. Tell her to telephone about ten-thirty.' And I would be off on another errand, but one which benefited myself as well as Julia.

It was Julia who had the idea that we should take a holiday together, the four of us. The winter was cruel to her incipient arthritis, and although she rarely went out, her flat, in which she spent so much of her time, was not quite warm enough. Actually I think – indeed I know – that she exaggerated her disability, as she exaggerated everything else. Once I saw her take a jar of marmalade that Maureen had been trying to open and give the lid a sharp wrench. 'Why, Julia!' I made the mistake of saying. 'Your hands!' She looked at me impassively, under the eyelids. 'I just fancied a little piece of bread and marmalade,' she said. 'But it doesn't matter. I'll go without. You can take that away now,' she said to Maureen, waving away the plate she had brought in. 'I'll have it later.' She also exaggerated the fact that she never went out. She would sometimes go out to take one of her many defunct clocks and watches to the jeweller's near South Kensington station, but these occasions were occasions for getting into character. She would take a wicker basket, like a milkmaid going to market, which she thought appropriate for the environs of the Fulham Road, and smile prettily at passers-by. The basket was always empty. She never seemed to have time to buy the more humble commodities on which a household runs. Members of her entourage – Charlie, Maureen, myself – would be used for this purpose.

She deplored the cold, which she said made her hands ache, but in fact she was antagonistic to most forms of weather. She liked the artificial climate of her dressing-room rather than anything more natural or more variable. She would sigh for the sun, but when it came it did not always meet with her approval. 'Just pull that curtain, would you? I can't stand a glare in my eyes.' This from a woman who could spend twenty minutes to half an hour examining her face in the light of the bulbs round her dressing-room mirror. But I have heard many women sighing for the sun, and I am inclined to take their longing seriously. What they are really saying is, 'I am weary, even frightened. I look tired, and plain. Why have I changed so? Is it age that is doing this to me, or is it just the winter? If only the summer would come! Then I might look young again!' For the sun is the symbol of all that has been lost, a great capricious god who might restore one to oneself, if only he were so minded. I too sighed for the sun, and I had reason to in those cruel dark rooms which I knew I could never transform into anything of my own. It was a relief to go to Onslow Square, although I found Julia's flat almost equally unwelcoming. She liked colours which contained no warmth, and the white curtains and the mustard walls, the white carpet and the white and yellow lilies in the enormous vases of clear glass seemed to reduce the temperature, which was always chilly, even further. She had some quarrel with the central heating, so that more often than not it had to be turned off completely. When it was stone-cold Maureen was despatched to the telephone to summon assistance. If none came, they would sit there, resigned, until Charlie came home, when all that was needed was someone to make the most minor adjustments, which they could easily have done for themselves. They could even fail to understand that they had to turn the knob and switch on the radiators. I myself have performed this function times without number. 'You're so clever, Fay,' Julia would say. 'What should we do without you?'

I was no longer happy, and in the restless state that this realization brought into being it was a welcome reprieve for me to sit in Julia's drawing-room, uncomfortable though it was, and cold as it even more frequently was, and to calm myself down in the atavistic pleasure of purely female company. It is a resource of women to exclude men from time to time, to take a break from being on the alert and looking one's best. It is a resource which can outlive its usefulness, as alliances are made and broken, and jealousies begin to peak. But at that particular period of my life, when Owen was away and winter turned the rooms in Gertrude Street into malevolent caves I would hurry round to Onslow Square as if to a sanctuary, a harem or zenana, where the half-maternal instincts of women could be deployed and the vagaries of men seen for what they really were. Women in such a situation will unite in deploring the childishness of men, their deceptions, and their frivolity, although, if questioned by an outsider, all would pride themselves on having such a fragile creature as their protector. Unmarried women come off worst in such company, and I began to feel sorry for Maureen, although I had never liked her, and I did not find that she improved on acquaintance.

Maureen, Julia's slave, was about thirty-five at this time and thus considerably younger than the rest of us – Julia, her mother, Mrs Chesney, Julia's former dresser, and myself. Maureen struck me as fairly hysterical in her devotion to Julia, who was dependent on her but who probably liked her as little as I did. Maureen was simply not very likeable, an eager hapless creature with permed hair and rimless glasses, usually dressed in a pair of shapeless navy blue trousers and a fairly juvenile

47

sweater which she had knitted herself. Maureen's furious knitting was an accompaniment to Julia's more tasteless revelations: bent over the needles Maureen could thus hide the blushes which rose in unison with her nervous laughter. One stubby finger, with a childishly bitten nail, would push her glasses back up the bridge of her nose from time to time. She was extremely religious, according to Julia, and I suppose it was true, although Maureen herself made no reference to anything of a churchly nature. Why did she stand such a life of slavery? She had a free room in Onslow Square, and I am sure that Charlie must have paid her quite well, but she had given up her independence, and also her profession, for although she had been a very minor sort of journalist, there was no reason why she should not have gone on and made something of herself. I think she was enormously frightened of the outside world, and instinctively took refuge with the strongest person she could find. This happened to be Julia, met, not entirely by chance, in the days when Maureen was working on the local paper.

I felt uncomfortable with Maureen, who blushed and writhed and laughed at Julia's remarks, although she must have heard them at least a hundred times: it occurred to me, in an idle moment, that with all her physical silliness and suggestibility, she was probably quite highly sexed, which made her doubly unfortunate. The thought surprised me, for in those days I was not given to speculating about other people's emotional lives. I assumed that they were all like my own: faulty. What I saw of Charlie made me think differently, but then Charlie was the exception. Whatever Julia was like as a wife, or even as a woman, she was successful in surrounding herself with an atmosphere of gallantry, and this had to be maintained by women as well as by men. In this respect Maureen was invaluable, and so, to a very much lesser extent, was I.

Nevertheless, I felt more relaxed when the five of us – Julia, Mrs Wilberforce, Mrs Chesney, Maureen and myself – were all present, because the absence of any one of us would encourage Julia to examine, with the others, some tiny fault which she would mention deprecatingly, and which only perverseness, it seemed, stopped us from rectifying. Thus, after an absence of a few days, when Owen was at home, I went round to Onslow Square, on one occasion, to hear myself accused of morbidity. 'It's such a little thing,' said Julia, smiling. 'But I had to mention it. I said to Mummy the other day, "Have you noticed how morbid Fay has become?" And Mummy was forced to say that she had. And Pearl (Mrs Chesney) was worried that something might be wrong. But I said, "Nonsense, I'm sure there's nothing wrong. Why should there be? As far as I know Owen hasn't got another woman, although of course he has plenty of opportunity, and no one would know if he kept a mistress in Monte Carlo or Málaga or wherever he goes, but I somehow don't think that's the trouble." ' She paused here and I trembled for Owen, though not as Julia would have wished. She continued. 'I think you've just developed a morbid outlook, Fay, and you've got to guard against it. Heaven knows I've got more to be morbid about than you have, but being on the stage teaches you to keep going, in spite of your feelings. That's what I try to do. With some success, I hope.'

These words were met with murmurs of approval from her audience, although I confess to feeling deeply annoyed, even as I recall the incident. At that time, of course, I was also a little fearful, for Julia had a speculative cast of mind, and it was difficult to tell whether she made such remarks out of sheer boredom or whether she really intended to make one lose one's temper and have a glorious row. 'We had a glorious row,' she would say with some satisfaction, after a passage at arms with one of her friends. There was another reason for my fear. Although I never mentioned Owen in company, conscious that I had much to hide, and also conscious of having to protect him, Julia was preternaturally aware of the sensitive part to which the arrow or goad might be directed. I excused this, as we all did, because we knew that her suffering was quite genuine and that it took some courage to transpose her sphere of influence from a full theatre to a group of silly women, although I think that each of us knew that the company of women held no charm for her and that she could turn her attention to each one of us and leave us unsettled as a result. Maureen, during one of her absences at Peter Jones, was convicted of gracelessness (difficult to deny) and Mrs Chesney was adjured to her face to lose some weight. 'You know how it ages one, darling.' I liked Mrs Chesney, whom I found a simple sympathetic sort of woman, and burned with indignation on her behalf. The fact of the matter was that Mrs Chesney, who was not well off, habitually wore a rather tight black suit which did nothing to conceal her ample hips, and the sight of this suit, which usually bore a little powder on the lapels of the jacket, was anathema to Julia, who continued, throughout her retirement, to be magnificently dressed. Although Mrs Chesney cheerfully admitted to enjoying her food I had caught an instant of helplessness in her smile, and hated Julia for mocking someone so defenceless. But in reality she mocked us all. Only Mrs Wilberforce, a tinkling fountain of appreciation, and Julia herself, constituted a protected species.

Why did I persuade myself that this sort of company was in any sense desirable? I believe that I had reached a low point in my life when I felt I could aspire to nothing good, when there was a kind of pleasure in accepting the second- or even the third-rate, as if that were all a person of my calibre could expect. There was in me an absence of volition which made me an easy prey for characters stronger than myself. And my motives in going to Onslow Square were not entirely noble, for the company of these women made Owen seem so much more interesting, worthwhile and laudable that I could hardly wait to get back to Gertrude Street in time to hear his key in the door. Owen, of course, was all in favour of my keeping in with Julia, for he thought that that softened Charlie's heart towards him, and in a sense it was true. Owen's motives were not noble either, but I had lost sight of Owen's moral strategies, and in any case the discovery of the money in the sock drawer made me willing to defend his interests, where once I might not have given these a thought.

The suggestion of the holiday, made by Julia, came as a direct result of her discovery of my morbidity. In fact she was not entirely wrong: I may well have been displaying some sort of symptom at that time, although I should have described this as unhappiness rather than morbidity. To save face – and because it is always bad form for a married woman of settled years to complain of unhappiness – I accepted the lesser charge. I mentioned the suggestion idly to Owen that evening and he surprised me by saying, 'Why not? You look a bit peaky. And I'm sure I could borrow a house for us. It might be rather fun.' 'Are you sure?' I asked. 'It might be a busman's holiday for you, with all your travelling. Wouldn't you prefer to stay at home?' 'It's time we spent a few days together, somewhere away from here. I've neglected you a bit, haven't I?' And he looked at me with a curious doubt in his eyes, and a sort of plea for trust, and I felt myself turn into his wife all over again.

The holiday in the south of France was our happiest time. The house was in the hills behind Nice and it had a terrace, and a long cool dining-room, and terracotta tiled floors on which tiny lizards palpitated in the sun. Each morning Owen drove me to the market, while Charlie and Julia were getting up, and I bought fish and vegetables for our dinner. Then we would go back to the house and collect the others, and go down to Nice. We would sit at a café, where Julia would have her whisky and Owen his *pastis*, and then make for a good restaurant for lunch. This was when I remember walking arm in arm with Julia along the Promenade des Anglais, in our white skirts, with Owen and Charlie chatting behind us. We would rest in the cool of the house in the afternoon, although no sun is too hot for me, and I would leave Owen and steal out into the garden. We went to bed early, leaving the car for Charlie and Julia, who liked to go back to Nice and did not get home till very late. Owen and I would be asleep by then, like children: like children we would fall asleep hand in hand. At those times I never thought that we could ever let each other go out into the world alone.

6

Memory begins to falter here, as if in anticipation of darker times ahead.

We took one more holiday in Nice, although not so successfully. We went one Christmas, the Christmas of the year which had seen our former visit, but this time Owen failed to borrow a house and we went to an hotel, the Negresco. It was ruinously expensive and not very nice, and although the weather was fine we did not really want to be out all day. Hotels make one self-conscious: one desires not to give offence, perhaps in the hope of being welcomed back with more deference than has been shown on the first occasion. We found the reception cool, or perhaps I am imagining it. Every morning saw me smiling placatingly at chambermaids anxious to do the rooms in which Owen still slept and Julia contemplated her wardrobe. Sometimes Charlie, who evidently had the same scruples as I did, would join me in the lobby. Finally we would leave a message for the other two and go out for a walk. It made me sad that Owen showed no inclination to be alone with me, as he had done on our previous miraculous stay in this part of the world, but of course Charlie was very agreeable, very kind, and did his best to make me forget my discomfiture. For that was what I felt. I knew that Charlie and I were blameless boring people and that we had left our more interesting partners behind – or rather that they had refused to join us. I think

Charlie always felt he had no individuality that could compare with Julia's, and so he kept mostly quiet when in her company, acting as her attendant, her protector, her perfect escort. Yet he was an attractive man in his own right, fit and bland and good-tempered, with an easy smile and excellent manners. It was only his silence, or rather his relative silence, that made him seem curiously out of the running, marginal, neutered, almost, as if his duties as Julia's husband precluded him from ever again fully engaging in normal human activity. His mode of address to me, on those slightly disappointing mornings when we took our walk together, was, 'All right, my dear? Let's try and find some newspapers, shall we? And then, I think, a cup of coffee.' We would sit outside a nearby café, sometimes for half an hour or so, reading and saying nothing, until the waiter came to be paid, and we would look up with a smile, fold our papers, and get to our feet. On our return to the hotel we would find Owen and Julia in the bar, nursing the first drink of the day, and realize that it was past eleven o'clock. 'Where on earth have you been?' Julia would demand. 'Only out for a breath of air,' I would say. 'It's so beautifully sunny, and quite warm.' Julia would stare at me under her eyelids. After a pause she would pronounce, 'How very odd.' She never failed to register surprise that we could voluntarily absent ourselves from her side. And then, losing interest, or reaffirming possession, or perhaps both, 'Charlie, run upstairs and get my glasses, would you, darling? The key? No, I haven't got the key. Well, ask at the desk. They must have a spare.' And so it went on.

I hated these time-wasting moments or hours. I could see the sun outside the darkened bar and longed for it as only one whose youth has been spent with the alarms and the distress and the heartbreaking cheerfulness of the war years can long for peace and beauty and brilliance, and that healing warmth. My eyes could not see enough radiance to satisfy me, for I remembered all too well the air raids and the broken nights and the shattered streets, and the endless dark. I should have been perfectly content to sit by myself all day on the front,

53

or in the little museum garden, doing nothing, perhaps reading a magazine, until the light began to fade and I would decide, reluctantly, to join the others. The palm trees, the dazzle of sun on the chrome of cars, the spiky plants, the crepitating earth would make me forget the house in Gertrude Street with its absurd appurtenances, its engraved wine glasses specially commissioned from an artist friend of Hermione's, its bed big enough for the birth of royalty, the winsome fresco in the bathroom. All this I would sacrifice for a bottle of cheap mimosa scent from the *herboristerie* or a bunch of blue carnations, magnificently vulgar, from the market. I began to discern depths of superficiality and bad taste in myself which I could see were not wholly regrettable. The sight of a simple plate of sliced tomatoes and olives, with oil and basil dribbled over them, made me think of the conscientious meals I cooked for Owen and his guests with something like contempt. I began to wish that the others would leave me alone so that I could eat pizza slices and sandwiches from street stalls. Instead of which, except for my early clandestine walk with Charlie, I was expected, as a matter of duty, to spend half my time in bars, and after that in restaurants, and only after that by the sea, until it was time to return to the bar again for the evening aperitif, which, to my mind, seemed to start earlier and earlier. Owen's drinking habits surprised me. He never drank like that when he was at home.

Next to being by myself I rather desperately wanted to be alone with Owen, although this seemed to be impossible, as Julia always insisted on a quorum wherever we went. It was clear to me that Charlie's gentle manners could not satisfy her natural avidity, although they were somehow necessary to set limits to her aggression. Sometimes I saw a distant look in his eye as if he too would like to escape, but it would quickly be replaced by one of attentive good humour: no one ever knew what it cost him. He could be called to order by Julia and frequently was; therefore he got into the habit of doing nothing in case he were needed. For such a man an office is a sanctuary, and Charlie was consequently known as an extremely hard worker. He was, I believe, very good at his job. Sometimes he spent Saturday in Hanover Square, 'going through some urgent papers', much to Julia's annoyance. His phenomenal patience seemed to wear out towards the weekend, especially when he knew that Julia liked her friends to call on Sundays, so that Saturday would really be his holiday, much as sitting alone in the museum garden was mine. He later told me that he would make a lonely and voluptuous cup of tea for himself, using his secretary's electric kettle. He would switch off the telephone and sit in absolute silence until his conscience told him that such licence must cease. Then, because of that same conscience, he would in fact do some of the work which could have been put aside for Monday, until the fading of the light outside his windows drove him home. When we came to know each other better we confessed that we were perfectly happy on our own, but that at a certain hour, usually at around five o'clock, we would begin to long for company. Now that I have all my time to myself I still feel the same, feel it more poignantly, even though I am no longer young, perhaps because I am no longer young. When the light goes, and the curtains are drawn, it is only natural to turn to one's companion. And if that companion is no longer there one feels his absence most cruelly.

Owen was my companion, and as the days drifted past in pointless trivialities – hunting for Julia's lost glasses, waiting politely with Charlie for the others to join us – I thought despairingly how these minute obstacles separated us, and of how they only did so because we were so separate already. I had never known Owen well, although I was now a seasoned married lady, one who had married late, and agreeably, and had settled down to be a traditional and if possible an honourable wife. I had never known Owen well because I had been infatuated with him and had therefore never seen him as a friend. If anything he was an enemy, an adversary, whom I would have to beguile and delay, distract and disarm. I came into these skills quite gradually, but they soon began to weary me. I was, however, too much in awe of Owen ever to contradict or ignore him. I never nagged, never provoked a quarrel, and so there was a vast distance between us that was filled with the formality of our life together. I endured the house and Owen's guests and Hermione's signature on everything because I thought, quite rightly, that this was what I had married. I thought in terms of paying the price for Owen's hand in marriage. That was how much I loved him at the beginning.

But love of this calibre is not easy to sustain or to prolong, largely because it is unrealistic, and in a sense inauthentic. Love is not the awesome prize I once thought it was but a much more daily commodity, penny plain rather than tuppence coloured. But I suppose women throughout the ages have felt dissatisfied with what is available, the friendlier varieties of love which are natural to the human race, and have broken their hearts and suffered mightily for unsuitable partnerships which were never meant to be consummated. My own was not quite in that category but it frequently felt uncomfortable; and I came to regard it as more duty than pleasure. This should have told me that something was wrong; in fact I knew that something was wrong, but I offloaded my suspicions on to the house or Owen's absences or even the length of the winter. I cannot say that I still loved him, as I once had done, but I still yearned for him, much as one yearns for a lost opportunity. I wanted to start again, but this time telling the truth, not smiling at inappropriate gifts or being nice to my mother-in-law or welcoming odious guests as if I were delighted to have the opportunity of serving them. I had reached that dangerous state in which I could see every fault that I had committed, and I desired an enormous confrontation so that I could cancel it all and begin again. This, of course, is impossible. Inevitably the false reading of one's own commitment has been supplemented by false readings on the part of everyone else. There is in fact no way back.

I mourned the death of my love for my husband, much as I think he mourned the death of his love for me. In that we were faithful to each other, and well matched. Neither of us, I am convinced, looked outside marriage for consolation; at least I never did, and I think Owen too was innocent in this respect. I considered this rather splendid of him, a badge of his original excellence, for he had many opportunities and was a fine-looking man to whom women were naturally attracted. As time wore on, and his permanently tanned face grew a little redder, and his body a little thicker, I would catch an occasionally puzzled look in his dark blue eyes as if age had surprised him, had taken advantage of his absence on other matters to install itself so insidiously. He did not care for my tender sorrowful approaches to him, and so I learned to suppress them. I think he loved me as much as he was capable of loving a woman, in conditions of intimacy, and for life. I am certain that he trusted me, and that the money left so ostentatiously in his sock drawer, where I should be sure to find it, was his way of confessing to me what was being enacted between himself and his so jovial and hospitable clients. I said nothing, not only because I was frightened and alienated, but because I knew that he would wish me to say nothing. I had by now realized that Owen was emotionally inarticulate – always had been – that the handsome and brazen personage with whom I had fallen in love was in fact in need of my acceptance, and more than that, of my care and protection, which I fully and freely gave.

Although we never recaptured the strange closeness – the almost uncharacteristic closeness – that Nice had previously bestowed on us, we did manage an evening walk or two, when Owen would catch my hand in his, or lay his arm around my shoulders, and when the middle years fell away from us and we felt that we had not done too badly after all. Now that I am old I like to remember that, and am proud to do so.

To Julia the holiday was a disappointment, loudly and freely admitted, and therefore Charlie felt distressed on her behalf. Julia deplored the money being spent, although none of it was hers, and Charlie, who seemed to be a wealthy man, would have spent more, unstintingly, to make her happy. Julia, I now see, and saw even then, was in the throes of such late middle age that it counts as middle age only as a matter of courtesy, and feared the onset of the time when she would have to acknowledge the fact that she was an old lady.

I could see that this was a crisis for a woman as beautiful and as prestigious as Julia, a woman, moreover, who had had a gallant past, but as I was ten years younger myself I simply thought that she was making an unholy fuss and could feel little genuine sympathy. I noted her irritability, promising mentally to do better when my own decline set in. Everything annoyed her, although a genuine expression of annoyance was foreign to her languid nature. If anything, she became more watchful, more acute, more dangerous. She referred more to her previous lovers, knowing that Charlie hated this; she became quite vulgar in her allusions to Owen and myself, when we announced that we were going to take an evening walk. Our wistful, almost elegiac closeness – a closeness which admitted its own lack of mutual understanding – gave her particular offence. She could not see how delicate, how fragile our contact was, or she did not believe in any closeness that was not of a sexual nature. She was a lewd woman, I think, and a cold one. At the same time she could not bear to be left alone, and would only be quiescent when the four of us were together in the bar of the hotel, which had become her salon. Even then she would express soulfulness, disillusionment. She would flap her hand in front of her eyes as if to chase away flies. There are few flies in Nice in December, but Julia managed to make one believe that she was beset by a small colony of them. She was not an actress for nothing. And her particular performances, relying as they did on pause and insinuation, could be used as an excellent instrument in any social game she chose to play.

I could see that she was forlorn, uncomfortable, unhappy even, but my own growing impatience with the boundaries that had been set to my life made me less than indulgent. Indeed, in my own mind I was scornful, convinced that I could do better. I felt what I can only describe as an urchin's irritation at the sight of all this upper-class distress. I had read the story of the princess and the pea, when I was little, and had felt no sympathy at all for the princess. 'But why didn't she just remake the bed?' I had asked my mother. 'Because she was too grand,' my mother had replied, 'and so she didn't know how beds are made.' This had turned into a lesson on how to make my own bed, which I learned very quickly, as I learned all domestic tasks: there was no servant in our house. Whereas Julia, who had never looked after herself, who would not even enter a room unless there were someone in attendance, began to strike me as importunate, faint-hearted, immature. I felt in myself a burgeoning scorn, not only for Julia, but for the acquiescent and mild-mannered Charlie, even for my own husband with his slipshod standards, which had become the standards by which we lived. I would, I thought, give them the slip for a couple of days: all it needed was a little courage. I would put on my walking shoes and tie a scarf round my hair and make for the hills, where we had been happy before. Of course this was a fantasy, destined never to be enacted, but it remained potent and served me well for many years to come.

What condemned me to inaction was my own desire to be liked, or if possible loved – lifelong, this, and hitherto unproblematic – and the attention I wished to give to Owen, to whom I felt myself bound in an entirely new fashion. It was as if I had set my former feelings aside, as if they were out of date, juvenile, even, in some vague way reprehensible. They had, in any event, died a long time ago. What I intended to be now was something more practicable, which was what Owen would have preferred all along. I faced the fact that he would rarely if ever make love to me in the years ahead, and that all I could hope for was his hand, in an unguarded moment, catching hold of mine, or his arm laid about my shoulders. The strange thing was that this realization did not frighten me or even make me indignant, for what was coming into being was a sort of pity. Owen seemed to me pitiable, unshriven. I thought, incongruous though this may seem, of mediaeval peasants, sinful and fearful, waiting eternally for God's judgment. Owen, all unconscious of this dilemma, nevertheless appeared to me in the guise of one who requires sanctuary, pardon. The occasional look of puzzlement in his eye, as if needing help from some unknown source, reminded me of a picture I had seen in the same museum through whose little

59

garden I walked every day: naked souls, their hands joined, the same look of discomfiture on their large-nosed faces, slipping out of the reach of God and His angels into the flames of hell. I had thought the picture naïve, applicable only to the century in which it was painted; now I was not so sure. I found myself going back to see it day after day, but after my first visit it seemed to rebut me. I tried to find out more about it, but even the information on the label seemed deliberately scanty, as if not available to one of so little faith. *Ecole française, XVe. siècle,* it said. And that was Owen to me, slipping away from good to bad, and the only role I was henceforth to play was as guardian, as curator. With this difference now: I could see the need for care. For vigilance, even. I would be Owen's keeper. I would see that he was not cast out.

The pity and sadness that I felt for my husband installed in me a detachment from him that was perhaps long over-due. Our frail closeness was a form of leave-taking: it was commemorative, valedictory. It held compassion for both of us. My task, as I saw it, was to cleave to Owen for the rest of my life, or of his, while acknowledging the fact that I no longer loved him as I would have wished to love him. In this way fate, which had denied me children, would see that my maternal instincts did not go entirely unused. I perceived the irony of this, but I did not appreciate it. There was no doubt in my mind that I could accomplish the task thus set before me but I felt a coldness descend on my spirit, the coldness which marks the recognition that equality in love will never be attained. I knew I was growing older, although I was only in my middle forties – forty-five, to be exact – and I remember that as the thought of my age struck me I got up and went to the mirror. To myself I was unchanged, merely a little heavier, but in the cruel light of the hotel bathroom I could see that my hair was duller than it had been, while my eyes looked strained and anxious. I could see no great alteration until I looked at my hands, which were now freckled with the marks called grave spots; the hands seemed larger, uglier than they had been, as if they had grown old while I was not paying attention. I was still active, still in good health, and it seemed absurd to think in terms of any kind of climacteric, but I knew that it had to come, and for a moment or two I sat in horror, knowing that love had gone and would never return. For I was not as ready to sacrifice myself as I had supposed, or rather I was ready in all conscience, but not with all my instincts: the body still retained its own longing, and I could see that with all the resolution in the world there might be sad times ahead.

We had been away for a fortnight, and it seemed longer. Christmas had come and gone, and New Year's Eve had been spent in a strange bedroom, with alien lights passing over the ceiling and cars hooting outside. On the morning of New Year's Day the hotel bar smelt of whisky and cigarettes, and porters were removing streamers from the lobby, where a party of revellers had come in from the street and had had to be removed. Outside, the sky was a pale blue and the sun shone, but it was colder at last, and I was aware of the immense and unbearable longing I still felt for gratification, plenitude, abundance. The prospect of going home to Gertrude Street almost frightened me into asking Owen if we might stay on for a while. I did not do so, because if Charlie returned Owen would have to go too, and Julia, whose complaints were now louder, had insisted that we leave almost immediately. So that on the morning of the day of our departure – our plane left at 4.30 in the afternoon – I really did give them the slip and went out on my own, not really caring that I had not explained to anyone where I was going or how long I should be. In any case I did not know the answer to either of these questions. I longed for company of an uncomplicated nature, and felt a sudden sharp distaste for the trickiness and compromise that had been our common language for the last two weeks, the dodging of Julia's criticisms, the finely judged reception of her tantrums, my own murderous desire for Charlie to display a little less fortitude and patience, and my longing for Owen to take me by the arm and say to the others, 'You won't mind, will you, if Fay and I escape for a while? We'll see you at the airport on the 8th. Or perhaps we could all have dinner together on our last evening here?' None of this had taken place. Instead there had been an aimlessness, of a kind to ruffle my practical nature, and I wanted, with all the spirit of the girl I had been, to enjoy myself just once, so that the entire fortnight need not have been wasted.

My wants were simple, and were timidly satisfied. I sat in the open air near the market stalls and drank a cup of coffee and listened to the market women greeting each other. How happy, how busy they sounded, and how I envied them! My unhappiness was slowly coming into higher relief now that I contrasted myself with these women, with their red hands and their coarse hair and their splendid teeth. I sat there neatly in my pale blue suit and my fine calf shoes, my bag and gloves on the rough wooden table beside my empty cup of coffee. Then, as I felt time running out, I got up with a sigh, and wandered lingeringly down the streets and back to the hotel. I bought some flower scents for Mother and some yellow hyacinth bulbs for myself. It was, of course, either too early or too late for bulbs, but I would plant them anyway. They would remind me of the South, to which I intended to return some day. I did not see how this could be accomplished, but, like the bulbs, the promise comforted me.

On the plane coming home Owen held my hand, which was unusual. When I looked at his face it was entirely self-absorbed, as if it had nothing to do with the hand that held mine. He had a look of wistfulness and constraint, as if he were waiting for bad news, or as if he were a patient in a hospital. He smiled at me briefly when he felt me looking at him, then turned away to the window. As the light passed over his face I saw a blankness in his eyes. It was gone in an instant, but I saw it, and it shocked me. I somehow knew that nothing in the past few days had happened to reassure him or to cheer him up, and I held his hand more firmly. Darkness filled the space outside the window. When it was complete I knew that we were nearly home.

7

My mother died in the spring of that same year, three months after I had made my decision to resign myself to a life for which I no longer had any taste. This death, on the morning of a cold day in late March, filled me with such despair that I suffered in a very real physical sense, and when I looked around the house in Gertrude Street I felt threatened by an overwhelming panic, as if I had been forcibly put down in alien territory, removed from home against my will, and left alone for ever and ever. This was ridiculous, because I was a middle-aged woman, and, as far as I knew, of sound mind. On the day of her death, after Joan Barber had telephoned me to say that she had found my mother when she went in at her usual time, I rushed out into the silent street, hoping that someone would come to my rescue, throwing myself onto the kindness of strangers. But there was no one about, only the sound of a distant car, which grew briefly louder and then quieter, until it disappeared altogether. I stood in the greyish silence, unable to believe that I should never hear my mother's voice again. After a while a 31 bus turned round the corner and stopped outside the café: the driver climbed down from the cab and went inside. That was the only human presence I encountered that morning, yet I stood there shivering, unable to face the journey and the house that awaited me.

Mother never got to live in the flat of her dreams, with the fitted carpet and the wall lights, and perhaps a few flowerbeds outside tended by a contract gardener. I found her more than one such flat, but she refused to move from the house in which we had all lived when I was young. By the end of her life it had grown very shabby, and although Joan Barber was good about clearing up she was not enterprising enough to see to things like getting the windows cleaned, which I had done, on a step ladder, on my now more frequent visits. I had performed many sad tasks, sad because they spoke of decay. When I went into the kitchen with the food I took over, I could smell stale dusters and dishcloths, hear the tap dripping into the new red plastic basin I had bought her, see that the clock had stopped, that she had not replaced last year's calendar, which still showed September, under a reproduction of Canaletto's *Warwick Castle*. Before taking off my coat I would note what had to be done. The little parcels of cold salmon, of tongue, of fruit tart, the hothouse peach and the madeira cake, would be put into the larder to replace the little parcels left over from my last visit, which had not been touched. Mother refused to eat, either out of genuine incapacity or of languor. I mentioned this to Joan Barber, who said, 'Oh, I see that she has a milky drink every morning. And she likes those biscuits I bring her.' The biscuits were the sort of chocolate and synthetic marshmallow confections that were designed to appeal to children. Thus my mother subsisted on what was not real food, or perhaps the sort of food that an impatient parent would hand out to stop a toddler from grizzling. The sight of an abandoned plate containing a biscuit from which a minute bite had been taken, as if by a child, and which my mother had felt unable to finish, affected me inordinately. It was the first thing I found when I entered the house after her death. It was her last meal.

I think we both knew that she was dying, although I was better at hiding the knowledge from myself than she was. I went on filling the house with factitious business and conversation, hoping to bring at least a faint smile to her face. My basket of morsels small enough to tempt her was unwrapped for her inspection and put away; I would at least be able to persuade her to eat some lunch, and I knew I should be with her every day to perform this little ceremony, although I also knew that the battle was already lost. My mother was not frightened. The discovery of her devotion to my father and his memory had made me jumpy, irritable, as if this were somehow a dangerous path to pursue. She wanted to join him, but I wanted her to live. That was not surprising: I wanted everyone to live – I wanted to live myself. But while I talked to my mother in a brisk voice, mentally noting that the kitchen floor needed cleaning and that I could just manage to do it, as well as washing the tea-towels, before it was time for me to go back to Gertrude Street, she would smile at me, as if in forbearance, as if to humour me, and go off for her rest.

While Mother slept, in her dark bedroom, with the looming old-fashioned furniture and the blue patterned carpet that my father had laid so badly, I scrubbed the floor and did the washing, trying to dispel the sad odours which had built up in that silent kitchen. Soon I was taking over bottles of bleach and disinfectant and going through the house, the whole house, which seemed to me redolent of desertion and neglect. I was like the sorcerer's apprentice, sweeping and polishing under some terrible compulsion, not because my mother wanted me to, but rather because she was now utterly indifferent to her surroundings, did not notice those sad odours, had become an old lady who wore thick stockings and wide shoes, she who had been so fastidious, so critical, so elegant in her modest way. I would make her a cup of tea and take it to her bedroom to wake her: I was anxious to get home before Owen, even anxious to get away from Mother. But she would awaken from her sleep with a slightly renewed sense of – what was it? Energy? Conviction? – and she would ask me about myself. I was too frightened to tell her. I kept up a bright chatter, which sounded too loud in my ears, and so she learned all the unimportant things about my life: what I cooked, what Owen was doing, who was coming to dinner. None of this was of any interest, either to my mother or to myself. Her eyes would be fixed on my face, although her expression indicated absence. 'Do you still sing?' she once interrupted me, as I was telling her about Owen's last trip. 'Sing to me, Fay.' So I held her hand and sang her some of my old songs. It was then that we both knew that she would die very soon.

She was barely seventy, not old enough to die, but her vitality had left her when my father died, and I was not enough to reconcile her to life without him. This was the grief that I carried, almost but not quite unnoticed, throughout my adult life. I could not imagine wanting to die if Owen died, and this too was in a sense forbidden knowledge. Although my mother had grumbled at my father, both of them knew that there was no anger in her reproaches, and she would never be in the slightest sense affected by them. As far as I could see, their life together was unambitious, unremarkable, yet I remember it as happy. The fact that this memory was so strong was crucial to my life, for against it I measured everything that happened to me, principally my marriage. I knew that I was not as happy as my mother had been, although the knowledge, which was ineradicable, took a long time to filter through to my consciousness. My mother thus laid a heavy burden on me without knowing it. But she was not to blame, nor was I ever crass enough to blame her. I can say with pride and gratitude that my mother and I loved each other without a shadow. And in the last two weeks of her life, when she could barely get out of bed, I was with her, going back to Gertrude Street only very late. 'Not up yet?' I had said to her one morning. I said it playfully, to hide my panic. She merely drew aside the bedclothes to show me her swollen legs and feet. So I let her stay there, although my instinct was to import nurses, doctors, even to get her admitted to hospital. I did none of these things, but it was a struggle to know how to behave in the face of the great separation which was soon to overtake us. I sang to her, and when I felt the tears rising in my throat I hurried out of the room and prepared the milk and the childish biscuits that she liked, or at that stage pretended to like. In the end she slept more and more. Once she woke up, looked at me, and sighed.

'Fay,' she whispered. 'Fay.' 'What is it?' I said. But she never spoke again.

When I left her that evening she was calm and smiling, although she said nothing, merely pressed my hand and held it to her face. I thought it safe to go home. Or did I? Perhaps I could stand no more. I left the house at ten o'clock, and she must have died in the night, because when Joan Barber let herself in on the following morning there was no sign of life: the tap still dripped into the red plastic basin, but that was all – no answer to her call, no stirring as she went up the stairs into the bedroom. She came down again and telephoned me. When I got there the first thing I saw was the abandoned biscuit with which I had tried to tempt her the previous day. Otherwise everything was in order. She had made a will some time before and had given it to me for safe-keeping. She had nothing to leave me but the house, and so it became mine. I think she still regarded it as my natural, my only home. In this she was prescient. But because it enshrined so much love, love that could never come again, I also knew that I would sell it when the time came. This I never told her.

I was surprised by the number of people who came to the funeral, for as far as I knew Mother saw nobody. Yet those of my father's friends who had survived her turned up faithfully. My father had been a popular man, and his easy simple conviviality had been shared by men like himself, small-time, respectable, in a humble way of business. They came, in their unflattering oblong overcoats and their trilby hats, old men now, eyes watering with the cold or with reminiscence, cigarettes lit with shaky hands. They kissed me as a matter of course: was I not in their eyes still a child? And they promised me their help if I should ever need it: I had only to get in touch. Business cards and pieces of paper bearing telephone numbers were handed over. Owen became impatient, as he had been throughout the ceremony. Once it was over he got in the car and went off to Hanover Square. I went back to the house and served sherry and seed cake to the old men and their wives. Then I cleared up, and carefully locked the front door behind me. 'Take a taxi, Fay,' I heard Mother say. So I took a taxi and went back to Gertrude Street. There was nowhere else to go.

Owen was furious at being exposed to my humble origins, for he had managed to forget them, or to overlook them. The tap dripping in the red plastic basin, the old men at the funeral, shook him out of whatever complacency was left to him. My preoccupation with my mother's dwindling life had been merciful in one way: it had helped me not to think about Owen's business affairs, which I now suspected were irregular. I surmised that he was keeping part of the money due to the firm and must have been falsifying accounts. Naturally I could not prove this, nor did I ever know whether or not my suspicions were correct. I think now that something was on Charlie's mind, and that Owen was questioned, but that he was able to give a reassuring account of himself. Owen had brought a great deal of money into the firm in the way of fees: he had a number of important clients, whose lordly manner, it was assumed, had recommended itself to him. Nothing was said, but I have an inkling that a mild word of warning was issued. Coming from Charlie it would have been deceptively mild, but Owen took notice of it. There were in addition one or two telephone calls from his uncle, Bernard Langdon, which left him red-faced and seething. I could be nothing but an additional irritant to him, and I learned to contain my grief, or at least not to display it when Owen was at home, which he was quite frequently then, not out of deference but out of prudence. For a few weeks he went off to Hanover Square every morning like a model employee. I never asked him what transpired there, nor would he have told me if I had. He merely asked me how the sale of the house was progressing. I think he considered it might be a good idea to have some money in reserve, in case any should be demanded of him. I had no idea how things were to be managed. Fortunately, or unfortunately, I was too taken up with my own sadness to brood for long on my husband's troubles. This was only one indication of the estrangement I had begun to notice.

I was very lonely during the weeks that followed my mother's death. I knew that I should never again be all the world to anyone, as it says in the song. Normally I despise women who claim never to have got over their parents' death, or who affirm that their fathers were the most perfect men who had ever lived. I despise them, but I understand them. How can any later love compensate for the first, unless it is perfect? My simple parents had thought me unique, matchless, yet they had let me go away from them without a murmur of protest. I tried to ask myself whether I could have done more – been more – than was really the case, but it was too late, and the questions seemed artificial even as I asked them. Parents do die, and children survive them: moreover I was in my fifth decade and had left childhood far behind. Yet at that time I grew wistful, thinking of all that I had lost or forgone. I had voluntarily entered a world in which a certain obliquity seemed to be taken for granted, pretty manners hiding a very real indifference. No one was unkind to me. But I felt a coldness in the atmosphere whenever my mother-in-law was present, and I was oppressed by the knowledge that I must continue to dance attendance on Julia, if only to please Charlie, on whose goodwill Owen depended. But I saw it for what it was; there was no question of love, or even liking. Even Owen, from whom I now expected little, disappointed me.

I remember at that time I went to the hairdresser's. I did this regularly, but I remember that visit for two particular reasons. The first was that next to me was a young mother with a little girl aged about three. The child, whose hair was about to be cut for the first time, screamed with terror and clung to her mother. The hairdresser stood by gravely, comb in hand: he recognized that this was a serious moment. The mother, blushing, tried to comfort the child who had suddenly plunged into despair; all around the shop women smiled in sympathy. What impressed me, and what I particularly remember, was the child's passionate attempt to re-enter her mother, the arms locked around the woman's neck, the terrified cries of unending love. So dangerous is it to be so close! I had tears in my eyes, witnessing that bond, seeing that closeness, of which only a sorrowful memory remained in my own life. One loses the capacity to grieve as a child grieves, or to rage as a child rages: hotly, despairingly, with tears of passion. One grows up, one becomes civilized, one learns one's manners, and consequently can no longer manage these two functions – sorrow and anger – adequately. Attempts to recapture that primal spontaneity are doomed, for the original reactions have been overlaid, forgotten. And so the feelings are kept inside one, and perhaps this is better in the long run. A child forgets easily, whereas it is an adult's duty to remember. But this proves hard, sometimes.

When it was my turn (and the child was soon smiling, and proud of her new short hair) the hairdresser – John, such a nice man – looked at my reflection in the mirror, and said, 'You've got a lot more grey coming through. Have you thought of a tint? I can introduce it quite carefully, while you've still got some colour. Then nobody will notice.' But I felt a little faint and was anxious to get out into the air. Possibly the child had upset me, or I was not eating enough. 'Let me think about it, John,' I said. 'I'll let you know next time.' He lifted the hair from my neck, ran his fingers gently through it, something my own husband never thought of doing. 'It's good hair,' he said. 'Don't let it go to waste.' It had been pretty, a light reddish blonde, the sort of natural attribute for which one was admired in the old days. Now it looked quite colourless, although still light. I gave no thought to my looks at that time and regarded the obligation to take care of them as one more of my duties. It was certainly not a pleasure. I was a middle-aged woman, and not making too good a job of it: loveless, mourning my mother, without children of my own, and beginning to regret my youth. 'Perhaps when you're feeling a little brighter,' said kind John, and because he was so kind, so discreet, I nodded gratefully, paid the bill, and made my escape.

It was a beautiful spring, so beautiful that even being out in the street was a pleasure. There were intimations of happiness in the mere fact that yet again fruit trees had blossomed, and after-noons were bright with the first strong sun of the year. I took to wandering, although I still found the district unwelcoming.

Solitude became important to me then, and has remained so. Mother would have said, 'Out of bad comes good,' and this realization gave me extraordinary comfort. There had been little comfort of any other sort. Vinnie had paid me a visit of condolence, although she had no time for me these days, and had not quite forgiven me for earlier reprimands. She sat at the kitchen table, swiftly eating a plate of bread and butter and evidently annoyed that there was nothing more substantial on offer. 'You'll sell the house, of course,' she said, poking at the corners of her mouth with her terrible handkerchief. 'What will you do with the money?' She seemed to think this quite a legitimate question, as perhaps it was. 'A little cottage somewhere? Owen has always wanted to live in the country, and of course I was brought up in Sussex. Etchingham. Near Eastbourne,' she added kindly. 'We could all go down in the car one day and look round. Perhaps *two* cottages,' she added coyly. 'So that I could be near my boy. And you too, Fay, of course.' I could hear myself making smiling sounds of interest even as I decided to ignore her.

And Julia came, one evening, on Charlie's arm. I thought that was decent of her. But Julia knew about mothers and was devoted to her own, that still pretty, rather silly woman, so appreciative of her daughter's looks and accomplishments that she was her most perfect audience. 'Have a whisky, darling,' one of them would say to the other; it hardly mattered which, for their voices were astonishingly alike. Mrs Wilberforce confined herself to the most general of remarks and was thus extremely easy to get along with. She had always appeared pleasant enough, largely, I think, because it was in her interest to do so, but also because she was not a reflective sort of woman. She was another of Charlie's pensioners, and as long as she had access to her daughter and to the amenities of Charlie's flat, which included his whisky and cigarettes, she was relatively contented. 'Too terrible for you,' said Julia. 'I came as soon as I heard.' This cannot have been true: my mother had been dead for over a month. But then why should Julia know that? As usual I was having to do battle with my own scepticism,

71

although I was curiously comforted by the visit. 'If Mummy went I don't know what I'd do,' said Julia in a melancholy voice. 'All the husbands in the world couldn't make up for her. Although of course Charlie is my prop and mainstay.'

She was right, I reflected; she was more daughter than wife, whereas I had had it in me to be more wife than daughter. My expectations had not been fulfilled, but that was in the nature of an accident. Owen had come along and I had fallen in love with him. I had not known then that it is not necessary to marry every man one loves. I know it now. Now I realize that it is marriage which is the great temptation for a woman, and that one can, and perhaps should, resist it. I should have resisted it, or rather I should have resisted it then and given it a chance to come along later. But as a young woman one loses heart so easily, and then one wants all the appurtenances of marriage, the excitement, and the security, and the promise of a new life. And it is so sad to go without. I think differently now. But old women have more courage than young ones. They have no choice but to be brave.

I put the house on the market and told Joan Barber, who had kept her key, to take whatever she wanted in the way of furniture or linen. I neither wished nor needed to have any reminders of my mother's life. I knew for a fact that the house had been run down, that the furniture, though comfortable, had always been ugly, and that her clothes, which had once been so pretty, were long out of date. I thought that perhaps Joan could use the material to make dresses for her little girl. My mother would have liked that, to see her floral prints and dark silks given a new lease of life in this way. Joan, to my relief, took a great deal; her husband went over in his van and moved out some of the easier tables and chairs. When I visited the house for the last time there was surprisingly little left, only the looming wardrobes and the shadowy dressing-table in my parents' bedroom, and the marks on the walls where the bookcases had stood. I visited each of the rooms, mentally saying goodbye, for I knew that I should never go back. Owen was again furious when he asked me, and I told him, what Joan had taken. 'You mean you just gave her the run of the place? You must be mad, Fay. I hope you don't think you're a rich woman now. That money should go straight into the bank. You can have your own account, if you like, but I think you ought to realize how much the upkeep of this house costs me. And it's not as if you're contributing in any way. I don't mean that,' he added wearily. 'It's just that my expenses are rather heavy at the moment.'

Millie came, bless her, and we had a lovely afternoon, sitting over the teacups as we used to do. Millie had known my mother and had accepted her as a natural part of our friendship. Some people, like my husband, allow one no access to their feelings, regard any enquiry as an encroachment. I had had to live with such people and I had not found it easy. But Millie reminded me that there were other, more fruitful ways of being. She cried easily, and just as easily brightened, her cheeks flushing with a lovely colour, to tell me how happy she was, married to her BBC sound engineer. He was some years older than she was, which we all thought rather exciting at the time, but he was a man who managed his life well and who adored his wife. He had a house near Oxford, to which he had planned to retire, and a bachelor flat in London, where he sometimes stayed overnight if he were working late. I asked Millie if she were content with a country life, for she had always been such a vivacious outgoing girl. (One could also be admired for being vivacious, in our day.) She told me that marrying Donald had made her happier than she had ever thought possible. She was radiant as she said this: there was no doubt in her mind. When she met Donald he had been a widower with two grown-up children, the least likely husband for a girl like Millie. But there had always been a certainty about their partnership that impressed me; there was a oneness between Millie and her husband that precluded any questions or comments.

The proof lay in the fact that she loved everything about him, and in turn loved his house, his children, with whom she got on extremely well, her new life away from all her friends, and even Donald's life, which meant absences in London, sometimes for the inside of a week, including nights. The mutual trust that existed between them gave her a relaxed wide-eyed appearance, and a permanent and charming half-smile. I have seen women who look like this – as if they were carrying on a conversation with their companion while going about their ordinary business – and they are usually married. If they have been really happy the smile will even survive widowhood. Divorce, never. I felt humble in the face of Millie's certainty, which I had never known myself. I had felt trembling gratitude, anxiety, exaltation, even fear: I had won Owen in the teeth of great opposition. And he had let himself be won, in a lazy but practical sort of way. My excess of feeling had amused him, for he had none of his own. Of the two of us he was the more passive, but also the more business-like; energy was for work, not for love. We had managed, somehow, although we both knew that this was a misalliance. For this reason we both deserved a little credit.

I said none of this to Millie; I had not spoken of it to anyone, and never should. I saw signs of age in her glossy complexion, now almost innocent of make-up, and the lines around her smiling mouth. She wore country clothes, a tweed skirt and a corduroy jacket. Yet she looked vital, viable, in a way which was no longer available to me; there was an energy there which had to do with plenty. She had brought a full basket with her, eggs from her local shop, jam she had made herself – Millie making jam! – and apples from their own trees which she had stored through the winter. She was in that blessed state of love that makes it natural to give. 'I go to church now,' she told me happily. 'Well, I've been so lucky, haven't I?' And she told me all about Donald's children with as much enthusiasm as if they had been her own.

Tying a scarf over her hair as she prepared to leave, she said, with a slight return to her old manner, 'Do you like this house, Fay? It gives me the creeps, if you don't mind my saying so. Those colours! Can't you persuade Owen to do something about them?'

'He likes them, that's the trouble. And he wouldn't hear of my spending money on something that doesn't need doing.'

'Well, why don't you move? Honestly, it's a bit quiet round here, isn't it? Doesn't it get you down?'

'Oh, no,' I said. 'I'm used to it.'

'I think I prefer our village. Why don't you come and stay? When Owen's away? Of course, we'd love to see him, but it's you I really want. Do come, Fay. You've only to pick up the phone, you know.'

'I'd love to,' I said, and I really meant to go, but somehow I put it off. I felt she should be shielded from my unhappiness.

After Millie had left I climbed the stairs, almost heavily for a woman of my age, and thought how the two of us were getting older. Owen and I were going out to dinner that evening, so I ran a bath, took off my clothes, and looked at myself in the long glass. That is when I saw the softness at my waist, the lines round my neck, the loosening flesh of my upper arms, the widening of the hips, the ashy hair. I had not felt these things happening. The process, so far, had been benign, but inexorable. I shed a tear then, not out of vanity but from some sadness that had touched me and that had to do with women who still thought of themselves as girls, even after their youth had gone.

My grief for my mother, which I had felt most acutely during her last illness rather than as a result of her death, affected me in a curious way. What youthfulness I had left deserted me: it was as if she had taken it with her. I felt a sad impatience with the childish memories that assailed me, for although the memories were insistent I knew that I was too old to succumb to them and not yet old enough to marvel at them. I felt drained of tenderness, of curiosity, of the emotions that sweeten existence. I was harsh, desolate, yet determined to protect my condition from the easy offerings of public sympathy. My mother's absence I reserved for my own contemplation and for such time as I might have the strength to mourn her properly. She was still too near to me. I should have to wait until I knew that each of us could survive without the other.

8

We had a wonderful summer that year, hot, steady and brilliant. Each day was like the last, so that, unusually for England, one could rely on a continuity that had something prodigious about it. The effect on our vitality was also prodigious. We woke gratefully to the sun before six o'clock and drank our early cup of tea at the window, gazing out at that astonishing light. I would see Owen off to work, rejoicing in the long day ahead of me: I could not wait to get out. My shopping gave me pleasure. The beautiful fruits of summer proved irresistible, and I bought more than I needed, for their colour and their scent; these I made into tarts and pies, which I stowed away against Vinnie's next visit. It was natural for me to cook for someone else, and possibly I regretted the little parcels I used to prepare for my mother, although Vinnie was no substitute in that respect. I tried to like her, but almost consistently came up against a watchfulness which I found unfriendly. She regarded me as a rival, and perhaps always had: she was one of those self-flattering women who convince themselves that they come first in their son's affections. Owen found Vinnie a bore but felt irritably contracted to her. I knew that he made her an allowance; I also knew that she was an impractical woman who frequently had unforeseen expenses. Owen was generous to her because he understood the impulse to spend money – they both had it. My feeling now is that they shared a vast boredom; they were terrified of nothing happening. Vinnie's haplessness came from a sort of despair, a conviction that no one would care for her or even notice her, while Owen's case was perhaps more serious. In the absence of distractions he foundered, became blank. That was why he put up with a way of life that would have exhausted many men of his age, why he pursued this fantasy of endless mobility, endless availability. I believe it gratified him even to know that he was expected in a certain place at a certain time. He had the fullest diary of anyone I have ever known. When things were going well for him there was an ardour about him that was still very persuasive. But I came to understand that he must not be balked or hindered, that nothing pleased him so much as pleasing himself. I also came to understand that although married he must be allowed to live as a bachelor. Women, I think, did not appeal to him so much as the opportunity to be someone's companion for a day, for a week, before flying off to the next bit of business, the next house party – for there was always a party when Owen was expected, or that is how it seemed to me. He feared permanence. Maybe he even feared the knowledge that he was committed to someone for life. It was, after all, against his nature, yet I think I made things easy for him. Once I admitted to myself that he should never have married me, or I him, we made a relatively good job of it. To think too deeply about these matters was not in my best interest. Owen, I imagine, took his marriage for granted and gave it no further thought.

I came to accept all this because Owen struck me as phe-nomenal and always had. If it was his desire to live as he did, it was no desire of mine to prevent him from doing so. I could not understand him, and so, to a certain extent, I felt lonely even in his company, but that was because after all those years he was still a stranger to me. But I was getting stronger. Exceptional circumstances, I knew, would somehow bring us together, and that beautiful summer, when we drank an early cup of tea sitting at the small table near our bedroom window, entranced us to such an extent that when it was time to begin the serious business of getting ready for the day we would look at each other and smile like children, for pleasure. I like to remember that. Sometimes in the evenings we would be drawn to the same window to watch the sky turn a light green and the first star appear. It seemed never to be dark. When we went to bed we slept, again like children.

Those summer days, smelling of fruit, were very kind to me, and I think I was as happy as I had ever been. I wore a cotton dress and sandals all day, ate a bit of bread and cheese for my lunch, and walked about in what I considered to be my private time, that fierce hour between two and three in the afternoon, when the sun was at its hottest, when the sounds of cars died away into the distance, and when men in shirt sleeves left pubs looking stupefied and happy, as if they were on holiday. Everyone seemed to be experiencing pleasure. My own pleasures were simple; I was a quiet person who needed few distractions. It was enough to wander the streets, knowing that nobody could find me. I felt an odd freedom, began to see that some of my obligations were self-imposed and could be taken less seriously. The cup of coffee I made myself when I got back home marked the end of that particular interlude and the beginning of the time when I was simply an adjunct to somebody else, Vinnie, Owen. But it was a good time. When Owen came home we ate early. We ate cold veal with a tunny sauce and strawberry tart. Owen was with me for quite a long spell that summer. Most people were away. We almost never went away because with Owen's schedule the only place where he could have a rest was Gertrude Street. Even during those rest periods he was always making telephone calls, then kissing me briefly, saying, 'Don't wait up,' and going off to meet someone. I got used to it. Most women married to ambitious and effective men do.

When he told me that he would be gone for a few days, that the Mulgroves were thinking of moving from their present house near Cannes to a larger one further along the coast, near the Italian border, I was a little sorry but not altogether surprised. An early morning cup of tea at the table near the bedroom window may have been pleasure enough for me but it was hardly the sort of thing to distract Owen for long. We had had a very nice couple of weeks, during which he had been slower than usual and I had been quicker; the heat affected us both in different ways, but in a manner which brought us into some sort of equality, levelling out the rhythms that separated us. Owen asked me, exceptionally, whether I would like to accompany him. 'Oh, no,' I said. 'The weather is so perfect here that it couldn't be better anywhere else. Anyway, you'll be back at the weekend. And you'll move more quickly without me.' He didn't mind; he never minded going off alone on his adventures. I was getting used to my own company, which I was discovering as a precious resource, and one which I desired to explore. I was looking forward to my few days on my own.

I sent him off in his pale blue seersucker suit in which he looked so handsome. He was still an impressive man, ruddy, solid, his blond hair thinning a bit, but with an air of indestructibility greatly increasing with the passage of time. Women have often envied me my husband, with his alertness, his shrewdness, his air of prosperity. In many ways I knew myself to be fortunate. The only trouble was that I never knew what went on in his head. I think he was probably driven by a daemon, since sex and affection played so small a part in his life. His energy, which was so far above the average, and which earned him so much appreciation from men and so many admiring glances from women, masked, I think, a personality which despised, which feared weakness. If weaknesses, misgivings, even loneliness were there, they must never be shown, must never be given a chance to manifest themselves. Anything less than a show of strength was forbidden.

While he was away I sat in the garden, which Hermione had had conveniently paved over, and when that seemed too uneventful I would walk up to the park, taking some bread for the birds. I knew that I was behaving in a juvenile manner but it pleased me to do so, and to talk to the mothers with small babies. How beautiful they looked! I no longer regretted not having children, although other women's children attracted me irresistibly. I was getting older, and I tried not to have regrets.

Perhaps not having been loved was one of them. But one gets used even to that. Perhaps the snatch of a song revives it, one of the old songs, but even then one learns to manage.

Everyone was away. Julia and Charlie were away, so there were no telephone calls beginning with the admonitory 'Now look here!'; no summonses to Onslow Square, no long, meaningless, decorative, but occasionally menacing conversations, no opportunity to discuss unsuspected or unnoticed shortcomings. These days alone provided me with perfect peace, and also the opportunity to be myself again, as I had been as a girl. With the light so bright I would get up early, have my bath, do the washing, all before breakfast. My shopping was finished by half past nine, my cooking completed and cleared away an hour later. Then the day was mine. Nothing to do except refresh my face, tidy my hair, take my purse and go out. My activities were completely inconsequential; they were simply a pretext for being out in that glorious light. Sometimes I wandered into town and had a sandwich and a cup of coffee for my lunch at inconspicuous cafés – one could still find them – counting the money out from my purse as if I were a schoolchild out alone for the first time. Then I would make my way back to the house, which did not seem so ghastly when the brilliant sun outside made the uncompromising colours look as striking as perhaps Hermione had intended them to look. Nobody bothered me. On two occasions, as I stepped into the blue drawing-room, I felt a vibration in the air, as if the telephone had stopped ringing. I took no notice; I did not wish to be disturbed. I assumed that the calls were for Owen, as they usually were. I could not have done much good if I had answered them: I had no idea where he was. I was alone and free, my last experience of these conditions. I have been alone ever since, and free, perhaps, as some would see it, but I have never been so unburdened as I was in those two or three days. Even now, looking back, I see it as a blessed time.

I was out for most of every day, and I was tired when I got home. I discovered the pleasures of going to bed early, with a book. I thought it might be quite possible to live like this, much later, when I was old. I was in bed, watching the sky deepen outside the window when the telephone rang. The call was from Bernard Langdon, Owen's uncle, who told me that Owen and Jack Mulgrove had been killed. They had been travelling towards Menton in Jack's new car, had taken an inland road to avoid the dazzle and glare of the upper corniche, and had come to grief a little way beyond Eze. A boy had found the curiously silent car smashed against a tree at the roadside. The road had been deserted; the fierceness of the sun had decreed a long siesta. The boy had reported the incident to the police. There was no uncertainty; Jack's wallet had been found and Owen's diary. At first sight it looked as if Jack had had a heart attack. The consul at Nice had been informed, and, failing to make contact with me – that telephone ringing in an empty room – had got on to the office.

'You'll have to go out there, Fay,' said Bernard. 'I've booked you on an early flight tomorrow morning. Frances and I will follow later in the day. There are certain formalities to be gone through. Knowing the French, there will be quite a few. The funeral, and so on. Unless you want him brought back here?'

'Dead?' I said. 'No, not true. Owen can't be dead.' But I knew suddenly that he was, and a great coldness spread over me, despite the heat of the night.

'Now listen, Fay,' Bernard went on. 'Your plane leaves at nine o'clock, there's no problem there. Your ticket is waiting for you at the Air France desk. Unfortunately, I've had great trouble finding you an hotel room. Everything seems to be booked; it's the height of the season. I've got you something, but I don't know what it's like. It's the Hôtel de Plaisance, in the Baumettes district. Rue des Baumettes. Are you writing this down? Frances and I will stay with the Spencers at Villefranche. I'm afraid you'll be alone some of the time. Stay at the Plaisance until we arrive in the late afternoon. Don't do anything until I get there. Just telephone the consulate and give them your number. Fay? Have you got that? I can't talk long, my dear. I'll have to go round and tell Vinnie. Just get yourself to Nice and wait for me.'

'Owen dead?' I repeated into a silent telephone. 'Dead?'
My voice became high, incredulous. 'Dead?' I must have said
it several times to the dialling tone. And finally, when no one
answered, I got up and stood at the window. I stood there for
most of the night, I think, seeing Owen in his pale blue seersucker suit, with his pigskin bag, ready, anxious to be away.
I felt unable to leave the relative safety of the bedroom and
that window. I sat, finally, at the table where we had had
our morning tea, and thought of the impossibility of Owen's
death, and how cruel it was that he should have died when he
was enjoying himself. The sun, the beautiful air, the friendly
proximity of the rich and powerful should not have ended
with heart failure and the impact of a car against a tree on
a deserted roadside. I knew that I had to see him, and the sudden
urgency brought me stumbling to my feet. I pulled a suitcase
from the cupboard and put in a nightdress and a hairbrush and
a dark blue dress. I had no black and would not have worn it
even if the perfect and appropriate garment had been available.
Despite the growing heat of the early day I dressed in a suit, a
cream-coloured linen suit, hopeless for travelling, and a cream
silk blouse. I have never been comfortable in that colour since.
I was out on the street before seven o'clock, unfed, desperate.
I got a taxi straight away.

During the flight I felt ill. I could feel real illness threatening.
The sleeves of my silk blouse darkened with sweat and my
head was hammering, with one of those migraines that came
to plague me in times of great distress. The stewardess gave
me a cup of coffee and two aspirins, and asked me if there
were anyone to meet me at the other end. 'No one,' I said. No
one would ever meet me again. I was alone, and now, at last,
I knew the true meaning of loneliness. The contentment I had
felt during the two or three empty days of Owen's absence had
been a lure: this was the real thing, and it was terrible. I doubted
my ability to get from the airport to the hotel, to sit out the time
until Bernard came. My linen skirt was already crumpled, my
feet swollen. I did not see how I could be expected to leave the
plane. Yet what I wanted above everything else was to see Owen

and to talk to him, to ask him how this thing had happened. I wanted to hear it from his lips alone. After a while this seemed to me entirely feasible.

'My husband is waiting for me,' I told the kind stewardess, who took a handkerchief from my bag and wiped away my tears. 'I was wrong when I said that no one would come for me. At least, not entirely wrong. I have to go to him.' 'Let this lady off first,' the stewardess said sometime later, shepherding me to the door. 'She needs to lie down.'

Then the true nightmare began, in comparison with which everything earlier had been a rehearsal. The heat, which had been beneficent in London, was ferocious in Nice. The leather seats of the taxi were scorching, the driver's cigarette a burn in my throat. The blinding sun entered my aching eyes like a sword. I had no dark glasses. I felt faint and sick in turn. All I wanted to do now was to reach the Hôtel de Plaisance and to sleep. Bernard could wake me when he came. And then I would see Owen.

The Hôtel de Plaisance was in a narrow corridor off a street dark in shadow, a populous commercial street now emptying for the midday lunch hour. I rang a bell on the desk, and a bulky looking woman emerged from behind a smoked glass door, wiping her mouth. She gave me a key, and I trudged up a narrow staircase, past a green plant in a brass pot on a tiny landing: the room I let myself into was small and dark and smelt of somebody else. Thick dusty tulle curtains covered a window which would not open. Two flies circled endlessly around the bulb of a central light. Outside, somewhere below me, empty bottles were being stacked, new cases being manoeuvred out towards the street entrance. I went downstairs and asked the woman if I could have a cup of coffee. 'On ne fait pas de cuisine ici,' she said. 'Vous avez le bistrot en face.' I gave up, went back upstairs, and fell on the bed. I must have slept, for the next thing I heard was the weak jangle of the telephone, which woke me. Bernard had arrived.

By that time, in the beautiful evening, with the lights blooming in the indigo sky and the air redolent of vanilla,

I was weak and shaking, and did not know where I was going. I sat next to Bernard in a taxi, my teeth chattering. He was enormously uncomfortable, muttered slightly to himself, clearly would have wished to perform this task alone. 'Vinnie took it very badly,' he said. 'She wants me to bring him home. How do you feel about that? Fay? Now, compose yourself, my dear. We have to formally identify him, you know. Will you be up to it, or do you want me to do it?'

'Oh, no,' I said. 'I want to see him.'

'He may be, how can I put it? Damaged,' he said, taking my elbow. 'We're here now. Be brave.' He was a ghastly colour. Why not? The dead inspire fear. But I rushed forward, my ankles twisting, into what I suppose was a mortuary. In a room in a basement, with strip lighting humming in a concrete ceiling, a man in a green cotton uniform pulled open what looked like the drawer of a filing cabinet. Inside was Owen, still in his pale suit, the right leg and sleeve of which had been cut away. There was a huge bruise on the side of his head. His feet, his beautiful marble feet, were bare. The expression on his face was strained, almost ecstatic, as I had sometimes seen it, as nobody else should see it. Bernard, a handkerchief to his mouth, nodded to the man, who slid the drawer shut again. 'No,' I said. 'I want to see him again. I want to stay with him.' Bernard pulled me outside, and then I fainted.

When I came round I was sitting on a wooden chair in somebody's office. 'Come along, my dear,' said Bernard. 'There is only one thing more to be done tonight, but it is important. This paper has to be signed by his next of kin. No one else can do it. It is important,' he sighed, pressing his handkerchief to his upper lip. 'Permission for burial to go ahead.'

'Here?' I said.

He nodded. 'The heat,' he said. 'They do not advise moving the body.'

I fainted again then. I fainted several times during the following two days, so that I was not able to attend the funeral and to see Owen put into the ground. I was not sorry. Frances came to me afterwards and talked to me as I lay on my bed in the Hôtel de Plaisance, still in my creased suit, one shoe fallen to the floor. I think she must have realized that I was better kept out of sight. Then, when there was nothing more to be done, they brought me home.

I arrived home in the early evening of a grey drizzling day in early September. The weather had broken in my absence and it was almost cold. I looked curiously at the house in Gertrude Street. Was I supposed to live here? I stood on the pavement gazing in perplexity at the silent façade. It worried me that Owen had left no message, no instructions. I did not know what he wanted me to do. I was so tired, so weak, that my inclination was to do nothing, yet even in my debilitated condition I knew that I should have to leave that house, which had never belonged to me and of which I had never felt a part. But I was no longer used to making decisions on my own, and in my mind I felt timid, uncertain. I even felt uncertain about entering the house and only did so when rain trickled from my hair on to my forehead. I managed to put on a kettle and make a cup of tea which I drank with lemon since the milk, which had been on the doorstep, was sour. The sharpness of the lemon made me wince. What I craved was sweetness, comfort. I would have welcomed the chance to regress, but none came; there was no soothing voice. I took off my filthy suit and the soiled blouse and put them aside to be thrown away, together with everything else I was wearing. Then, naked, unwieldy, I crossed to the bedroom on painful feet and fell into bed and slept. I slept for nearly twelve hours and aged several years in the course of that long night.

I awoke clear-headed, rational, even cold. It was a curious state of mind; I felt fatalistic, reduced, even slightly mean-spirited. I felt bitterly towards Owen for the frivolous circumstances in which he had died. I even – and this was a shock to me – saw him as what he was, a not very ideal husband. The ultimate frustration of not knowing what he wanted or thought or intended was with me very forcibly. I was conscious of the fact that he had left me alone – for ever, this time – and I resented it. I was dull, rancorous. I did not know then that one frequently fails to live up to the enormity of death. I even felt hungry. I had not eaten much for days, and there was no food in the house. I glanced out of the window at what I could see of the grey wet street, then I swung my legs out of Hermione's outsize bed and went downstairs.

After I had drunk another cup of acid tea, had bathed and washed my hair, and dressed in a grey skirt and a grey cardigan – for this seemed the nearest thing to black – I took my basket and prepared to go round to Vinnie. I glanced down the hall, looked at the silent telephone. Silence was to be my burden, my portion. I did not expect anyone to care what happened to me in the future. It occurred to me that I was free, as I never wanted to be free. I experienced this freedom as a sort of shame. If I was free it was because nobody needed me, because there had been a failure of some sort. It would be a matter of discretion to disappear from the lives of Vinnie and Bernard, and of course, Charlie and Julia; no one, I thought, would press me to stay. In fact the partners at Hanover Square might be relieved that I made no further demands on them. There was the little matter of the money in Owen's drawer, which I thought I might hand over to Charlie, together with an account of Owen's death. Fortunately he was away and not due back for a week. I would give him my new address as a matter of courtesy but I did not expect to see either of them again. For I had known, even in the fatigue of the previous evening, that I must move.

I am a simple woman, and always was. But my life had become complicated, and I had actively encouraged the process. My husband, his friends, my mother-in-law, this awful house, suddenly seemed extraneous to me. I even longed, as my mother had once done, for a little flat somewhere, with a tidy kitchen and a cosy bedroom, and perhaps a balcony. I could live there unnoticed for the rest of my days, tempting my appetite with modest delicacies, watching television, following serials on the radio. I should not be missed: I had been too marginal. It was my duty now to be obscure and self-sufficient, as befits all widows. I felt no great surprise at my decision. My only concern was that I might not have the strength to find that flat, to go through the wearisome process of selling the house and storing the furniture, which I did not want. I would ask Bernard to handle the legal side of things for me. He might even like the house for his son, whose wife was expecting her third child. I longed to hand it over, and to disappear.

When I saw Vinnie I knew that she had been dealt a blow from which she would never recover. She sat huddled in her chair, in her pink suit, oblivious to her ruined face on which all the colours had run. She clutched a man's handkerchief, and there was a glass of whisky beside her, but her hands were shaking too much for her to reach for it. I went into the kitchen and made her some hot coffee, knelt beside her while I guided the cup to her mouth. She did not seem to resent me, although I could not cry. This, I knew, she would remember later, when she recounted the story to her friends.

'Let me put you to bed, Vinnie,' I said. 'You're shivering. It's the shock.'

'Fay,' she said, smearing the colours on her face with the handkerchief she held to her shaking mouth. 'My heart is broken.' Those were the simplest and the truest words she had ever spoken to me, and I put my arms round her and held her tiny body to mine. Then I put her to bed and sat with her until she slept. On my way out I alerted a neighbour, a Mrs Bliss, who promised to keep an eye on her. I reminded myself to get keys cut, for Mrs Bliss and for myself. Then I went back to Gertrude Street and sat in a darkening room until it was late enough for me to go to bed as well.

On the following morning I made an appointment to see Bernard at the office. This, I thought, was the correct thing to do. I did not want to embarrass him further after my inadequate behaviour in Nice, and in truth what had we to discuss other than business? At Hanover Square I met serious faces and condolences; my hand was shaken, my shoulder patted several times by people I hardly knew, for I had only seen them at Christmas parties. Bernard looked old and tired. He seemed to be in a worse state than I was. I was still cold and clear-headed, although physically weak. I knew that I should not feel better until I could get into that little place of my own, where I could live my own small life, undisturbed.

'Bernard,' I said, rather quickly, for he looked ill and this was a strain on him. The journey had upset him; these days he did not like to move farther than his house in Wiltshire. 'I'll have to sell Gertrude Street. I was wondering if Paul and Caroline would like to have it.'

His face brightened. 'I know they would,' he said. 'They were looking for something bigger. And Caroline is having rather a difficult time,' He paused. 'I'll have it valued for you, if you're sure.'

'I'm sure,' I said. 'And I don't want a great price for it. Just enough to buy me a little flat and to provide something for Vinnie. I thought you might handle the money for her. Bernard, I think she's very poorly. I must pay someone to look after her.'

'Yes, yes.' He sighed. 'When would you want to move?'

'I'll start looking for a flat. There's no need for a valuation.'

He looked shocked. 'Things must be done properly, Fay. You want to get it all over now, I know, but there's the future to think of. How will you live, my dear?'

'Quietly,' I said, and at last I could feel the tears beginning. He saw me to the door, patted my arm, and turned away. Later that day Frances called on me. I thought that nice of her. She had always been vaguely pleasant, like someone I hardly knew, but she had cared for me in Nice. Without her I doubt if I could have got home. I managed to assemble some tea, and she tactfully rose to go when I was shaken with hiccoughs and racking yawns. She had brought me a sleeping pill, which was an incredibly sensible thing to do, and I promised to take it, even though I knew that sleep, which I craved, would come easily. When she left I realized that that part of my life, the married part, was over. I stood at the window watching her get into her car, then following the car mentally on its way to Egerton Crescent. Then there was nothing left to do but take my pill and go to bed.

9

'It's too dreadful,' said Julia in a broken voice, which never-theless held an undertone of fretfulness. 'Too dreadful. That poor poor young man.' Owen had been fifty-two at the time of his death. 'So dear to us all.'

The difficulty, as I saw it, was that she was trying to manage a public self whereas she was by nature a miniaturist who excelled at drawing into her field of activity nuances, intimations, unspoken thought, the most tenuous of personal statements. She was better at the glancing criticism than at spon-taneous magnanimity. Magnanimity was too big, too grand a concept for her to make anything of it: it went with statues in public places, Beethoven symphonies, the condescension of rulers. Julia was essentially a creature of insinuation, the eyelids lowered and then flying open, request and accusation mingling, retribution to follow. None of this bothered me, or rather my irritation was tempered by the knowledge that after this visit I could withdraw from her little circle of acolytes and live my own small life somewhere out of reach. I had no time for her tragic attitudes, for I knew that whatever pain she felt was always confined to her own preoccupations; I had sensed the impatience in her tone at having to defer to me – her audience, her inferior – on this occasion, at having to displace herself from Onslow Square, with Maureen in attendance rather than Charlie, to pay her visit of condolence. In fact we both felt a certain impatience, but the ritual had apparently to be observed and by the same token endured.

'But then it's all so dreadful,' Julia went on. 'Mummy getting older and Gerald in difficulty at work, poor darling. Of course, that job is simply not good enough for him. To think of a Wilberforce working as a car salesman! Those people never did understand him. And now Owen,' she went on, remembering why she was here in my drawing-room and plunging her head into her hands in a pantomime of grief. It may even have been genuine: there was certainly something like a tear in her eye when she raised her head.

'Your tea, Julia,' I said. 'Maureen, do let me give you some cake.'

'You must be brave,' said Julia bravely. 'We must all be brave. When I think of how the world has changed! As I said to Charlie, only last night, it's not my world any more. No beauty, no elegance, no distinction. Not a gentleman in sight. We're all supposed to be cockneys now, aren't we, all mucking in together. And this hatred of the upper classes! Well, I'll never be anything else. I'm out of touch. I'm finished. My day is done.'

The melancholy smile that accompanied these remarks demonstrated the true source of Julia's grief, which, as usual, was very close to her own concerns. It was only with an immense effort that she was capable of abstract thought, and then she only managed it for a second or two at a time. Maureen's role on this unique occasion was to mimic sympathy – for Julia, that is – and to attend to her as if she were extremely frail, an invalid in comparison with whom I was perceived as coarse-grained. I even perceived this myself. I was aware of my humbler and simpler background; I was aware of the likely verdict of a man like my father on Julia's social observations, and I could feel the years dropping away and myself reverting to the naïve and optimistic girl I had once been, if only as a counterweight to this salon performance, this essay in the higher cliché.

'A little whisky, Julia,' I said.

'Thank you, darling.' She stretched out her cramped hands, rubbed them, and returned them to her lap.

'Your pills, Julia,' warned Maureen. 'It's better if she takes them with a drop of milk,' she confided to me. 'That way they don't upset the stomach.'

'I'm sure you can find a clean cup in the kitchen,' said Julia. 'No, let her go, she's quite capable of finding her own way. And frankly, her voice gets on my nerves,' she said, without much lowering her own voice. 'I've tried to train her, but it doesn't seem to take. "Juli-erre," she says. "Juli-erre." I've tried to tell her that it's light, short. "Julia." ' Her face lit up, as with glad tidings, as she pronounced her own name. 'Yet God knows I couldn't do without her. I wish I could. But I'm a poor old woman now. My day is done.' She took the two pills handed to her by Maureen and knocked them back like a sailor taking a tot of rum.

I reflected that Maureen paid a high price for her room in Onslow Square, but I could also see that she was extremely irritating. On this particular afternoon she wore a pink track suit, with a pattern of teddy bears on the sweater. Under her frizzy brown hair – her perm always on its last legs – her rimless glasses shone forth with goodness. She had dainty manners, which did not quite conceal a voracious appetite. I wondered if she got enough to eat. Unless she cooked it herself there was unlikely to be a meal waiting for her if Julia were not hungry. They ate irregularly in Onslow Square; sometimes, it seemed to me, they hardly ate at all. Charlie went to his club, and Julia would only eat a sandwich for lunch and sometimes again in the evening. 'Plenty of calories in whisky,' she would say, and Mummy would give a delighted laugh. I wondered whether I should invite Maureen for a meal, the meal she so obviously needed, and then reflected that my new life would be devoid of people like Maureen, at least if I could possibly help it.

'You're lucky in a way,' said Julia. 'At least your mother's dead. Whereas Mummy will have to go into a home, if Charlie can find the right one. I can't look after her. I'd love to, but these silly hands of mine . . . ' She surveyed them once more. 'What are you doing about the house?' she asked.

'It's sold,' I said. 'To Paul Langdon, Bernard's son. I'm glad it's going to remain in family hands. And to have children in it. Something I could never provide.'

'So that means you've sold two houses. Well, we shan't need to worry about you any more, shall we, Maureen? You'll be extremely well off,' she said, adjusting her glasses and gazing at me through them, as if I were momentarily capable of arousing interest. 'Did Owen leave much?'

'I don't know. Bernard is looking into all that for me. I may get some sort of pension from the firm.' I thought of the money I had found in the drawer. 'There are some things that ought to go back to Hanover Square,' I said. 'I wonder if Charlie would take care of them?'

'Ring him up,' said Julia, nodding towards the telephone. 'Ask him. He's coming here to pick me up anyway.'

'In that case,' I said, slightly confused, 'perhaps I could explain to him . . . ' What I had to explain made me reluctant to face Charlie, yet I knew that something must be managed. I regarded it as one more obligation, perhaps, as I hoped, the last.

I had put the money into an attaché case of Owen's, and I longed to be rid of it. On reflection it seemed to me disloyal to Owen to bring it into the light of day and hand it over to Charlie. I felt uneasy and superstitious about it, so uneasy that I had not even wanted to count it. I longed to lose it, yet I did not want this action to be witnessed. As long as it was in the attaché case I could forget it. So strong was my desire to forget it, mixed with the stronger feeling of loyalty to Owen, that the attaché case was now in the cellar, where I should have liked to leave it. If the house and its contents were to go to Paul and Caroline Langdon, could not the money in some confused way go with the house? At least Owen's family would benefit. I resolved to find a solicitor on the following day – no one I knew, of course – and to will the contents of the house to the Langdons' children. It was, after all, by way of being Owen's money. And if they never found the case (which for safer keeping I would put into the attic) so much the better. The whole matter would be out of my hands.

In the meantime I had to drill myself to keep awake in Julia's presence. The sort of fatigue I normally experienced, and which I associated with her, was gradually giving way to something more open, less sympathetic. I reflected that I had never really got on the right terms with her. She was a fascinating but difficult woman whose affections were beyond me: I took it entirely for granted that she found me dull. I fell into a hazy receptive mood when I was with her, not quite knowing the right responses, my own identity in abeyance. It sometimes occurred to me that this was the last thing she wanted. 'Let's have a discussion!' she would say, meaning an argument, and when I smiled steadily and said, 'No, Julia,' I simply confirmed her earlier impression of me as a suburban bore. 'Suburban bore' was her favourite term of abuse for a woman, and after it there was no appeal. Men were never suburban bores. At their worst they were merely common. Even this was preferable.

'And how will you manage?' she now said. 'It's not easy for a woman without a man.' The eyelids came down suggestively. 'Of course, I'm lucky. Charlie is devoted to me.' She spoke as if his devotion to her made him immortal. 'I expect you'll be lonely,' she added.

'Don't worry about me, Julia,' I said. 'I'm a sensible woman. Of course I'll be lonely. But I shan't do anything melodramatic. I'll find myself a little flat, and then perhaps I'll look for a job. I've got time, time to settle down. It's been a bad shock, a bad year. I need some time to myself.' I thought with longing of the rest I could have, in my own bed, my own small bed, the early nights, the unhurried mornings. I felt anxious to get back to something resembling my girlhood, even if that meant paying the price of loneliness. I did not think that it would frighten me. The only thing that made me uneasy was the fact that I should have rather a lot of money. Camberwell Grove and Gertrude Street were both becoming immensely fashionable, and I should have enough for myself for life, if carefully managed, and enough for Vinnie too. I pushed the money to the back of my mind, because I much preferred to think of myself as a working woman. I would work for nothing, if necessary: there must be something I could do. Meals on Wheels, perhaps, or voluntary work at the library. Something practicable, reassuring, down to earth. I could not wait to get out of this drawing-room, away from people like Julia.

'You are a funny little thing,' said Julia. 'Aren't you? Isn't she a funny little thing, Charlie?'

Charlie, lately arrived, assumed a smile for both of us, but I thought I saw a light of intelligence in his eye as it met mine. 'Don't take offence,' it seemed to say. 'It simply isn't worth it. I shall hear about it all the way home. And of course this is not an opinion I necessarily share.' I ignored this, although I complied with his wishes and said nothing. It was all one to me what they talked about on the way home. I simply wanted him to take Owen's briefcase and not ask me any questions. Like Julia, I wanted someone to do my bidding. Charlie had always seemed to me intensely biddable, or maybe he had been reduced to this condition. It occurred to me to wonder whether he had a mistress. I should not have blamed him. Men who undergo a forced training in tactfulness have to break out somehow. Or was Charlie so beautifully himself, so naturally kind and self-effacing, that his inner life was not a place of betrayal, as my own had so often been? His eye, as it sought mine to enjoin me not to take issue with Julia, was not mean, not weak or pleading, but rather manly, compelling, as if he knew what was right for both of us. He seemed to be telling me that it would not be in my interest to make a fuss, and certainly not in his, if I did. As for Julia, he seemed to imply, he would deal with her later, but only if the matter arose. He had a horror, I knew, of anything less than perfect manners. I doubt if Julia ever satisfied her desire for a discussion with Charlie.

I did not tell them – nor did they ask – that I had my eye on a flat in Drayton Gardens, comfortingly near the cinema. It was not the flat of my mother's dreams, being large and roomy, with big windows, but it had a homely feel to it, and it was on the ground floor, with a view of the street. There were shops around the corner and a hairdresser's right opposite: a perfect flat for a widow. One walked up seven ochre-coloured steps to the building's liver-coloured façade, and once inside the black and white tiled hall it was extremely quiet. My flat, if I took it, was on the right of the entrance. From the sitting-room I should be able to see people passing, see the bus at the end of the street, whereas the bedroom, which overlooked a small communal garden, was completely private. I had gone back to this place three times now, and the agent was getting bored. I had come to the conclusion that it would do. No home is perfect, except the home in which one has been happy, and that, somehow, is the home one leaves for ever.

I could not wait to leave Gertrude Street. I felt now a chill, a revulsion for the evenings I spent alone there. I did not feel this chill in the flat in Drayton Gardens, even though it was empty. I planned to make the colours light, pretty: pale blue and white, with a flowered paper for the bedroom. I would have lots of flowers and plants in pots: I would not bother about good taste. Good taste was something I could now leave behind, without regrets. I wanted a setting for my own little life, for I did not think that I should know too many people. There was a spare room for Millie and Donald if they ever wanted to stay, although this was unlikely since they still had Donald's flat in Great Portland Street. It was just that Millie had said something about the lease running out: I wanted to be sure that she had a base in London, if she needed one. It would be so lovely to see her again. In her absence I should simply have to make new friends. I should not mind if they were all women. I was as yet, and possibly for ever, unable to face a life with men in it. By the same token I did not exactly miss my husband. I merely wanted a respite from the sort of life one lives with a man. I do not think that this was particularly unfeminine of me; on the contrary. Women often take refuge from men, or feel in need of a rest from them. They seem to want to be restored to more innocent days. I could see myself in Drayton Gardens, going out with my basket on wheels, tempting my own appetite, keeping up appearances, and doing no harm, not even to myself. Lonely? Yes, I should be lonely, but in time I should see that this was to my advantage. I should be training myself for old age, which takes a certain amount of training; better to start as I meant to go on. And there was the cinema, the library. I could even take a holiday. But in truth I doubted if I should need one.

It was Charlie who wrote down my new address. 'But I haven't quite decided,' I said. I knew, however, that with the writing down of the address in Charlie's diary the decision was made. Grey carpet, I thought. White walls. China blue and white curtains and covers. I saw the letting in of the light as imperative. There had been a pleasant-looking woman coming up the steps as I had left to go, on my last visit, and I thought we might be friends. Not necessarily intimates, but we could look out for each other, make gentle enquiries if we had not seen each other for a few days. I would manage. I would become the optimistic person I had once been, but this time with my feet on the ground. After all, I was nearly fifty and looked nothing like my younger self. I decided to instruct the agent the following morning, for which I was now anxious and impatient. With the prospect of my own home before me Gertrude Street, and the years that I had spent there, became irrelevant, an interruption, an error. Some memories of Owen, now strangely absent from my thoughts, would, I hoped, come back to me. But he was in the past and I was impatient for the future. Or perhaps not impatient but wistful, as if the future might still be snatched away from me. My hold on things was weaker, because of what had happened to Owen. I did not trust in fate or circumstances, as I once had, although I was aware of unused energy. I would have to make that energy work for me. And then, I thought, with a burst of relief, I can have a piano again.

'If there's anything you need,' said Charlie. 'Anything at all, just let us know.'

'But of course we shall be seeing a lot of Fay,' said Julia, winding a silk scarf round her throat. 'Maureen, why don't you run on ahead and put a light under that soup of yours? We might as well eat in tonight. Not that I'm hungry.'

'Could you take this briefcase of Owen's to the office, Charlie?' I said. 'It's nothing to do with me. I don't know about Owen's business affairs.'

This was true. I hoped that Charlie would dispose of the briefcase – rather a handsome one – and regard it as a memento. I actually felt too tired to say this, although I had every intention of doing so.

I stood under Hermione's chandelier, which Paul's wife, Caroline, would now have the problem of cleaning, and said goodbye to them, expecting never to see them again.

'Poor little Fay,' said Julia, touching my cheek. 'Poor, poor little Fay.' She was overdoing it again.

I could hardly condemn her for insincerity since I had displayed a certain insincerity of my own. I was shocked by Owen's death, but not grief-stricken. In fact my own feelings told me nothing; it was as if I had got rid of them all in Nice, as if they had knocked me out, taking away my consciousness once and for all, as I had fallen into faint after faint. I had recovered as if from a physical illness, and, like all sufferers from violent afflictions, only convalescence interested me. Health was what I wanted, and I looked forward to it eagerly. Julia was not the only one who was play-acting, although I tried to say as little as possible, or at least as little as was compatible with the circumstances of her visit. This visit had made us both impatient. I was simply not of her world, nor she of mine. And I had lost my meekness, my pliability: I was an independent woman. I think the money annoyed her too, although Charlie kept her in some state. I did think it hard for her to be deprived of her former visibility, for I knew that this was almost impossible for her to bear. She had become futile, and she knew it. She saved her pride by underlining my own loss of status, but was further annoyed by the fact that I was quite comfortable without it. Indeed I seemed to be settling down into a state which was mysteriously denied to her. She was shrewd, clever, able to penetrate one's unspoken thoughts. She knew instinctively that I was anxious to be free. And I think she determined then that she would never let me go. Although she found me uninteresting, I would do as an adherent, or, if I did not conform, as an adversary. She would get her discussion at last. I resolved once again to disappear. If it had not been for that address in Charlie's diary I might have done so.

I bought the flat the following day, and as soon as I had done so a certain desolation fell on me. It looked so empty, so abandoned. Fortunately I found a nice woman who had set up as an interior decorator, and I handed the whole thing over to her, simply telling her what I wanted. She was nice, but she was slow. Evening after evening I went round to the flat to find it devoid of any activity, just a few dust sheets on the floor and wires sticking out of the walls. This made me very restless and even frightened to go back to Gertrude Street. It was a fine late autumn, but a cold one: people foretold a hard winter, as if in punishment for those astonishing days of summer. There was a café on the corner and I tried to eat a meal there, but I felt self-conscious, was aware of the dark night outside, and of the lights of the cinema, where crowds gathered. I became nervous of the dark. I told myself that this would pass as soon as I got into the flat, but the evenings were wretched. As soon as I could I got into bed, but I did not always sleep. My energy left me: I was permanently tired. I haunted the flat as if it did not belong to me, as if I were asking permission to occupy it. Men turned up eventually, cheerful noisy creatures for whom I ran to the café to buy tea and coffee. Gradually the walls became white, gradually the washing machine and the cooker were installed, and then I was not needed even to run to the café. Clouded milk bottles accumulated on the step, and there was a smell of crisps and hamburgers. It was better once I had been to Peter Jones and bought dustbins and kettles and tea towels. I wanted everything to be new. Even then the flat did not satisfy me as I had imagined it would. In my mind I had got to the stage of renouncing Drayton Gardens and planning to move on; perhaps I could do better somewhere else. When the grey carpet arrived and was laid I found that I had chosen too dark a colour. But by then the main work was completed. All I had to do was await the curtains and covers and then I could move in, with the new furniture – comfortable, undistinguished – ready to be delivered on the day I took possession.

I was standing in the empty flat one evening, a cold evening, already misty, with an orange street lamp shining through the window, when the doorbell rang. I hoped it might be a neighbour, perhaps the woman I had noticed at the entrance, but it was Charlie, in his dark overcoat, with Owen's briefcase in his hand.

'I tried Gertrude Street,' he said, stepping over a roll of superfluous carpet. 'And then I thought you must be here. This is a pleasant room, Fay. Show me round, if you've got a moment.'

He murmured appreciation in all the rooms and I began to warm to the task once more. Sometimes it only wants a little whisper of approbation to set one on one's way. I was at that moment excessively grateful to him.

'Would you like a cup of tea, Charlie?' I asked. 'I'm sure the men have left some, although they seem to drink it all day.'

'That would be fine,' he said, examining the doors. 'Will you get all your stuff in here? It's much smaller than Gertrude Street.'

'Oh, I'm leaving everything. I shan't want much. Anyway, it's all ordered.'

He felt the radiators. 'Beautifully warm, at any rate.'

'Do you like it?' I asked him.

'Very much.' He drank his tea in one swallow and put his cup on the window sill. 'You'll want Owen's briefcase, I suppose? I've removed everything relevant. Not that there was much. He left his files more or less in order.'

There was a pause. I held my breath, wondering how much he knew. But it appeared that nothing was to be said, whatever Charlie knew or did not know.

'If the briefcase is of any use to you, Charlie, please keep it. It was my last Christmas present to Owen. I really don't want to see it any more.'

'I should like to have it, my dear. I'll take it back with me then, shall I?'

I nodded gratefully. That, I thought, was the end of the affair, but he seemed reluctant to go. With the minutes that passed a very slight awkwardness could be felt, but only, apparently, on my part. Without Julia, Charlie seemed more resolute, more purposeful.

'How is Julia?' I asked.

'Oh, she has her difficult days, you know. But we survive, we survive. She needs company, mostly. So do go round, won't you? She was saying the other day that she hadn't seen you.' He kissed me then, and I stood in his arms, astonished. It was only kindness, I told myself, although it did not feel like that. There was certainly no excuse for anything else. Yet instinctively we moved away from the light of the street lamp and into the empty bedroom, where he kissed me again. Now there was no room for doubt. Neither of us said anything.

After this he left, still without reference to what had taken place. I put my hand to my throbbing cheek, and stood in the flat, uncertain, but not uneasy. In fact I laughed. It was only a gesture, I thought. He was an opportunist, like most men. Nothing would come of it. Indeed, I did not want anything to come of it. And yet I was not indignant. I was, if anything, amused; I experienced a lightening of the heart. I felt newly capable. But not deluded. I was grateful that a man had found me attractive, pleased that it should have been Charlie, whom I had always liked; nothing more. What more could there be? Like Julia, my day was done. I was a woman in late middle age, no candidate for romance. Even my mind, normally so naïve and sentimental, no longer lent itself to fantasies and self-indulgent imaginings. I told myself that I had had my share of love, and I was able to acknowledge that it had disappointed me. There is an age at which not telling the truth is fatal and I had reached that age. If I still looked forward hopefully to some experience that remained vague in outline, if I still dressed with care and was fastidious about my appearance, I was nevertheless quite resigned to spending the remainder of my life alone. I even took a certain pride in the prospect. No more unwelcome hopes and disappointments, no more wild anticipations, brooding let-downs. I was of an uncomplaining disposition, had never nagged or belaboured my husband, was good at disguising my cares. It seemed to me a better thing to suffer than constantly to accuse. Yet all this good behaviour, if that is what it was, had left me a little sad, a little passive, and that occasionally seemed to me unfair. But I put such thoughts out of my mind when they occurred and on the whole they did not bother me unduly.

Looking back I am impressed by two things. Firstly, that we moved instinctively out of the light of the street lamp and into the darkness. And secondly, that so slight a pretext should have set me thinking about myself in a way that I had not done for years, if ever. Idle conversations with Millie, when we were girls, had left me untouched, unstirred. I had had no other confidante. All I knew was that on certain summer evenings I felt a pain of longing which no one person – or no one that I knew – could assuage. This pain had its origin, perhaps, in my nature as a woman, dreaming, passive, so far unexamined. I felt none of this longing, this nostalgia, as I walked home to Gertrude Street that evening. On the contrary, I felt alert, slightly cynical. Thus does Nature prepare us for the practicalities. I felt no guilt, no concern for Julia: I had already decided not to see her again. In any event I knew how she regarded me, as almost someone of the servant class. I felt free of her, free of everyone. A lifetime of freedom seemed to stretch out in front of me.

Then nothing happened for three weeks. The curtains were hung, the loose covers fitted on to the chairs and sofa, the bed made up. It looked very pleasant, but for some reason it did not gratify me. I ordered newspapers, contacted the laundry, made an appointment at the hairdressers, yet failed to feel at home. I suppose I was lonelier than I had anticipated. And there was so little to do after the big house that time passed very slowly. The woman whom I hoped would be my neighbour had not acknowledged me again; the porter was surly. The weather was too cold for me to spend much time out of doors, and I soon had little need to go to the shops more than once a day, sometimes not even once. I always woke in the dark, long before I needed to get up. Certain evenings I sat in the sitting-room without bothering to put on the lights, looking out at that street lamp. I was perplexed that I was not able to comfort myself more, now that there was nothing to torment me. The prospect of this sort of life continuing indefinitely caused me the occasional intake of breath. My good sense told me that I was fortunate, that I had no possible cause for complaint. Nevertheless, I could not help noticing that nothing pleased me.

I was sitting by the window, in the darkened room, one evening, when Charlie came the second time. Already I felt embarked with him. He handed me a parcel, and said, 'I brought you this. I thought it had your name on it.' It was a flowered Victorian cup and saucer, gilt rimmed, capacious and confident. I loved it. 'How is Julia?' I asked. He looked at me with a certain amusement, showing a side of himself not naturally seen. 'You know Julia,' he said. 'She is my wife. She will always be my wife.' I felt disappointed, as if this heralded the start of something that could only be nefarious and was thus signalled from the outset. 'Why are you here?' I asked him, almost antagonistically. 'You know why,' he said, and took me in his arms.

That was all that he said, but possibly not all that he felt. The collusion was avoidable, and it did not occur to me to avoid it. I never made claims for it in my own mind, although it was real enough, and seemed right enough at the time. Yet shame, and a kind of irritability steal upon me even as I write these words. Adultery is not noble. Adulterous lovers are not allowed to be star-crossed. Anna Karenina and Emma Bovary are not really heroines. Even when there is real love, authentic love, it is not the sort in which one rejoices. That night I began a long training in duplicity, in calculation, in almost continuous discomfort, but also in confidence and expectation and effectiveness. Years did not diminish any of these feelings: they constituted my apprenticeship.

10

One tries to make light of these things, for to make anything else of them is somehow unseemly in the circumstances. I look back now in amusement, surprise, and only occasionally despair at my love affair with Charlie, which was a love affair, although fatal words were never spoken. We were a recreation to each other, and this made the time we spent together permissible. How could it hurt? Whom could it hurt? Only one person was thought of as a victim, and her name was only pronounced airily, socially, normally. 'Julia says she never sees you these days.' 'Yes, I must go round.' But I could not quite do this. I telephoned instead, concerned myself with her health, her needs. 'I'm not quite defunct, you know,' she would say. 'But I dare say I'm too dull for you now. That's why I never see you.' This saddened me, the necessary deceit. But that in any case was part of my involvement.

He was a good-looking man, tall, broad, well set-up, perhaps putting on weight, as I was. We reconciled each other to growing old, for this was the last thing that would happen to either of us. He came to me on Saturday afternoons or looked in on his way home. Retirement, which was looming for him, would pose a problem about which we declined to think. We both assumed that the affair would end when that happened, when he had to take his place as Julia's full-time companion. With me he demonstrated a levity which I would never have suspected; in Onslow Square he was always resigned, mild, tactful. His nature was, I think, reserved, quiet, not given to confessions or complaints. His enormous control suited us both well, keeping me within bounds when I might have been tempted to be foolish. He never mentioned his marriage; this was, in a way, honourable of him. I understood discretion had been professionally bred into him. As far as I was concerned I was his permitted luxury, after a lifetime of endurance. I think he loved Julia. She was his wife; she was innocent. And he respected the conventions.

I never got a job. He was my sole occupation. Not knowing when he would be able to visit me kept me alert, presentable; time no longer hung heavy. Each day I would prepare for him. I took my bath and changed after I had made a cup of tea, and on the whole I was quite happy to sit in the darkened room, looking out of the window. When I heard the car door slam – and it was a door I never confused with any other – I would draw the curtains and light the lamps. Sometimes days went by in this dreamy fashion. The tension of the waiting tired me and it was almost with relief that I would realize I was free to turn on the radio or the television, eventually to go to bed. On occasion I was surprised by a terrible sadness. This I did not fully understand. I would catch my breath in amazement: why so sad? I had what few women of my advanced age could lay claim to: a man who did not bore me and who never made me suffer. For he never did make me suffer; my unhappiness, of which I was barely conscious, had to do with a certain disappointment. I had been a conventional wife, and now I was a conventional mistress, docile and agreeable, little treats always to hand. I felt a certain pride, a boldness; I was not pathetic. I could hold up my head. I grew older more or less successfully, refused to dye my hair, chose my clothes with a new care. I would try to dress up for him until I realized that this was the last thing he wanted. I made him feel younger, for which he was grateful. He was amused, indulgent, overwhelmingly fond. The cup and saucer he had given me became his cup and saucer. I would serve him coffee in it.

I never sang again. Who would want to hear a fifty-five-year-old woman singing love songs, which were the only songs I knew? But I did ring Harry, the agent, my father's friend, who had been at my mother's funeral, and who was retired but eternally present in his son's office, making a nuisance of himself, and it was he who got me the engagement to read the story on 'Woman's Hour', which I did for a fortnight. This suited me very well, for it meant that I could get home in time for Charlie's expected visit, and it was nice to be back at the BBC, although it now seemed to be staffed by convivial young women in jeans. To them I was a relic of olden times, and they were enormously kind to me, bringing me glasses of water, begging me to sit down when I would have been quite happy to stand. I think they were surprised that I managed to last the course.

Julia rang me after that. 'Now look here! You simply can't abandon me like this. You say you're busy, although I can't see how you can be. The least you can do is spare an afternoon or two. I feel very lonely now that Mummy's gone to this home of hers, although of course she's madly comfortable there. The other two are complete fools. I don't know how I put up with them.'

'I've been on the wireless,' I said, really just for something to say.

'I know. I heard one of them. An episode, or whatever you call them. I thought your diction quite good, surprisingly good; in fact I meant to listen today, but Maureen forgot to switch it on. Perhaps when you've finished you could come and tell me all about it. All your adventures.'

I think she meant nothing by this. I think she was lonely. She had maintained her rigorous nun-like existence until she was fitted for no other. With this in mind I went round to see her, aware of all she must not know. I found her seated in her yellow chair, wearing an immaculate white suit with an orange and black blouse. All at once I felt plump, clumsy. Mrs Chesney later told me that getting dressed was the main event of Julia's day. She would survey her banked wardrobes, sit at her dressing-table trying on one pair of earrings after another, then take her place in the drawing-room, sighing with languor, as if she had just completed some wearisome task or duty. She still thought in terms of her public, of living up to it, of never disappointing the people who had bought tickets for her performance. She looked older, thinner. She was now having trouble with her back, had to control a tendency to lean forward. 'Posture, Wilberforce, posture!' she would say, straightening herself. The eyes were still fine, impassive. They contemplated me at leisure. 'What a lot of weight you've put on,' she observed. 'And you shouldn't let your hair go like that. Standards are so important.' But her heart wasn't in it. I, on the contrary, found myself eager to please, but as usual I disappointed her. She found me dull, as dull as Maureen, as Mrs Chesney. When I got ready to make my escape she did not try to detain me. This made me plead a multiplicity of things to be done.

'Anyone would think you had a lover,' she said, which brought obedient laughter all round.

'I saw Julia today,' I said to Charlie that evening.

'Did you? Good.' He drew a dark green silk handkerchief from his sleeve and brushed a crumb from his mouth. 'Excellent toast. Any more of it?'

Seasons changed, years melted into one another. I no longer walked the summer streets; in fact I spent more time in the flat than out of it. There must have been hot weather and cold weather, but I remember those years as being mainly dark, late autumn, with a little mist curling round the orange street lamp outside the window. I went out early in the morning to do my shopping, not because I was constrained for time, but because I liked to see the children going to school. I knew one or two of them by name, and I would have lingered with them had I dared, but although I am a respectable woman I was aware of a certain impropriety in doing so. I also feared the onset of a particular morbidity, that morbidity with which Julia had once taxed me. From the children I turned my eyes to the young men and women going to work. On some days I longed to join them. They looked so fresh-faced, so smart, with their briefcases and their morning papers. They made me think of certain Strauss polkas.

These young people were my main reason for going out so early. I would be home by nine, with a whole empty day in front of me. My duties as a housewife were minimal: I had no family to take care of, no garden. I never exactly regretted the big house but I did sometimes wonder what to do with my time. Once a week I went to see Vinnie, now looked after by a student nurse, who was glad to have a rent-free room near her hospital. Vinnie could be left alone in the daytime, although her mind was no longer intact, and she rarely spoke. I would take her the little parcels of food that I used to take to my own mother, the cold salmon, the tongue, the fruit tart, and it was almost a relief to do so; it made me feel purposeful, dutiful again. She recognized me but lost interest almost at once; with advancing senility old grudges were coming to the surface. I spent little time with her; my company, I knew, did not please her. I simply provisioned her, looked for any messages that Sandra, the nurse, might have left for me, and went on my way.

Those who stay at home all day live in a world of women. The only men are those who have retired; one sees them going for their newspaper, domesticated, smiling at their freedom, wearing cardigans instead of jackets. The women of the same age seem more thoughtful, as if bearing the heat and burden of the day. Some still wear gloves and even hats, navy blue berets to go with their coats and the silk scarf that their son or daughter gave them for Christmas. Age can be detected here in the length of a skirt, the turn of a collar. I was at one with these people, whom I saw in the late morning when I went out again, for flowers, or for fresh bread, or perhaps just for company. We were out of it, somehow, although our preoccupations were surely weightier than those of the young men and women with their briefcases. We knew our time was limited, even though we were still healthy; we had the same desire to see and hear the young, in whom we perceived true beauty. We were courteous with each other. The women smiled, the men lifted their folded newspapers in greeting. On days when the sun shone words would be exchanged, of an extremely formal nature. 'Isn't it lovely? Spring is really here at last. Keeping well?' For it was essential to keep well.

There was a pleasantness about these exchanges that eased me into the afternoon. Since this could have been lengthy, empty, I took to lying down on my sofa, as my mother had done, to rest, sometimes to sleep. I seemed to resemble her more and more, in my own imagining at least, for I could not help but be glad that she had died knowing nothing of my present behaviour. In her mind I had always been her marvellous child, her prodigy. Now I was old and deeply flawed. When had this process begun? It was not entirely recent. Perhaps it began when I moved out of my milieu, married above myself (and unwisely, I now saw), started to watch my words, censor my reminiscences of harmless but homely relatives, of being spoiled by the boys in the orchestra, and closed the door on memories of the Blitz, of evenings in the cinema, all the paraphernalia of a suburban upbringing. It seemed to me that once I had left my world nobody had loved me. Until now, perhaps. But in order to bridge the gap between then and now what adulteration had taken place! I thought of it as adulteration rather than adultery, adulteration of my original essence. One does not grow up in innocence, I told myself: changes are bound to take place. I reflected along these lines throughout that hour on my sofa, then I closed the matter off. I cancelled the afternoon, cancelled the experiences of the day, took my bath and changed, and sat down to wait for Charlie. Even when I knew he was unlikely to come I waited for him.

There was the time when he took Julia away to the sun, Majorca, I think it was. He came round in an official capacity, with the keys, and a request that I should keep an eye on things. Even when the flat in Onslow Square was empty, Maureen also being away, I hated to be there. The yellow and white drawing-room seemed so impregnated with Julia's essence – acid, heartless, virginal – that I felt it accusing me. Nothing would have made me enter their bedroom. I aired the place, opened the windows, then closed them again, and left as silently and as hastily as any burglar. On the eve of their return I took round some food, a chicken and a tub of potato salad, and put fresh flowers in the vases. This went down wonderfully well. It was in my capacity as a servant that I best pleased Julia. Her fortnight in the sun had left her as white and as immaculate as ever. Later Charlie told me that she had hardly moved from the hotel. He, on the other hand, was bronzed, expansive. They looked a handsome couple.

'We must see more of you,' said Julia. 'Do say you'll be round soon.'

'Why, yes,' I said. 'As soon as I come back.'

'Back? Are you going away?'

'Yes. A brief holiday.' I had only just thought of it, but it seemed as good an idea as any other. Occasionally I found myself on the edge of panic when anyone – not just Julia – asked me about my affairs. Taking a holiday seemed the only thing I could do that was halfway respectable and had the added advantage of being something I could talk about. I would talk about it endlessly, if necessary.

So I went to Saint Paul de Vence for a week and it was a disaster. It was a disaster shrouded in mystery for I had managed to give the impression that I might be away for much longer. As soon as I got there I wanted to come home. It was late September, and the mosquitoes were still active; I was bitten immediately. The heat I could tolerate, but the light bothered me, the hard cloudless sky under whose brilliance it was so difficult to get one's bearings. I found myself sunburnt, dazzled, fearful, and unoccupied. My hotel, a modest one, had a café on the ground floor, and I would take my breakfast there and try to make it last. Then came the expedition to buy the *International Herald Tribune*. Then the walk, during which I would be engulfed by tourists pouring out of coaches and into souvenir shops for that bottle of lavender essence or that cake of brown soap to take home. Then more coffee. And then the walk along the terrace, hearing the cars speeding on the main coast road far below, trying hard to tolerate the noise and the glint of the sun on every surface. I was aware of excess; everything seemed excessive, and I could not accommodate it, not the olive oil in the food, nor the deeply sensuous smells of sun lotion and caramel that came from the tourist shops, nor, of course, the pitiless sun which kept up its strength all day until it declined briefly and all at once into darkness. I thought with longing of my flat, of which I was in reality not all that fond, and of the view from my window, the cinema on the corner. I had never been so lonely in my life.

Suddenly it was all too much for me, the duplicity, the endurance. I doubted my ability even to make the journey home. I was shocked, I suppose, at this revelation of my solitariness which I had thought banished for ever by the circumstances of my life, however irregular these might have appeared. I thought of Charlie and Julia, so very much together, and myself, so very much apart. And not only apart, but exposed as being apart by the unyielding sun and my own lack of occupation. In the end I gave up pretending to be on holiday, pursued my daily round cynically and mutinously, defying the charming place to charm me. This moment of revolt served me well, made the days seem unimportant. But it also showed me how vulnerable I was, so vulnerable that I found myself buying bottles of scent – the modest flower waters they have down there – for Julia, for Vinnie, for Sandra, even for Maureen and Mrs Chesney, as if theirs were the only friendship on which I could hope to count. When I got home I stood in the hallway of the flat and closed my eyes in gratitude. I made a vow never to go away alone again. I would stay with Millie, I told myself, or take her with me. With a friend beside me I would be impervious to the pity or the curiosity of others. Or even to their indifference. Then I reflected how my life had been designed, with my fullest co-operation, so that I was accountable to no one, not even to a dear friend. My life was my secret and that was how it had to be kept. Millie would not approve, would look at me sadly and with surprise if I confided in her. I would spare us both that. I would get used to my routine again, would simply school myself out of certain imaginings, certain

longings. Fortunately, Charlie came round that evening. I had
caught the earlier plane, hoping that he might. He had missed
me too.

I delivered all my bottles of scent the following day. I
put a few drops on Vinnie's handkerchief: she stared at me
haughtily and let it drop. In her ancient eyes was a look of
outrage, of rejection. The afternoon saw me at Onslow Square,
where Pearl Chesney and Maureen murmured gratefully, and
Julia said, 'You'll have to open it for me. My hands are too
bad. That's why I always use an atomizer. Charlie keeps me
supplied.' I found myself apologizing. 'But there's one thing
you can do for me,' she said. 'And that's get me something
to read. You're near the library, aren't you?' I was not, particularly. 'If you could just change my books once or twice a
week, that would be so kind. *Really* kind.'

'But Julia,' I said. 'I don't know what you like.'

Unfortunately I did. She liked particularly violent and slap-
dash crime novels, the kind recognizable by the colour of the
jacket. I knew she liked these because she extolled their merits
and attempted to explain the plots, all of which seemed to be
interchangeable. Her former gifts were of no use to her on these
occasions. Hopelessly confused and confusing, she had no idea
of what made a book good or bad but judged it by the actions
it contained in the first and last chapters. She liked stories about
confidence tricksters, small-time crooks, weak young men who
preyed on weaker old ladies. She liked lags, con men, in an
English village setting. She liked rural detective sergeants and
aristocratic policemen, but infinitely preferred the criminals to
either of them. She liked the classes to be distinguished by
their names, humorous or hyphenated. She had a weakness
for lovable rogues who got away with murder, to try it on
again in another novel of the same kind. Unfortunately there
were a great number that she had not read, or claimed not to
have read, until Maureen brought them home from the library,
eight at a time. She used Charlie's tickets as well as her own.

I found this aspect of Julia's reduced life unbearably pathetic.
That a woman of her quality should spend her time on these

productions, should take them seriously, should actually discuss them, made me see the emptiness of her days. I was probably wrong, or my conscience may have made me more susceptible. Julia regarded a novel as she regarded a glass of whisky or a cigarette, as something to be consumed and endlessly renewed. She got through one a day, or rather a night, for she was never tired, and kept her light on long after everyone else was asleep. A shabby plastic-covered pile waited on the table.

'I thought Maureen got them for you,' I said.

'Maureen, I'm afraid, is quite hopeless. And anyway she's always round at that church of hers. God knows what she does there.'

'Maybe God does,' interrupted Maureen merrily.

Julia closed her eyes, as if in pain. 'Or at Peter Jones,' she said, as if this were the same thing. She seemed to regard both establishments as derogating from her own pre-eminence.

'Nevertheless,' I demurred. 'Maureen is more on the spot than I am.'

'That's your fault,' said Julia sharply.

'And anyway I've taken on the parish magazine,' said Maureen, who seemed in the best of humour. I had often had my doubts about Maureen, could find no cause for dislike, but felt it all the same.

'No earthly use asking Pearl,' said Julia. 'She's never read a book in her life.'

Pearl Chesney flushed. She was aware of her uncertain status in this little group, aware of her past years as Julia's dresser, her devotion to her, which may not have been repaid. She turned up regularly and faithfully, but I suspected that she came for the cup of tea and the glass of sherry, the touch of glamour conferred by Julia's superb appearance, the professional pride she felt in seeing her so beautifully turned out. I know that from time to time she took some of Julia's clothes home to wash and press, and that she was useful about letting down hems. Charlie, I am sure, paid her handsomely.

She was a homely looking woman who wore a lot of make-up, rouged cheeks and cherry lips in the style of the

1940s, above which large eyes the colour of oyster shells looked out humbly at a world which had changed too much for her. Over seventy now, she still laughed appreciatively at Julia's every sally and could be counted on to come up with a loyal and flattering reminiscence. I think she adored Julia, hoped only to be useful to her for the rest of her life. Julia was tired of her, except for her skills as a dressmaker, and was increasingly cruel, in a reflective throwaway style which seemed to have no malice behind it. Pearl Chesney was not unaware of this, as she was not unaware of her physical gracelessness, her increasingly stout figure, her lack of all the attributes that Julia admired. Yet sometimes she took away a whole suitcase of Julia's clothes, which she would bring back, minutely repaired, on her next visit. She would insist on travelling by bus, back to St Maur Road, in Fulham, although Julia would say in a bored tone, 'There's no need for that. Charlie left you money for a taxi.' Mrs Chesney was uncomfortable about taking it, I could see. It occurred to me that these matters could have been more gracefully managed.

I believe that she was a good woman, rather lonely, more sensitive than anyone understood.

'I'll help you with those, Fay,' she said, bundling four of the books into her basket. Her face was red with unhappiness. It was her eagerness to be gone that weakened my resolve not to have anything to do with Julia's wretched books.

'I'll change them, Julia,' I warned her. 'But this is the first and last time. I'll bring you some paperbacks the next time I come. I've got dozens in the flat.'

'Quite useless,' she said. 'With these silly hands of mine I can't keep them open.' Paperbacks were dismissed, along with my bottle of scent.

'I believe they have a better selection at the Kensington branch,' she said. 'Or there's Brompton Road, if that's nearer for you. There's no need to put yourself out on my account.'

I felt angry and helpless as I left and could sympathize only too well with poor Pearl Chesney, who trotted beside me manfully, although her heavy breathing should have told me that I was going too fast for her. I was too angry to slow down, but when we reached Drayton Gardens, with our four books apiece, I asked her in, as I should have done a long time ago. I never invited anyone to the flat if I could help it. I thought of it as a place reserved for shadowy meetings, not to be exposed to the light of day. Looking back this makes me groan with irritation: I see it now as one of the traps into which women fall so easily. But really I had divested myself of my friends in the interests of this love affair. If I had fallen ill I should not have known whom to call. Only the doctor, I suppose. Fortunately, I am never ill.

'Oh, Fay,' said Mrs Chesney. 'What a lovely flat! How happy you must be here. Although of course you must be lonely without your husband.'

'Sit down, Pearl,' I said, ashamed. 'I'm going to give us another glass of sherry. And I've got some little biscuits that would go nicely with it.'

'It's very kind of you, dear,' she said. 'And I'm glad of this opportunity to have a word with you. There's something I've been meaning to say.'

I all but paused, but managed to hand her her glass.

'The truth is,' she said, 'I shan't be seeing you again. I think my days at Onslow Square are over.'

'You're not ill, are you, Pearl?'

'No, I'm fine, except for this chest of mine. Julia doesn't want me there and that's the fact of the matter. Oh, I'm useful to her, I know, but I'm getting old; women of my age are retired. I can't keep it up, Fay. I may be an old fuddy-duddy, but sometimes I think Julia forgets how long we've been together. I bore her,' she finished simply, but her eyes were wet.

'I think we all bore her,' I said. 'She strikes me as a woman with an enormous capacity for boredom.'

'And perhaps a tiny bit selfish from time to time,' said Mrs Chesney, putting away her handkerchief.

'Perhaps,' I said.

She had been badly hurt, I realized, over a number of years, probably all her life, and she did not possess the resources to deal with what others would have construed as contempt. She was weary, and fatally badly dressed: her nylon raincoat, with the nylon fleece collar and cuffs and the useless trimmings of synthetic leather, spoke even more eloquently than her words had done of slights received and misunderstood.

'So I'm going to live near my son,' she went on. 'He's found me a little flat. He's a good boy. He says it's my turn to be looked after. Out Surrey way, it is. It'll break my heart to leave London, but I dare say I'll get used to it.'

'I didn't know you had a son,' I said.

'Well, I don't talk about him. My mother brought him up. I wasn't married, you see, that's why I went on working. I wanted him to have the best. He went to university, you know, won a scholarship to Queen Mary College. Engineering, he did. He's been with British Rail ever since he left, on the administrative side, of course.'

'We'll miss you,' I said. 'Julia will miss you.'

'She's got her husband, hasn't she? That's more than I ever had. *And* he spoils her. Well, he's been good to me, so I won't say a word against him. But they don't know the half of it, really, either of them. How other people have to live.' There was a little silence, in which I could think of nothing to say. 'I must go, dear. It's been so kind of you, and I hope you won't pay too much attention to what I've said. We've all got our feelings, haven't we?'

She fastened her creaking raincoat, put on her gloves, picked up her basket. I did not suggest a taxi, thinking that at that moment her independence was her proudest possession. I gave her my telephone number, kissed her, and waved to her from the window. For the first time in all the evenings I could remember I wanted to be alone. There was a tiny knot of uncertainty, even of bitterness, somewhere inside me, and if Charlie had come I might have been unwise, disappointing. I might have asked for assurances which would not, could not be forthcoming, and I was glad that there was no opportunity for me to do so. A suppliant is never popular.

II

Uncharacteristically, I came down with some sort of virus and had to tell Charlie, when he telephoned, not to come. He always telephoned at some point during the day, or, if he missed a day, or even two days, shortly afterwards, never leaving me for too long without some contact with him. I knew better than to telephone him. I had done so once, and having to speak to his secretary had filled me with shame and confusion. I had reflected then, as I had done on subsequent occasions, that what I was doing was too difficult for me. I think concealment is difficult for a woman, unnatural even. Most of the time I felt confident, lighthearted, but when I look back I realize that this too was unnatural. I was like someone on a euphoric drug, not giving a thought to eventual withdrawal symptoms. Those timid mornings, those empty afternoons were all part of my adventure: after a time I stopped noticing the loneliness and congratulated myself on having arranged matters so well. No interruptions, no unforeseen visitors, no telephone ringing at awkward moments, for I had managed to anticipate and to ward off unwelcome callers. Most people took notice of this and left me alone. Even Julia, it seemed, had become more passive, less peremptory. Now that she had annexed me into changing her books – and how could I deny her something to read? – her famous 'Now, look here!' was relatively rare. The always uneasy compromise with my own conscience was resolved, or partially resolved, time after time by my leaving the books with Maureen or Mrs Wheeler and pretending to be on my way to somewhere else. I thought this quite a successful ploy, and somehow persuaded myself that it was temporary: I was performing a service which I might revoke at any time. Julia, slowly trying on earrings in her bedroom, would hear my cheerful voice at the front door, but be too preoccupied to call me in. In any event she had never expressed much desire for my company. Attendance was enough.

With the slight illness that had brought me down my euphoria vanished and I realized just how isolated I had become. Dark silent days in the muggy warmth of my flat set my head aching: I was wretched and rather frightened. I even called the doctor, something I had never done before, and the action filled me with terror and relief. I was voluble when he came, thanking him and apologizing at the same time. 'It's probably only a cold,' I said, and in my head I could hear Julia saying, 'Fay is hapless. Don't you think Fay has become very hapless recently?'

'No, not a cold.' he smiled. 'One of those opportunistic viruses. Have you let yourself get run down?' He looked round the room, which had shadows in its corners, although it was only midday. 'Live alone, do you? What sort of things do you eat? Do you cook properly?'

I was shocked. I had always cooked properly, but it had seemed so silly to buy joints of meat for one person and I had gradually stopped doing it. Pies I made for Vinnie, and cakes out of an old housekeeping habit, but I rarely touched them myself. There were other meals, and I cooked them and ate them, or perhaps I just ate one dish, as one does when one is alone. I shopped normally, I even cooked normally; perhaps what I did not do was eat normally. But in my own eyes I was so far from being that elderly self-neglecting patient that doctors have in mind that I shrugged off his questions and resolved to buy a chicken as soon as he had left. I calculated that I could walk as far as the shops, although I felt weak. I was anxious not to appear weak, at least as long as the doctor was there.

Afterwards I should probably sink back on the sofa and sleep. I felt too nervous to go to bed, in case I should never get up again.

I did nothing else for a couple of days. I felt strange and light-headed; more than that I felt uneasy, as if there were no help for me in all the long lonely mornings, now as long and lonely as the afternoons had always been. Illness distorts, but that distortion can serve as a commentary. I now saw the days for what they were, hours of simply waiting for the evening to arrive. And then suddenly came the unbidden thought: this is intolerable. And having once allowed it, the word re-echoed in my head. Intolerable! I was too old, I was too tired, it was all out of character. Those children, those young people I admired so much in the early mornings – they were the proper occupation for a woman of my age. Sometimes, these days, I dressed myself defiantly, as if challenging unknown and unseen onlookers to criticize. I believed those who maintained that a woman is as old as she feels, but these days I surprised myself by feeling older than I looked. All my hopefulness had vanished. I thought of myself as I had once been, naïve, happy, and obedient. Or perhaps just happy to be obedient. In the films of my youth when the heroine married the hero that was the end of the story, and life was justified and fulfilled. But when they both survive the ending the story changes. And when one of them survives or outlives the other the story changes again, and not for the better. For the worse! I saw that now. In the dim light of a February afternoon, with the grey carpet a lake of darkness, I saw all too clearly that some changes have to be resisted. I had thought that I was resisting them in the right way, the only way for a woman who is growing older. I had thought to outwit the changes, to defy them, but in fact I had fallen into a trap, one that had narrowed my life, diminished it, so that I sat here, stranded on my sofa, wondering how I was to continue. For continue was the only thing I could do. There was no other course open to me.

'No, don't come,' I said to Charlie on the telephone. 'I'll be fine in a couple of days. And I don't want you to catch it.'

One pays too dearly for love. It seemed to me then that I could have managed without, although now I think differently. Now I know that one must accept everything in order to prepare some kind of harvest. Maybe that is why one is drawn so blindly into what is patently unwise. At that bleak moment I envisaged life free of the fate I had devised for myself, and myself free to come and go as I pleased. For although the day was dark I knew that spring was coming, when I would recover my former lightness. I would tell him, I thought, and suddenly my mind was made up. When I was recovered, and could trust myself not to be tearful, I would tell him that it had to end, that he must not come any more. Then I should be free of them both, for Julia inevitably came into this equation. I could refuse obligations that I had accepted out of pity or guilt or terror. For I was frightened of her, always had been. Although I did not like her any more than she liked me, she was always in my thoughts, in a way that I hoped, I trusted, I was not in hers. She was impervious to me; what I did was of no interest to her. That was the mark of her ascendancy. That was how I had managed to keep my secret for so long.

With Charlie it was different. Charlie was so schooled in discretion that nothing untoward would ever escape him, and thus he persuaded himself that his loyalty was intact. Maybe it was. With Julia he espoused a mode of being that was the one perhaps best suited to his nature. Soft-footed, smiling, attentive, it was natural for him to care for her. 'You are the woman of my life,' he had written to her. 'There will be no other.' I saw now that this was true, that what happened when he was away from her troubled neither of them. So solipsistic was Julia that it would not occur to her to wonder what he did when he was not with her. When he handed her her drink in the drawing-room in Onslow Square he would be as he had always been: the essential, the eternal lover and husband. I had often wondered at the unthinking way in which she issued her orders, and the unthinking way in which he obeyed them. He would never leave her. He had never left her. I was marginal. I had always known this and had not resented it, perhaps had not examined it, as I did now. What did he feel? Probably what I felt, pleasure and regret.

Fortunately I had never told him of my feelings and the shadow they sometimes cast. To do that, I knew, would make him sigh, but would bring out something defensive in his nature. The citadel of his arrangements was not to be breached. That much had always been clear, but was now becoming clearer. As for me, I had reached the limit of my ability to dissemble. Perhaps I had somehow thought that the dissimulation was also temporary, as temporary as my attendance on Julia. Perhaps I had never wished for either. This, however, was now irrelevant. Now that the end of the affair had apparently been reached, and so swiftly, almost easily, I was willing to concede that he had almost loved me, but that what he had felt had been a fraction out of true, something that he could manage only by withholding it, keeping it out of my reach, lest I should take it into my head to lay hands on it and do damage. I wiped my eyes, got up and made a cup of tea. I would end it as pleasantly as I could, so that we both had a decent remembrance of each other. And when it was done (here I trembled) I would telephone Harry and ask him to get me some more work, or I would push a tea trolley round the hospital, or join the WVS. There must be several things a woman can do other than think of love and marriage. The young, of course, know this, or they seem to nowadays. My generation was less realistic. It seems to me now that my own youth was passed in a dream, and that I only came to see the world as it was when it was already too late.

I was about to do something prestigious, something I had never done before, and I felt a very slight return of energy. Professional pride had never meant anything to me: it was as natural for me to sing as it was to breathe. It had never occurred to me to think of singing as an heroic enterprise, whereas breaking off a love affair seemed to demand of me a certain prowess. It called for style, and I doubted that I should be equal to the occasion. It was my lack of style that had made me fear Julia. Still she came into my mind, had in fact never left it. We could never be friends; the idea was abusive, perverse. Acquaintances perhaps, whose acquaintanceship was dwindling. I should in effect be taking my leave of Julia, as well as of Charlie. It was strange how they now appeared to me to be indivisible, as if I could not know one without partaking of the other. That had been the position and I had ignored it, and had paid the price of ignoring it. If I had been discreet, uncomplaining, it was out of shame as well as a sense of what was fitting. And I was not really qualified for the task. It seems to me now that a mistress is a kind of prodigy, that this particular calling is not within the reach of all. The young can manage it, but such is their innocence that they do not even use the word, which is lurid, old-fashioned, with connotations of little black dresses and scarlet nails and evil ways. The young can manage anything, and perhaps they should: it is their prerogative. But a woman like myself, conventional, a widow, which somehow makes it worse, has no business to be engaging in these matters. Yet to say goodbye to someone – anyone – is such a terrible thing that it should not be undertaken lightly. One shrinks from such finality, and if one does not there is something wrong. Nature gives the warning here. But then Nature has also provided an unwelcome commentary: tiredness, a wrinkled skin. These are harsh verdicts on what is unsuitable, inappropriate. My weakness was to wish for consolation, when, properly speaking, there could be none.

I was not quite prepared to act on my great decision, and so I did something that I had thought of doing for a long time: I telephoned Millie and asked if I could come down for a day or two. She was delighted, and her pleasure moved me, made me think of simple days to come, or at least of simple days in the past when I seemed to have achieved the wholeness I now desired. It perturbed me slightly that I was not able to let Charlie know that I should be away; I had never done this before, and had always been there to speak to him, to greet him, to serve him his coffee. I thought of the telephone ringing in the empty flat and felt a disappointment that I should not be there. For some reason it reminded me of the telephone ringing in Gertrude Street and my not being there to pick it up, my preferring to be absent in the sunny streets. There was no lightheartedness in my present projected absence, no sense of escape, as there had been that last time. There was no summer to beckon me away from my duties, for now I had no duties to abandon. I had difficult work to do, preparations to make for a new life, one for which I suddenly had little taste.

I felt weak and incapable of getting to Paddington, so I ordered a car to take me down to Millie's, or at least to Moreton-in-Marsh, where she would meet me. From the back seat of the car London frightened me as it never did when I was on foot; I seemed to enter a world of traffic from which there was no exit and all I saw was ugliness, thundering lorries, overpasses, meek houses, seedy private hotels, factories apparently sited in vacant lots, and everywhere noise, confusion, urgency. England seemed to have turned into one huge road system while I had been living my sleeping life. Reading passed me in a flash, then Oxford, and then the sounds diminished and we were in the open country. Charlbury, Kingham, Moreton. I told the driver to drop me outside the station, where Millie was to collect me. I had an hour in hand. On weakish legs I wandered down the handsome high street, found a café and went in. I sat at a table in the window and drank excellent hot coffee. I wondered what it would be like to live in such a place. There could be no life more circumscribed than the one I had devised for myself, and it might be better for me to have a change, or rather make one. Shops here sold the same products, the same newspapers. And the place was handsome. Pale buildings faced each other across a carriage road; there was a porticoed hotel, and a couple of estate agents, and a particularly fine bank building. There were souvenir shops for the visitors, and discreet pubs with an air of reserve about them. There was nothing to stop me living here, near to Millie, but already I felt the ache of the town dweller displaced into an atmosphere which will never become famili-ar. I should never become a native of this place, never accept it as my own or myself as part of it. Yet it was beautiful. As I walked back to the station I noticed a lightness in the air, a powdery hazy quality and a colour somewhere between grey and blond, a trembling of leaves waiting to emerge, a watery lightness to the clouds, a white brilliance held in check. Spring, so much more noticeable than in London, where only the cut flowers changed and where one made special detours to view flowering trees. Spring was also unsatisfactory in London, pale mornings leading to long pale days in which nothing seemed to happen, and bird-song sounding forlorn in the long late twilight. In the country spring seemed sturdier, more an affair of men and cultivation than of women and girls, and their vapours. Distractedly I scanned the pleasant street, and at last I glimpsed Millie, waving. I waved back and ran towards her, as fast as my newly fledged condition would allow.

She had aged too. The skin of her face was shiny and seamed and her hair was now pepper and salt and tied back carelessly with a velvet ribbon. She had worn it like that when she was a girl, when we were both girls, and were slim-waisted in the pretty cotton frocks of the day. Now she wore an olive green waterproof jacket and a tweed skirt, thickish stockings and flat shoes. Her legs, which had been magnificent, were still beautiful, as were her hands, white, straight, without loose flesh. The full body, sloping down into those beautiful legs, had been Millie's greatest attraction, and even now that the body bent a little forward at the waist I could see her as she had been when she was a girl. We had never quarrelled, had never shocked or disturbed each other with unwonted confessions or unwise accusations. Some instinct had kept us true friends. We had preserved each other's modesty. That was how we came to greet each other with such a rush of feeling; we knew that there were no spoiled memories behind us. Each saw in the other, perfectly preserved, a picture of her own girlhood, and with it all the Edenic simplicity of a life which can never be prolonged or duplicated. Growing up means growing away, and everyone is eager to begin the work. It is only halfway that one begins to look back, and by then it is already too late.

Her house was small and dark and smelt of apples stored for the winter. The windows of her long low sitting-room looked out on to the single street of a small village. I was glad to see that she still had her piano. We bumped out through the kitchen with my overnight bag and into a garden bounded on one side by a miniature wing, just one room on top of another, which was where she housed her guests. 'We've had both children staying here, *and* their families,' she boasted, but it looked too small for me, used as I was to the flat where I could roam all night on bare feet if sleep deserted me. I sat down on my bed and gazed at the white sky out of the window. It was colder here and silent, yet I was not unduly dismayed. Rather I was bemused, in abeyance. How much so I saw when I looked in the silvery mirror of the little dressing-table. A pale wary face looked back at me, with a drained lifeless appearance, the expression watchful, stunned, as if at the receipt of bad news.

Over tea Millie asked me all about myself, but what I longed to tell her I could not, out of a sort of respect, both for her and for myself. But when she said, 'You must miss Owen,' I started, and said hurriedly that I did not, that it had been a mistake in so many ways, not to marry him, but to imagine that he could be happy with a woman like myself. 'I am so dull,' I said to her with a smile.

'Dull?' she said indignantly. 'I never heard such nonsense. Why, you could marry again tomorrow if you wanted to.'

'Why no,' I said, bending down to fondle a little white cat. 'No, I shall never marry again.'

'Fay. I hate to think of you on your own. You were so gifted, so happy. Do you ever sing these days?'

'Never.' I smiled.

'Well, you're going to sing now,' she said, going over to the piano, which was open.

'I couldn't possibly,' I said, feeling a forbidden ache in my throat.

'I'll start.' She played a few bars, hummed a few notes, then began to sing, and stopped. 'You see?' she said. Her voice had become thinner, whispery, like an old record. 'I've lost it. All over. Fortunately I'm so happy in other ways that it doesn't matter. I can still carry a tune, but I haven't the breath. And do you know, Donald still boasts about me, as if I were in my heyday. "My wife's the musician," he says, when anyone asks him to play – and he's a good pianist, you know. And his wife can't sing a note these days. But I'm sure you can, Fay. Won't you try? For me?'

So I sang. I sang 'Only Make-Believe', and 'You Are My Heart's Delight', and 'I'll Be Loving You Always', and, of course, 'Arcady'. Sometimes my voice broke on a high note but I sang on, for those songs said better than I could the emptiness and longing of my life. Singing reminded me, weakened my resolve. Why end what was there, why cancel it? What right had I to think it the correct course of action? Those songs were somehow too much for me. When I was young they did not move me so much: I sang them unaffectedly then, unshadowed by knowledge. Now, even the words seemed unbearable. But I sang on as if I were giving my final performance, as if all that mattered was to get through the programme, and then to say goodbye. My breathing was still good, and I sounded quite well, even to myself, although by now there were tears in my eyes.

Millie closed the piano with a bang. 'You can still do it,' she said, but she eyed me sadly, aware that something was wrong and that I would not tell her. 'If you would only come down here more often,' she said, walking me through to the kitchen with an arm round my waist. 'I could introduce you to so many nice men. You'd never be lonely. And who knows? You might fall in love again. It's never too late.'

Smiling, I shook my head. When we were girls we had often introduced each other to nice men; there were so many of them then. There had never been any jealousy between us.

Donald came home to dinner. He had come home specially, for he had to be back in London the following day. He was an easy happy man, rather plain, rather large, pleased with his life and charming to others, all of whom were outside the close communion he had with Millie. The evening passed pleasantly. I drank a couple of glasses of wine, and all at once felt tired and ready for bed. At ten-thirty Millie said, 'Shall I put the kettle on, Fay?' for we always used to drink a late cup of tea. 'I'll do it,' I said, as I always did, and we both laughed. We drank our tea, while Donald looked on indulgently, and then I left them and went to bed, and slept.

I woke early, too early. With nothing to do until the rest of the household was awake I stuck my head out of the window. Still that white light, that impression of brilliance withheld, immanent. A misty hazy morning, with sudden fitful brightenings, as if spring might really break if only one could hold one's breath for a while and not interrupt it. Attentiveness seemed to be called for, the strangest kind of caution. But suddenly it was all too much for me to wait, and on impulse I bundled my clothes into my bag and determined to ask Donald if I could drive up with him. I wanted so desperately to be at home that I almost overlooked my rudeness to Millie. Almost, not quite; I knew she would be hurt. But I felt beyond help, beyond courtesy, beyond normal exchange. All I wanted was to be back where I had been for the last six years, back where I – however mistakenly – belonged. To belong is a state of mind, not a state of possession.

I was ashamed, yet I was driven. Now, looking back, I feel the same. I had failed Millie, and I had failed myself: my freedom had proved illusory. Yet at the same time I knew I was in the wrong place. Whether I would have felt this had I not been unwell, had I not been unhappy, and unhappily aware of what was to come, I do not know. In a sense I was tragically disappointed, without knowing exactly why. I had been in search of some completeness and I had failed to find it. Ordinary life, real life did not seem to contain it, although Millie remained my dearest friend, her husband the kindest of men, their welcome as warm as could have been desired. Perhaps I was really ill, as Millie seemed to think. At least she accepted my excuses, although she looked concerned. I had sung for Millie, yet I was conscious of lacking a voice, or perhaps my own words. It seemed to me that I had something to say, or rather that something was left unsaid, and yet I did not quite know what it was. The image of that white empty sky stayed with me, and the mute garden down below, in which nothing stirred. I was conscious of the lengthening days ahead and of the need to fill them before I completely lost what little identity I had left. I felt a sense of danger, and yet I am really a very unimaginative woman. I chattered away to Donald in the car in what I heard as a rather high voice, conscious of extreme anxiety, and the need to get home.

Yet when I reached Drayton Gardens everything was normal. I put my key in the lock, went inside, unpacked my bag, and made myself some coffee. Here too the light seemed different. Of course it was darker in the flat than it had been at Millie's, but I was strangely conscious of that whiteness, that absence that I had previously noted. Crocuses had been out in the park. I had pointed them out to Donald, acutely aware that I was taking him out of his way, that I was making him late, that I was being a nuisance. Yet the crocuses had made it seem less odious of me to force this detour on him: I offered them up. It was a fine morning, sun struggling through mist: it would struggle until about three o'clock and then gradually begin to fade. That fading would be the most characteristic part of the day. Now, when I look back, the English spring seems to me heartbreaking. I dread it every year, although nothing more can happen to me. I associate it, still, with a certain panic, as if events are moving at their own pace, not at mine. I think of spring as the most impervious of the seasons. Nothing in me responds to it: I simply bow my head and wait for it to be over, wait for it to deliver me into summer, when, for a little while, I can relax.

There was nothing to do, no one to telephone. I was so jumpy that I nearly called Julia, but decided, on reflection, that this was unseemly. I was in fact waiting for Charlie's call and was eager to explain to him why I had been absent, and to tell him that I was back for good. My eagerness was such that all thoughts of renunciation had left me, or rather I had postponed them. I could not give him up without his full attention, and I needed his presence, and more than his presence, I needed him to concentrate on my situation, something which I doubt that he had ever done. I needed to know, from him, how fatally he would miss me when I was gone; I needed him to plead with me, since he had never done that either, had had no need to do so. The grudge that women feel against their lovers is really a desire to be taken seriously, and a suspicion that they have passed into the realm of familiar things, on which no great thoughts need be expended. The yeasty drama that rises in a woman about to end it all may simply be a desire to be talked out of it, but in the same high-flown terms. This desire is rarely satisfied and should probably be resisted at all costs. I most urgently needed Charlie's presence so that I could say various unpalatable things to him. It was no longer a matter of doing what I wanted, but of obeying some compulsion. To make him listen to me was my overriding concern; what I had to say was somehow of lesser importance. Indeed, I hardly knew what it was.

It was therefore frustrating when he failed to telephone that evening. When I calculated that the time for a call was past I took my coat and went out, walked in the still light streets, looked in shop windows, bought an evening paper. I had a few sleeping pills left out of the small number the doctor had given me, and I intended to take one, so that there should be no trace of tiredness on my face the following day. I walked on, in order to tire myself further, still conscious of a tremor of the nerves. In the event I slept badly. I put this down to anticipation.

I was thus unprepared for the fact that he did not call the next day, Friday. I was irritated rather than concerned, for he would surely be with me on the Saturday, which seemed to me appropriate for what we had to discuss. In order to make sure of this I did something that I had vowed I would never do again: I rang him at the office. When Gaynor, his secretary, said, 'I'm afraid he's not here at the moment. Can I take a message?' I said, as lightly as I could, 'No, thank you, no message,' telling myself that there was no reason why she should recognize my voice. I sat looking at the humming telephone, and then, very quietly, put it down. Another sleeping pill would get me through to Saturday, but I thought I might not make my great speech until we had re-established some sort of continuity. I was faint-hearted suddenly, and like many about to commit themselves desired only not to do so. Time seemed to be in abeyance until Charlie manifested himself. I gave up trying to distract myself and surrendered to the business of waiting for him. It was something I had learned how to do.

Looking back from my present vantage point, I feel pity and distaste. What certain self-made characters feel about their humble beginnings I feel about my prosperous and secret middle age. I refuse to blame anyone: I alone am to blame. If there is any profit in it I fail to see how it has come about. The opinion of my friends (for now I have them) and of the ladies at the WVS is that I am delightfully sympathetic: I refuse to believe it. I have no sympathy for women who make fools of themselves, boast of their sexual prowess, or inquire into that of others. Sex now seems to me a book so firmly closed that I am taken, I believe, for a faithful widow. 'Such a pity,' I heard one woman say to another. 'I'm sure she could have married again. But she just didn't seem to have the heart for it.' I accept all this as part of my punishment, for it is quite right that I should pay a price. For not being sufficiently loved, perhaps. For knowing this. Yet how does one close the door on feeling, when there is still time to use it? I can do it now, of course, but it was truly impossible for me to do it then. And although I now look back with sorrow I really had no qualms, no scruples. I behaved, I think, naturally, and to outwit nature would take a stronger character than mine. I never pretended to be anything out of the ordinary.

When the telephone rang I leapt from my chair, aware of sensations of alarm and bewilderment: how was I, in my extreme state, to behave naturally? The fact that it was a woman's voice made me slump with disappointment, one hand to my beating heart.

'Fay? Is that you, Fay? It's Pearl here, Pearl Chesney.'

'Hello, Pearl,' I said evenly. 'How are you?'

'Not too badly, dear. Just packing up my bits and pieces. And yourself?'

'I'm fine,' I said.

'I'm sorry to ring you like this, but I wondered if you'd been in touch with Julia?'

'No, I haven't. I've been away for a few days.' As usual, my absences from home were stretched to fit the time expected of them.

'Then you haven't heard the news,' she went on.

'What news?'

'Charlie. A stroke. On Wednesday morning, at the office. They called an ambulance. They managed to get him into the Harley Street Clinic.'

'I see,' I said, through numb lips.

'Do you know how to get there? I expect you'll want to slip in and see him, won't you?'

That use of the word 'slip' told me that Pearl Chesney knew, and had always known, exactly how matters stood. She was a good woman, unable to judge, probably too experienced to be shocked. The knowledge would have made her own situation delicate. It may even have had something to do with her decision to leave. Or not, as the case might be. In that moment I cared nothing for anyone who was not Charlie.

'How bad is he?' I asked.

'Not too good.' She sounded uneasy, her breathing hard.

'When does Julia go to the hospital?' I asked, for there was no pretence now.

'Well, she went on the Wednesday, but she says there's no point because he doesn't know her. She says she's waiting for him to come round. She has every hope, she says. Of course, I've been keeping her company while all this is going on.' She paused. 'I think she said she was going tomorrow.'

'Did you say he doesn't know her?'

'Well, yes, dear, but they're very confident. It's wonderful what they can do these days, isn't it? I expect you'll want to give Julia a ring. She needs a lot of support at the present time.'

'How is she?' I asked.

'Very brave. She was always brave, marvellous, really. "I can't let Charlie down," she says. "I shall be there when he's ready to see me. I shall always be there." She's made a big hit with the nurses. But then Julia knows how to talk to people.'

'Yes,' I said. 'Thank you so much for letting me know, Pearl. We'll be in touch.'

'Or I'll see you at Julia's,' she said. For she thought it inconceivable that I should not be at her side. But I knew that Charlie was going to die, had always known, had seen the message in the white sky, had felt it in the tremor of the nerves. So strongly did I know this that it seemed to me useless even to ask for further news of him. Dully I rang the Harley Street Clinic, but they refused to tell me anything. 'Are you a relative?' they asked. 'Just a friend,' I said, and put the receiver back before they could say that he was resting comfortably.

12

'Of course, it was different in the old days,' said Julia. 'When I had staff. Then I could just have a tray sent up.' A powdery tear, like a very small pearl, made its way down her cheek, leaving no identifiable trace behind.

We were in her ultramarine bedroom, and Julia was in bed, wearing an ultramarine satin nightgown with cream lace insertions. Her hair was more rigidly set than usual and her eyes a little frightened. These were the only signs of her grief, which she experienced as an enormous discomfort. She had talked more about the loss of her former cook and maid than she had about the death of her husband. At least we had no wild outpourings to contend with, although her decision not to get up was slightly worrying. I doubt if she knew what she felt, apart from helplessness. Her feelings were so far from the surface, so deeply buried, that they gave her no information. This conferred an undeniable dignity, for she never lost her composure, or, more accurately, her command. There was, to me, something shocking in the expanse of white shoulder and arms, left on view for visitors: her flesh looked cold, preserved in its marble chill from unwonted surges of the blood, ageless, in its way perfect, remarkable by any standards. I shrank from the intimacy that this seemed to signal, but to Julia it was entirely natural to appear in this manner, as if she were receiving in her dressing-room. I did not want to see her in this way, yet she was apparently set up for the day, in her large cane-headed bed, and would remain there until the last sympathizer had taken his or her leave. The remains of a breakfast – a sticky plate, a cup and saucer – could be seen on one of the bedside tables. It was eleven o'clock in the morning, and no one had quite managed to clear this away; hence the lament for absent staff. The room was very hot; through the window a tiny silver plane was a point of brilliance in a cloudless light blue sky. Pearl Chesney and Maureen sat on either side of the bed, attempting to hold Julia's hands. There was no reason for them to do so; she was quite calm. But she was fretful, and her eyes kept turning towards the window, the heavy eyelids falling from time to time. I stood at the foot of the bed, forcing myself to look at her.

What I myself felt was as indistinguishable as Julia's grief. Where she was plaintive, helpless, I was simply conscious of an enormous disorder, a chaos in my thoughts, which were dominated by fragments of popular songs and the remnants of terrible dreams. The previous night I had dreamt of returning home to find the place flooded: sodden books floated in pools of water, tiles had fallen from the walls into cracked and ruined baths and basins, shelves sagged and buckled. The blotched and discoloured walls were being surveyed by a team of impassive men who had got there before I had, may even have been there all the time. I was mysteriously absent, returning to this place only when the damage was irreversible. To rebuild and redecorate would take months, yet the men, who became increasingly indifferent, could not even give me a date when they might start, seemed unwilling, reluctant to take it on. To begin with I did not recognize the damaged rooms as belonging to the flat in Drayton Gardens, which gave me a sense of relief, until I saw that it was my parents' house in Camberwell Grove that had undergone such an assault, such a letting in of alien waters. My grief at this revelation was immeasurable. In panic I had woken to find that only an hour had passed since I had turned out my light. The whole night stretched before me, and although I slept voraciously no sleep was devoid of its succession of bizarre and disruptive images.

Awake, I hardly knew how to think or feel. What was clear to me was that I must defer to Julia, whose loss was greater than mine, not only in the eyes of anyone who might know the story but even to myself. There is no appropriate attitude for a bereaved mistress, although she is spared the Job's comforters who attend the wife. The best thing she can do, or if not the best then certainly the most expedient, is to turn into one such comforter herself, aware of the hypocrisy involved, finding some relief in the savage alienation she feels. Rage is better than grief, especially where no atonement is possible. Seeing Julia stranded in her large bed made me profoundly thankful that my passage through her life was of so little interest to her. Infidelity seemed too ponderous a word to use of Charlie's behaviour now: diversion seemed more accurate. He had been discreet, practised. In any event his feelings had died with him; there was no evidence left, apart from the insistent refrains in my head. 'Just A-Wearying for You', an appallingly wistful song which had always moved me, now erupted into all my thoughts, so that I almost had to turn my head to listen to it. This made me seem absent, and I failed to produce the correct condolences and reassurances.

'You're very quiet,' Julia remarked, surveying me from under her eyelids.

'I'm sorry, Julia. I simply don't know what to say.'

This was nothing more nor less than the truth, but it sounded crude. I was afflicted with a terrible weariness, which was intensified by the sight of Julia in bed. It occurred to me that she was old, however ageless she seemed, and that what had originally been a matter of choice was now one of necessity. I doubted whether she would ever leave the house again. Maureen was there, of course, and there seemed to be no further talk of Pearl Chesney leaving London. These two were acting as official mourners, were flushed and anxious and ready with all the futile phrases one utters on such occasions. Only Julia and I were dry-eyed.

'I shall be next,' said Julia. 'I can't tell you how I look forward to it.'

'In the meantime,' I told her, 'I very much hope you intend to get out of that bed.'

'I may. And on the other hand I may not.'

'Come along, Julia. Get up, have your bath, get dressed, and eat some lunch. I've brought enough food for a couple of days. It's all over, Julia, there's nothing more to be done. Try to take up your life again. After all,' I said roughly, hating myself, 'you wouldn't have wanted him to linger, incapacitated as he was. This way is cleaner.'

She turned her head slowly towards me, as though I were some sort of secondary audience, a matinée audience, perhaps.

'If you've got nothing better to say or do,' she said, 'you might change those books.' Most of her requests were framed in this way. 'You might throw those flowers away.' 'You might pull that curtain.' 'You might fill my glass.'

'Yes, I'll do that,' I said. 'But if you want anything to eat you'll have to get up. And if you drink instead of eating, your arthritis will get far worse. I'm not scaremongering. I'm telling you the truth. If you stay in bed you'll soon become too stiff to move. And, as you say, you no longer have staff to wait on you.' Whereas if she got up she could manage with Maureen and Mrs Chesney, who, I had no doubt, would be there to the end.

My one fear was that she should declare herself incapable of further movement. That, however, was my only fear. Julia no longer terrified me. I felt for her pity and repugnance, as someone who had darkened my life and was now a victim herself. My condolences were inadequate because I was now seeing the two of them, Julia and Charlie, as despoilers, rich and idle, and more expert than I could ever be. And of the two of them perhaps Charlie was the more to blame. He was younger than Julia by a few years, had no doubt made discreet arrangements, of which I was one. I doubted the value of his feeling now; it seemed to me of lesser significance than his discretion, of which I was assured. It even occurred to me that he had thought of me in the same dismissive terms as Julia was inclined to use, but I cancelled the thought. There had been feeling there, but there was no clue to it now. I should have to live with its absence for as long as I remembered him. It had disappeared, along with his fine smile, his air of ease. That air had misled me into confusing it with intention.

Yet below the rage and the hopelessness that I now felt was a certainty (or was it a hope?) that my own feelings were not affected. I preferred to examine them later, alone, not ever to consider them in company, in any company at all. I knew they would not stand the light of day. What I wanted more than anything in the world at that moment was to get out of Julia's bedroom. I really wanted never to have to face her again, but I knew that this would be impossible. I should have to be very brave in order to contend with this, and to deal with it justly and competently, without undue favour or guilt. Again I felt engaged in something that was too difficult for me. In the absence of comfort I longed to be alone, if only to listen to the songs playing in my head.

I think I truly believed her to be a terrible or at best a tiresome woman, so what was my difficulty? Why was I, at that moment, planning to buy out of season asparagus and raspberries in order to tempt her appetite? What was the nature of the peculiar obligation she cast on me, almost without any exertion on her part? Why did she make everyone feel responsible, not just myself, but Maureen and Mrs Chesney, who had almost abandoned whatever plans they might have had for their own lives in order to attend to Julia? Why was it impossible to enter her presence without a full quota of compliments, almost as if she were the object of some religious cult? Why did she, without doing anything for anyone, inspire such devotion, while humbler, clumsier people like myself seemed doomed to do without?

I did not envy her her power and never had: indeed it seemed to me monstrous, particularly as her mind was so undistinguished. It was the force of her character that was so overwhelming. She was the still centre of a web of pointless intrigue, of disobliging gossip, yet should one's attention falter for just a minute she would divine the reason why. She was a loss to the stage, no doubt of that. Her pauses, her irony, her nervelessness gave her full command, while her inflection gave her utterances a scurrility of which she seemed innocently unaware. Yet over and above all this – and I truly believe she had no heart – she was a solitary figure, too beautiful and too unready for the ways of this coarse world. Hence her willingness to cast blame and doubt on everything, good intentions included, as if she could not quite tell what was good from what was bad, and therefore decided that there was no good anywhere. A prize for any man, though one who might weary him in the end, would remain a cult object throughout the most humdrum circumstances, and require worship at all times. She had uncommon strength, never caught cold, never tired unduly, yet employed nursery terms for her habits and functions, as if Nanny were still in attendance. I never saw her drunk, yet frequently heard her belch. 'That's better,' she would say, with evident pleasure. She had tales to tell of being taken short in various expensive or exotic places; never once did shame or confusion enter her voice. Rather, she felt a schoolgirl's zest for the sort of dilemma which normally only schoolgirls faced, but which Julia welcomed as normal throughout her adult life. Constipation was a well-aired topic, followed by wind. She seemed to feel a certain fondness for both, took vast quantities of patent medicines, washed down with whisky, yet never had a headache, barely suffered from the heat or the cold, but claimed to suffer from everything else. 'Don't speak of it,' she would say. 'I'm a martyr to it. The pain kept me awake all night.' She deplored exclusivity on the part of anyone else. I once heard her rebuke Maureen, who had intemperately turned her ankle. 'If you only knew the pain I suffered in my hands,' I heard her say, 'you'd keep quiet about that ankle of yours. Anyway it was sheer clumsiness on your part.'

I wavered between clear-sightedness and confusion, aware of many things I did not claim to know. I had not gone to the funeral, which had been in Hampshire, where his sister lived. I did not know that he had a sister. 'Catherine and I have never got on,' said Julia, as if that explained everything. There was to be a memorial service: I should not go to that either. I was conscious of the tangled nature of human affections, as if, after childhood, nothing could be deemed pure. I was devoid of blame, but also of pity. For our own good, it seemed to me, we had better be discreet about our feelings, our sufferings. I did not wish to know the nature of Julia's pain – for pain was what she claimed, no doubt truthfully. Her hands were undoubtedly giving her trouble and these seemed to be her main concern. We were all used to this, but I knew that for once she was understating the case. Lying there in her courtesan's nightgown, she seemed quite satisfied that she was playing her part, yet from time to time the great eyes were turned absently towards the window. I nodded, almost grimly, as I registered a state of grief. I supposed that I was in the same state myself. Yet I could walk out into the sun and know that I was free. This freedom appalled me, but I knew that it was mine. In dying, Charlie had removed an impediment. I could go away, book a cruise, sail round the world. All this was dreadful to me, but true. I was a rich woman, with no one on my conscience. My only responsibility was Vinnie.

For Vinnie lived! Eighty-eight and almost senseless, she no longer spoke, hardly ate, never left her bed. I had had to install a housekeeper during the day, though Sandra was still there for the nights. Fortunately these were quiet; indeed sleeping and waking were almost undifferentiated. When I went to see her the small clouded eyes opened and stared at me accusingly. I was to blame, it seemed. I was to blame for everything, for Owen's death, for her own decrepitude. All this was far from my thoughts, yet so insistently with me. My visits gave her no pleasure, but if I stayed away she was agitated. 'She missed you yesterday,' Mrs Arnold, the housekeeper, would say. 'We wondered what had happened to you.' I was terrified that she would leave, and so I continued to go round, with my basket full of food, which was much appreciated by Mrs Arnold. She was a woman of a certain age, with a badly mended broken hip, glad to sit down all day, to read or listen to the radio. When she moved it was with a painful lurching gait that hurt one to watch. Yet she had to work, for her husband was retired and some years older than herself. I paid her well. She smiled kindly at me, sighed at the end of the day, rolled up her knitting, and left reluctantly. Yet it was an irksome, wearisome job of work, and although Vinnie was now light as a doll it was not easy for Mrs Arnold to lift her. Vinnie herself seemed to me faintly unclean, as she had always done. I thought her better off in her own bed, however dubious, than in a home, though that too would have to come. Fortunately, there was enough money to take care of her for the rest of her life.

It occurred to me to wonder how far worthy actions compensated for a lack of true virtue. I had always wanted to be good, yet had turned out to be flawed. Julia, though impossible, was somehow uncompromised. I could almost have wished for these positions to be reversed. Throughout my — what was it? association? affair? — with Charlie I had felt conscious of being in a false position, yet had been stimulated, amused by the very unexpected turn events had taken. Women feel this dangerous amusement when a lover approaches: it eases the way forward into an emotion which is not amusing at all, which is in fact melancholy, uncertain, nearly always uncomfortable. Periodical attempts are made to cancel everything, turn the page, resume a measure of good conscience, although innocence is always out of reach. Respectability is as much as can be hoped for; there is no woman so respectable as the one who has rediscovered virtue. In this spirit, and profoundly tired, I sought to make amends. I turned away almost irritably from my own feelings, aware that once I was alone, a kind of longing would descend on me, for that presence which had been so intermittently mine, and for that reason so heightened. At times it had seemed to me that men and women who lived together enjoyed a lesser intimacy than the one I stole; the very flatness of Julia's conversation, her malice, the regressive nature of her references to the body I took as proof of boredom. Now I was not sure, and the revelation was unwelcome. It bothered me to see the accoutrements of that bedroom in which an ordinary life could be lived, cigarettes smoked, the events of the day discussed, books picked up or discarded, pills taken, idle speculations entertained, and lights eventually put out. No haste, no compulsion. Haste and compulsion are what make a woman guilty, no less – perhaps more – than a man.

Trying to repair the ruin of my life I forced myself to look outward. There were, to say the least, those less fortunate than myself. Although I was sure that Charlie had made a careful will, had left life insurance policies, I doubted Julia's ability to deal with any of this. The task would fall to Maureen, for Julia would immediately declare herself incapable – had already done so – and poor Pearl Chesney would ultimately be released to her little flat in Surrey, Kingston, I think it was, although she was no longer enthusiastic at the prospect. Julia's prostration gave her a chance to assume her former ascendancy: she looked altogether more purposeful, more gainfully employed, wiping easy tears from her tawny cheeks, bustling in with glasses of water, offering a highly elaborate négligé and laying it reverently at the foot of the bed, even rearranging pillows. It seemed odd to me that with all this attention being paid no one had managed to remove the filmed cup and saucer and the plate with its traces of marmalade which was now being used as an ashtray. A degree of uncertainty was one of the tenets of their housekeeping: not knowing where to start or how to finish, so that one intention was always colliding with another. I was there one afternoon when they had discussed the making of a cup of tea, although none had been produced. 'Hardly worth it now,' Julia had said. 'Might as well have a drink. Oh, you don't drink, do you? Well, if you had come earlier we could have had it together. I rather look forward to a cup of tea. Never mind, another time.' 'It's no trouble,' Maureen had said, appearing in the doorway with a tea towel in her hand. 'I can easily make a cup if Fay wants one.' 'No, come and sit down, Maureen. You've done quite enough,' said Julia. 'It's too late, anyway.' There would follow the usual lament on demise of staff, an affirmation that her day was done, and a condemnation of the changing world. All of this was quite predictable. Food seemed a particularly uncertain commodity, owing to the extreme incompetence that prevailed. Frequently discussion about a meal, or reminiscences of meals in the past, would be called in as partial substitutes for the meal itself. 'I'm not really hungry,' Julia would say. 'Is there anything left over?' For she was a fearless eater of ancient cooked meats, congealed sardines, cold rice pudding, cheese with a greenish bloom on it, none of which affected her in the slightest. 'If there's one thing I can't stand it's waste,' she would say. She had the digestion of an adolescent at boarding school, whereas the mere sight of such food made me feel ill. 'There's a lot of nonsense talked about cooking,' said Julia. 'Not that I can taste it anyway.'

The greater part of this incompetence, this helplessness, was due to the character of Maureen, that mysterious and apparently ageless devotee who, twenty years earlier, had come to interview Julia for the local paper and had stayed ever since. She had not grown weary in her devotion: if anything she had grown more devout, but in a general sense. From being once exclusively concentrated on Julia, her goodwill now reached out to embrace the universe; she was tireless in the service of the church, though what she actually did remained obscure, possibly because no one could bear to ask her. She seemed to clock in to St Luke's twice a day, once for worship, and later for a rather excited discussion of parish business, which included the magazine and what she referred to as 'the rotas'. To my mind putting Maureen in charge of anything was asking for trouble, but in the way of certain Christians she regarded her muddleheadedness as God-given, laughed forbearingly over a hopeless mass of papers which someone else would have to sort out, and further burnished the ready and rather mad smile which she bestowed on the world at large.

'Now look here!' said Julia. 'This love affair you're having with God.' In so saying she adopted the pose of a forthright downright no-nonsense Englishwoman: I think she even leaned forward and grasped her knees with her hands. 'It's all very well, darling, but where's it getting you? As you know, I've always been religious myself.' (This may have been true, although one was inclined not to believe it.) 'But I've always looked for God outside the church. In nature,' she said, her hands describing a poetic curve. 'Whereas you closet yourself inside that awful building, with those awful people, and life passes you by. It's not as if you were a girl any more.' Maureen must have been about forty-five, having been a fledgling reporter on her first arrival. 'If only you'd let Bobby do something about your hair you'd at least be more presentable. Not that there's any chance of your meeting anyone, the way you carry on. I suppose it's all quite harmless. But remember, Maureen, God is outside as well as inside. The sun,' she said vaguely. 'Trees. Look up,' she added more vigorously. 'Look about you. That's what I've always done. And I don't think anyone would say I was a bad woman,' she said, with a fine smile. 'At least, nobody ever has.' Certainly not in your hearing, I thought. No one would dare.

My heart ached for Maureen, whom I did not, could not, like. In the full flush of middle age she looked like a girl, unadorned, clumsy, touching, and irritating. An overall impression of paleness was highlighted by her eager smile and her habit of pushing her glasses up her nose. She had fine teeth and indeterminate features, surmounted by too much badly permed hair: hair met glasses and was occasionally trapped behind them. She wore track suits in baby colours of pink and blue, and white socks and sneakers. The body thus hidden appeared to be healthy and undemanding, for she was essentially virginal. She was like one of those very early martyrs who cheerfully embraced their doom in the Colosseum without ever tasting the alternative. Julia was Maureen's doom, and her smiles grew ever more radiant, her laughter ever more hearty as Julia became more unreasonable. The suspicion grew in me that she regarded Julia as her cross and personally offered her up to the Almighty every time she suffered a rebuke or broke crockery on her behalf. It also occurred to me that Julia would not care to be annexed in this way, but had no idea that this was the case, being totally unconcerned with and certainly uninterested in Maureen's feelings. Some justification is needed for certain actions in this vale of tears: Maureen had perfected a euphoria that kept her immune from Julia's hints and excused the curious calling of parasitism that had come her way.

My uneasiness with Maureen stemmed from my suspicion that she was highly excitable, and that if she did not look for God in nature it was because her relationship with nature was on the sneaky side and occasionally overpowered her with headaches and deep blushes, leaving her paler, more mirthful, and more devout than ever. Julia's advice to her was cruel, but unintentionally so. Maureen was in fact tormented by nature, or rather by Nature, her instincts always on the alert. She should have married young and had a baby every year for four years. As it was, her fecundity had lost its original character, and now manifested itself as hysteria. Maureen's laughter, these days, was almost continuous, as she dropped and broke things, or alternatively praised and cosseted Julia. Julia thought her a fool, but had, I think, no real understanding of Maureen's tragedy, forced as she was to make do with this simulacrum of a life, when she possessed the makings of an earth mother. I had watched, pitying and slightly perturbed, as she exclaimed with pleasure over some titbit of food that I had brought, how pleasurably the teeth had closed and the mouthful tipped down the yielding throat. The key to Maureen was the voracity of her appetite and the mincing ways with which she sought to disguise it.

She had never cared for me, although so all-embracing was her love of humanity that I doubt whether she realized this. The normal and perhaps more limited passions were subsumed into her gigantic and indiscriminate goodwill. I wondered if she was still capable of knowing whether she liked or disliked any one person: she accepted everyone as a matter of principle. Although this is undoubtedly an admirable trait it depressed and inhibited me, since it made the truth unavailable; one could never judge Maureen's mood or even her character, since her defensive laughter seemed to put her beyond criticism. Yet once or twice I noticed her eyes on me, and when I returned her glance she immediately made her face a blank, as if in embarrassment. I could not tell whether the cause of the embarrassment was myself or her own thoughts. She gave the appearance of being sexually null, since she devoted no thought to her hair and clothes, but my impression was that she went to great pains to curb unused energies, and that once alone in her room she performed all sorts of spiritual exercises before embracing the loneliness of the night to come. I hated to see her living the life she had devised for herself, yet she was a blameless woman, eager, and no doubt generous. Her good qualities were immediately compromised by the fact that although willing she was almost always unhelpful. This moral clumsiness was a trait as ineradicable as tone deafness or colour blindness.

I wondered how Julia could bear to rely on her ministrations, until I reflected that Julia's days were long and trivial, so that being subjected to excited discussions as to the advisability of making a cup of tea struck her now as entirely normal, and may even have responded to something genuinely unschooled in Julia's make-up. A mixture of the convent and the dressing-room, the atmosphere in Onslow Square seemed to be redolent of the company of women. If they had been men, Maureen would have been Julia's fag. But what had always constrained me was to see them so happy with their own female company. Pearl Chesney, I think, had felt the same constraint, and so was not a true member of the little clan. I, of course, was a renegade; I should have been one in any case. What I loved and prized was the steadiness of a man's affection, his indulgence, his company. I had known this in childhood, and even during my brief career, when the boys in the band had looked after me as if I were their little sister. In adult life, unfortunately, this affection had been fitful, limited, doled out in unpredictable instalments. Even so it struck me as the greater prize, greater by far than the intimacy of women. This may be an indication of my lesser nature. To Julia, primarily to Julia, though I think to Maureen as well, female company was a rule of life, and one deserted it only through stupidity. Julia often cited her first husband, Hodge, as an example of this desertion. 'I should never have left Mummy,' she would say, with what seemed to me brazen

144

innocence. Lovers did not impair her fidelity to her own kind in the same degree. Indeed mother and daughter seemed to look on the taking of a lover as licensed naughtiness. 'I'm afraid I was rather naughty,' Julia would say, of her various lovers. 'But he *was* very good-looking.'

This sort of talk had gone on in Charlie's presence, although her gallant days were over by the time Charlie met and married her. My impression was that she did not miss them, those lovers of hers, but regarded them much as she might have regarded the various performances she had given, in a detached and semi-professional sense. I have no doubt that she would have revealed all to a biographer, had one been forthcoming. For the essence of Julia was an untroubled conscience, a conscience so limpid that wrongdoing, detectable in others, was always excusable in herself. This conferred on her a certain girlishness, which, combined with the authority bestowed by great beauty, made her enigmatic and irresistible to men. But I wondered how companionable it might be on a daily basis. To my mind too much caprice obscures affection. To Charlie, I could see, she was still a prize. He respected her, feared her, certainly loved her, and perhaps hardly noticed his reduced role as supporter and protector. She accepted his tributes, valued him for the quality of the life he had enabled her to live, may have loved him, but looked to him mainly to love her. She did this without presumption, as if she found it natural that people should love her. As far as she knew, they always had.

We had thus both known a certain indulgence, Julia from her theatrical eminence, I from my singing days. The difference was that I longed for it to last, registered and mourned its absence, whereas Julia assumed that the source and supply would never dry up. While I, all longing, all loving, had made of a meagre portion my entire diet, Julia was able to remain indifferent to circumstance in the knowledge that she would be eternally protected. I even regarded her indifference to food as proof of the fact that she was always confident of being eventually fed, that she could go through the day on one of her revolting snacks and a couple of glasses of whisky, secure in the knowledge that when Charlie came home he would cook her an omelette and generally look after her.

She believed in the rights of women, she told us, but what she really believed in was the right of women to behave capriciously. There was a distinctly masculine side to her, in her refusal to entertain weak hopes and fears, her judicial appraisal of her gifts and attributes, her professional competence and objectivity, her hardy egotism. She was an unreliable mixture of the calculating and the obtuse. In comparison, I felt stupid, clumsy, vulnerable, and now tired to death. Yet I saw in dwindling perspective the nature of Charlie's feeling for me. I had thought of him as an opportunist, and maybe I had been right. I had come to welcome every sight of him, and he undoubtedly took pleasure in the extent of my welcome. Was there more? Did it occur to him, ever, to regret his role of complaisant husband? This I should never know, for I had never asked him. Nor did it much matter now. For it seemed to me regrettable, and always had. Only Julia's monstrous vanity had provided a partial justification, had obscured my part in the affair. I viewed her with a cold eye: nothing would alter that. I resented the pity I felt for her as she lay in that bed, smoking cigarette after cigarette. That very slightly haggard expression gave me pause. Yet when I saw how little of Charlie was left in that flat, how easily his trace had been effaced, how total was Julia's presence, my heart hardened again. Dead, he was as discreet as he had been in life. There was no trace of him in my flat either. The Victorian cup and saucer I had put away, never to be used again. I had nothing by which to remember him. It was perhaps fitting that I should now take my leave, since no ties bound me to this place, where I had failed to entertain or be understood.

'I'll go now,' I said to Julia, not expecting her to protest.

She turned to me, her eyelids raised.

'Did you say you had brought some food?' she asked.

'A lovely rice salad,' said Maureen.

'I see. Not a dish I normally like. Never mind, it won't hurt me for once. You might just put some on a plate and bring it in.'

13

I became nervous now in the evenings, particularly when rain threatened, as it did frequently after the hectically bright days of late April. Standing at my window I would nervously count the hours that remained before I could go to bed. There was nothing to stop me, of course, but I felt unwillingly expectant from about five o'clock onwards, as if someone were due to look in and ask me how I had spent my day, or perhaps in the hopes that such a person would arise. I knew no one like that; I was generally judged old enough to look after myself, but not yet old enough to require care or at least a cheerful enquiry from time to time. Eventually I would become an object of pity, if I were lucky enough not to become an object of derision, one of those mad old women in broken shoes who mutter to themselves in public places. Whenever I thought of women like this I would take a deep breath and pull in my stomach. Even standing at the window became an improving exercise, and any uncertainty I felt almost benign. But it was an anxious time, and nothing seemed to allay my uneasiness. As the light faded, and it took longer to do so in the lengthening spring days, I would scan the street for signs of life, watch the hairdresser over the way locking up for the night, hear the home-going traffic in the distance, and reflect with sadness that the children would all be gathered safely in, watching television, and that none would pass my window, waving, as they sometimes did.

I no longer liked the flat, which had always seemed to me appropriate rather than endearing. I disliked the orange street lamp outside the window and the dark lake of grey carpet; I disliked the brilliantly lit bathroom, and the bedroom from which the sun was always absent. The liver-coloured exterior, the clammy tiled entrance hall now filled me with dread as I returned with my shopping, but this may have been because I always returned too early for my liking, having mentally seen the children off to school. The whole blank morning stretched before me, and yet the mornings were not as bad as the unforgiving evenings, when I longed for the sound of a friendly step turning in towards my doorway. Oddly enough it was not Charlie that I missed, but rather the person for whom Charlie had always been a substitute, whoever he was. Charlie had been, and had remained, too clandestine for comfort: his fine smile had concealed a certain brutality, so that the agreeable and no doubt authentic face that he presented to the outside world, to his colleagues, his associates, his clients, and of course his wife, would be revealed to me as false, for I would see the grinning face of desire, the face that would be easily relinquished and left behind, as he resumed the easy lineaments of his superior and public self. I did not want this back. I was tired of, even disgusted with, my role in this matter, for it was only with my collusion that certain pretexts could be acted upon, and although I knew that desire had been authoritative, even if the relationship had been rudimentary, I renounced it all in the name of a virtue which would in any event soon be imposed on me by age and which I now embraced with the fervour of a convert.

The irony of the situation was that it had been quite foreign to my nature. I was not born to be a mistress; I doubted if I was even born to be a wife. In my own mind I existed as a hopeful adolescent in a tight-waisted cotton frock, practising my scales, or as a young girl, singing all those touching old songs with dedication but without sorrow. Maybe, like Julia, I should never have left my mother. I am aware that no woman of any sense thinks like this today, but, perhaps because of recent experiences, because of the disappointment I was bound to register with my life, I had to confess to feelings of longing for earlier days, days of confidence and high expectation before the realities of life closed in. From those early days I had retained my disastrous simple-mindedness, which guaranteed that I should do the wrong thing, know the wrong people, enter into associations through sheer ignorance, and be forever haunted by the outcome. Women of sixty – nearly sixty-one – are supposed to be experienced, prudent, tough, yet I felt as wistful as I had always done since I had left girlhood. It was this wistfulness that would descend on me in the early evenings, when I stood at the window, my hands idle, and listened for that imagined friendly step. When the street lamp came on, later and later now, it was my signal to turn away in despair, like Mariana at the moated grange. '"He cometh not," she said.' Yet there was a measure of relief in the knowledge that no conceal- ment would be necessary. I need never draw my curtains now.

So peculiarly distressing were these evenings that when Paul and Caroline Langdon invited me to one of their dinner parties in Gertrude Street I accepted without hesitation. They were a pleasant couple, with whom I had remained on distant but friendly terms. They had been generous with invitations, but had taken my refusal to be reclusion after Owen's death or a general reluctance to visit my old home again. Caroline was a good woman, punctilious with Christmas cards containing family news and signed by all the children, although we were no relation to each other and had so very little in common. I sometimes saw her in the local greengrocer's, a tall thin woman with an interesting melancholy face, which was quite mislead- ing for she was habitually cheerful. She would be dressed in a ruffle-necked blouse, a long bright skirt and a suede waistcoat: work-worn hands, adorned with two splendid diamond rings, would grasp the six carrier bags containing provisions for the evening's dinner, for she liked to entertain at home, and man- aged it all quite effortlessly, as well as teaching deaf children, running a house in the Dordogne, and skiing with her husband every February.

She was obviously just back from the annual trip to Villars

when I met her, for her face and hands were brown and her hair long and lank. The usual amalgamation of shopping bags was grouped around her ankles as her large and bony hands selected oranges and cradled chilly nests of grapes. 'Please do not touch', said a notice, but Caroline was tolerated as a particularly splendid type of local womanhood. 'Hello, Fay,' she said, flashing her tired smile. 'Keeping well?' 'I'm fine, dear, thank you,' I replied. 'And you? Paul and the children?' 'Yes, we're okay, much better now that the two big ones are away at college. Only William at home now. You must come round and see us, Fay. I'll give you a ring,' she shouted as she negotiated the door with all her plastic bags. She wore large flat shoes on her stockingless brown feet. I was glad to see her, as I was always glad to see anyone who accepted me at face value in those days, although she made me feel prim and elderly in my blue tweed coat, with the pink scarf at the neck. Even the thought of her busy life gave me pleasure, as I turned with a sigh to buy the pint of milk and the lettuce and half-pound of tomatoes that constituted my own meagre shopping.

I rarely cooked for myself these days, which was a pity, for I had always enjoyed it. The preparation of food seemed to me to be of worth only if one could provide it for others, which I did, in a sense, but not in any sense of which I could approve. Vinnie picked malevolently at what was on her plate, managing to spoil the food without actually consuming much of it, while Julia deplored whatever I took round to her, although I noticed that it all disappeared. Maybe Maureen ate it. It hardly mattered; its function, for me, was automatically lessened by the mere fact that only an irritable conscience had spurred me into what had originally been a gesture and now seemed to have become an obligation. And so when, contrary to all expectations, Caroline did telephone and invite me to dinner, I astonished her by accepting. To be treated as a guest, and to be out of the flat for the entire evening, suddenly seemed the most desirable thing in the world. I had a long black silk skirt which I had hardly worn, and a white silk blouse with a high neck and full sleeves. I had my hair done, and felt as excited as a girl at the prospect of being treated like a real person, by kind young people who had no reason to denigrate or to distrust me. I believe, in fact, that they remained eternally grateful to me for letting them have the house, into which they all fitted comfortably, as though they had been designed for it, or it for them. When I looked back on my own uneasy days there I could only congratulate myself on having done at least one thing right.

But I felt nervous just the same, my social muscles all unused. Also unused were my reactions to the pleasantries of men met on such occasions, for I did not doubt that Caroline, who was correct to her very fingertips, would have invited someone suitable as my partner. I felt the lack of such a partner very forcibly as I made my way, in my narrow shoes, through the blue evening to Gertrude Street. I felt something of my original unhappiness – which I now recognized as such – as I approached the house and felt the peculiar quietness of the landlocked street descend on me. Men in pinstriped trousers were locking their cars for the night and going in to the dinner parties that their wives had no doubt arranged, for this was the sort of urban landscape in which dinner parties were a twice-weekly affair. No children played in the street. Basement kitchens were brightly lit; television sets banished to nurseries or master bedrooms. The house looked to me as uncomfortable as it had always done, but now at least it was convincingly populated. I had been wrong for it, inadequate, seeking to fill the house with my own girlhood dreams, whereas what was demanded of me was an altogether adult appreciation of my duties and a perception of the demeanour that a man like my husband would have chosen for his wife. I had given dinner parties but I had not enjoyed them, had thought Owen's guests either too dull or wholly unsuitable. I had always hoped for much more than those occasions seemed to deliver.

As I stepped inside the house I noticed with a pang, but a pang of deliverance, that the old harsh colours were still in place. 'Not that we like them,' Caroline had said. 'But those papers will last for ever. She had them specially made, you know, Hermione, I mean. Hideous, but wonderful quality. At least we've obliterated all the decoration in our bathroom, all that fake Rex Whistler stuff. You don't mind, do you Fay?' 'My dear,' I had told her. 'The house is yours. I said goodbye to it when Owen died. Do whatever you please.' I had left the furniture there as well, and I think that they were happy with it. As I made my way into the drawing-room I greeted various chairs and tables as if we were old friends at a memorial service.

To my surprise the man who rose from his chair and held out his hand was the doctor who had treated me for whatever had been wrong with me a few months earlier. 'Do you know Alan Carter, Fay?' asked Caroline. 'Only professionally,' I said, giving him my hand. 'And are you better?' he asked, peering into my face with what seemed a worried look. I had noticed that he appeared excessively worried for a doctor, as if he himself, unlike most doctors, were subject to the ills of the flesh. This reassured me. I thought the ideal doctor should be a bit of a hypochondriac, ready to test his own remedies, or, better still, having already tested them.

'Really better?' he asked, taking my hand in both of his.

'But you mustn't ask me that,' I said. 'Or rather I mustn't tell you. If I want to tell you how I am I should make an appointment.'

'Oh, don't worry about that. I can hardly sit down to a meal these days without someone telling me about their back. Headaches are commonplace. "I suppose it's a virus," they say. I've even had bunions: would I recommend the operation? I was eating smoked salmon at the time, I remember. It tends to ruin one's dinner.'

'You must be very susceptible. I thought doctors were made of iron. One thinks of riotous medical students.'

'Youth, you know. Not that I ever rioted. And I was ill an awful lot as a child. After that one becomes more wary of it.'

'In that case,' I said, 'dealing with illness must be something of a trial for you.'

'It's got better, actually. Illnesses can be treated, you know. I think I can just about manage it now. I remember you,' he went on. 'You were Fay Dodworth, weren't you?'

I blushed with pleasure. 'How did you know?'

'Oh, you haven't changed all that much. I used to listen to you when I was in the army, doing my National Service. We all did. It was a lovely voice, but why were the songs so sad?'

'I didn't know how sad they were at the time. I was young, you see; nothing had happened to me then. It's strange how the words come back to me now.'

'Fay, do you know the Finlays? Alison and Richard? And Louisa and Anthony Cope? Fay Langdon, our cousin by marriage.'

I thought that was nice of her, as it was nice of her to keep the party small and manageable. I exchanged a few remarks with the Copes and the Finlays, and I was glad that I had taken a certain amount of trouble with my appearance, as the wives were resplendently dressed, with pearl chokers and tiny diamond earrings, but my attention was monopolized by Dr Carter, who now had me by the arm, as if he were shepherding me to a safer place. 'I really am most tremendously hungry,' he said in a confidential tone of voice. 'I do hope the pleasantries will not be unduly extended. I like to eat early and then go home and play the piano. It's the only chance I get.'

'I rarely come out myself in the evenings these days,' I said. 'This is quite an adventure for me.'

'Never fear,' he said. 'Stand your ground. You may be required to protect me, for unfortunately Mrs Cope is a patient of mine and rather a regular visitor to the surgery. A complicated condition, but far from serious. I won't tell you about it, if you don't mind.'

'Please don't,' I said.

'No, my worry is that she may give me the latest news of it. She believes in keeping me in the picture. So awkward, particularly when I am hungry. That's why I accept these invitations with misgivings.'

'Do you live alone?' I asked, slightly rattled by his apparently compulsive desire to tell the truth.

'Completely. A woman comes in every day, but she doesn't

cook. That is why I have to go out to dinner. What you mean is, am I married? I was. My wife divorced me, on the grounds of her adultery and my incompetence.'

'I see,' I said, as thoughtfully as I could.

'One daughter,' he went on. 'Rather a nice woman. Ah, I think we are about to go in.' He grasped my arm, as if to shield himself from Louisa Cope, who now bore down on him. 'Alan,' she said flirtatiously. 'Those new pills you gave me are hopeless. Quite hopeless. What on earth are they supposed to do? Well, whatever it is they're not doing it.'

'You seem quite well to me, Louisa,' he said, his eyes furtive.

'Hopeless, quite hopeless,' she went on, but she said it with an amorous look on her face, as if she had other plans for him. It occurred to me that to some women he might appear attractive.

'Perhaps you could look in tomorrow morning before surgery,' she went on, as we moved to the dining-room.

'I'm afraid I shall be running round Battersea Park,' he said, regretfully but firmly. 'I always do, you know.'

I stole a look at him as his head bent reverently over his mozzarella salad. His looks were cadaverous, more suited to a funeral director than to a doctor, I thought, though that might be explained by his evident hunger. He had a long dark mournful face, punctuated by two startlingly blue eyes: hair was strenuously trained over a high and otherwise sparsely furnished head. It seemed to be agreed that no one should speak to him while he was eating. In the interval of the plates being changed he sat back as though exhausted.

'If you are always hungry,' I said. 'Perhaps you would like to come for a meal one evening?'

'I should like that very much. Mind you,' he added, 'I shall never marry again.'

'No,' I replied, rather annoyed. 'Neither shall I. Did you think I was asking you to marry me?'

'I seem to be the target of women,' he went on, 'as I expect you are of men. After all, you are attractive, as I am not. Are you on your own?'

'I am a widow,' I said primly.

'I look upon widows as ordinary women,' he said. 'I have your telephone number in my files. I will get in touch.'

After that he turned heroically to Mrs Cope who was on his other side, and I to Richard Finlay who immediately began to tell me about his latest holiday in the Seychelles. Across the table a long and involved story was going on between Paul and Anthony Cope. It seemed as if the ladies had been paid their quota of attention for the evening. Cautiously I began to relax and enjoy myself. The room still looked hideous to me but was softened by the white candles in Caroline's Georgian candlesticks. Upstairs I knew that I should find the terrible bed, but the thought no longer disturbed me. I drank my wine and felt comfortable. Lemon mousse succeeded fillet of beef. 'And of course the car was an absolute write-off,' said Anthony Cope.

'I will see you home,' said Dr Carter. 'You'll excuse me if I don't come in. I try to put in my forty minutes at the piano.'

'What do you play?' I asked, imagining a well-tempered clavichord.

'Oh, all the old music hall songs,' was the reply. 'I collect them. A hobby of mine. Do you know one called "Our Clara's Clicked Again"?'

'My father used to sing it,' I said wonderingly.

'That's a particular favourite. A marvellous antidote to what I have to do in the daytime.'

'Doesn't it wake people up?'

'Not really. At least, no one's complained.'

They would hardly do that, I thought. A doctor is still held in high esteem, even in, perhaps undoubtedly in, our secular society. They would tolerate his eccentricity, for the privilege of having him next door, in case they needed him, although with all this running and piano playing and dining out he did not seem to be particularly available. But I remembered that when he had come to me he had looked entirely normal, rather impressive, in fact. I had not known that his anxiety was habitual. I had assumed it was something to do with my condition. I had felt anxious myself, with good reason, it now seemed. All that was now over. For the first time in ages I felt normal, as if I were starting with a clean slate. Charlie disappeared, as though he had never been.

I took my cue that evening from Dr Carter. If he could be an eccentric bachelor, I could be an eccentric widow. We might have an eccentric partnership. Or not, as the case might be. Caroline had obviously thought he might 'do' for me, and although this was ridiculous it was nice to be included in people's thoughts, after my long exile. For the first time in what seemed like years I felt as though I were among people who approved of me. It even became apparent that Caroline was offering me as a sort of attraction, for after dinner, as we sat in the drawing-room, she encouraged me to tell the others of my early days, and of life at the BBC in the stringent years after the war. None of them remembered me, of course; they were that little bit too young, even though they looked prosperous and substantial enough to be my age, yet women's liberation and a mistaken nostalgia for the war years had made me an object of some interest. 'I never thought of myself as a feminist,' I said, to an enthralled Alison Finlay, 'but I earned my own money from the age of seventeen and gave some of it to my mother. You see, it was Mother who saw to it that I had a good training, and so I really owed it all to her. My father would have approved, whatever I did. There was none of that antagonism between the sexes that there seems to be now. Even women don't get along with each other as well as they might. But we were all friends then, quite shy and trusting by contemporary standards. I never had the slightest difficulty, although I went out into the world so young. Everyone looked after me.'

'How *interesting*,' said Louisa Cope. 'But why did you give it up? It sounds delightful.'

'I married,' I said. 'And I thought it right to be a full-time married woman. That's where my age tells. No woman today would give up her career in that particular way. But I couldn't have managed both, and I didn't think it right to try. The thought simply didn't occur to me.'

'She had a lovely voice,' said Dr Carter, from what seemed to me a remote part of the room. 'But the songs were lugubrious.'

'But you see we were far more sentimental in those days, far less inhibited about feeling, although we were shy. We used those songs to do our courting with: they were about longing and loyalty, very big feelings that simple people can't bring themselves to name. And the war made them that much more important.'

I felt flushed, confident. No one had ever asked me about my career before, not Owen, not Charlie. To be in the company of someone who had heard me sing was a deep pleasure for me. And Caroline was pleased with me too, for entertaining her guests in this novel way. I was a relic to them, almost a celebrity. It somehow pleased them, I sensed, that I was now an elderly lady and yet still presentable. Caroline kissed me warmly as I left, and said, 'You must come again soon, Fay. You've been a tremendous hit.' I said, and I meant it, 'It was one of the nicest evenings I can remember. I'll telephone you tomorrow, dear. Thank you so much.'

Dr Carter took my arm and strode off at an athlete's pace. After a moment I unhooked my arm and stood still. 'Are you unwell?' he asked, walking back to me.

'I'm perfectly well, but I'm wearing rather frail shoes,' I said, 'and I can't keep up with you. And anyway, it's such a pleasant evening. Why hurry? Oh, of course, your piano playing. I'm so sorry; I don't want to hold you up. Would you like to race on ahead?'

'I'll see you home, of course,' he said. 'I dare say I need not play the piano tonight. I'm not a slave to habit.'

'It is so nice and mild that I'm enjoying this breath of air. Indeed, I enjoyed the whole evening.'

'Pleasant people, yes. And here we are, Drayton Gardens. I am further on, Lowndes Square. Well, I'll be in touch. By the way, are you comfortably off?'

'Yes,' I said firmly.

'That's good, so am I. Well, good night.'

No dreams that night, not much sleep either. Louisa Cope

and Alison Finlay would have been perturbed and not a little disconcerted to learn that pleasurable anticipation can persist even in a woman of my age. It did not worry me, but it did make me laugh. I felt scandalous again, seeking an age-old remedy for a wounded heart, and finding it. I had no illusions about Dr Carter's desirability.

In truth, I thought he was impossible, but he amused me into thinking fresh thoughts. An original man is a rare and valuable thing, and as I get older I appreciate humour more than the kind of seriousness that usually attends these affairs. It now strikes me that seriousness is misplaced, that it is all a joke, a sport of the gods, that eventually wears out and fades away. Sometimes not even a memory is left. That is what I saw in the course of my sleepless dreamless night, that I had been granted one more touch of humour in my life, one last joke, before the dark. The best of it was that I had no designs on Dr Carter, none at all. I simply warmed to the idea of having him as a friend, of cooking him the odd meal, of claiming him as a person of my acquaintance, of occasionally being his partner at some kind of social function (this last was vague to me). My long loneliness disappeared in the course of that night, and when I got up to make my tea the following morning I felt as fresh as if I had slept for ten hours.

I watched the sun come up, bathed and dressed carefully. I had already decided to do something that I had been thinking about for a long time. It seemed appropriate to expend some of the energy that had been restored to me, and to cancel the last remnants of my idle life. I had passed the little headquarters of the WVS on one of my evening walks and my intention must have been fixed even then, for I remembered where it was. It was a brilliant morning, good for a new beginning. In the WVS office, which was really the front part of a shop, the sun streamed through dusty windows on to a desk covered with papers. Beside the desk, and occupying a large area of the carpet was a huge dog covered in very long hair. A striking white-haired woman in a heather mixture suit appeared from the back room, carrying a cup of coffee. 'Harding,' she said. 'Letty Harding. Can I help you?'

I explained that I wanted to do some voluntary work and she seemed delighted, although when I explained that I could not drive a car she looked a little more dubious. 'I'm afraid that means office work,' she said. 'Not what you're used to, I'm sure. How do you feel about sitting here answering the telephone?' I said that would be fine. We arranged that I should work from one-thirty to four-thirty on four afternoons a week, sitting at that desk, in the dusty sunlight, in the shop window.

'By the way,' said Mrs Harding. 'You won't mind if I leave Doggie with you? I called him Doggie because I couldn't think of another name. He's very old, and he sleeps all the time, but he hates being left at home.' I said that I should be quite happy with Doggie, who already had a dish of water and a tin plate beside him. So many new things seemed to have come into my life so suddenly that I hardly recognized myself. Perhaps it was all a mirage and I should end up like Maureen with her rotas. Either way, it seemed to me, my fate had been decided.

As it turned out, office life suited me wonderfully. There was very little to do, which may be the case even in real offices among unskilled women like myself, but one has the complacency of belonging and the excuse for dressing up and the tremendous cordiality of one's own kind. It strikes me that women in offices find the same sort of peace as men do in clubs. I took a book along with me, made coffee as soon as I got there, gave Doggie some fresh water, and prepared to answer queries about Meals on Wheels. Women like Mrs Harding did marvellous work, taking old people to hospital for their appointments, seeing that the housebound got properly fed, arranging for the visit of the chiropodist or even the hairdresser. I learnt there about being old, and how terrible it is. I determined to work for these people for as long as I could, until I was old myself. With a little grace I should be better prepared to deal with my own decrepitude, when it came.

I felt well, I felt buoyant, but there was no doubt that I was ageing, and quite comprehensively. I was stiff in the mornings and getting more shortsighted; my once pretty hands were now quite gnarled, and, of course, the hair was silver. I looked attractive for my age, but I looked my age: there was no danger of my being mistaken for somebody younger. I was glad that Dr Carter had seen me at my best. Behind the daytime mask the cruel body goes its way, breeding its own destruction, signalling – blatantly – its own decay. I knew all this. That was an additional reason for my gratitude to Mrs Harding, for giving me a little work to do, and a reason to think of others, and an agreeable way of passing the unforgiving time. 'You've fitted in so well,' she said. 'We're really very grateful. And Doggie is devoted to you. Quite devoted.'

With my afternoons taken up in this way I could no longer put in time at Onslow Square, a fact for which I felt the purest gratitude. I had never been in any doubt that Julia was an obligation, and one that I had come to shoulder with distasteful feelings of guilt and shame, but the truth now burst upon me that I need no longer bear the burden. Naturally, I should have to sign off, as it were, go to see her to explain my new circumstances, but although I could imagine her staring at me, the eyelids fully raised, and then going into one of her pantomimes of incomprehension, the spectacles on their silken cord slowly raised and adjusted on the nose, I could also see that I should have to talk my way out of it, be bluff, reasonable, if necessary unforthcoming. She would resent it, as if I were slipping out of the theatre before the house lights went up, but really, was there not something unseemly, something masochistic in continuing to visit a woman who at best was bored by one and at worst antagonistic? It was just that I had always had what seemed to me good reasons for doing so, and not only that, because I pitied and admired the woman, difficult though she was. Antagonism was the climate of her chilly nature; she found it hard, perhaps impossible, to love, whereas I found it all too easy. For that reason I lost caste, while she consistently gained it. On no account must Dr Carter's name be brought into this, although I felt dangerously tempted to share my delight. This was another of my lower-class attributes, this silly and unwarranted trustingness, in promises which were not promises at all, but only forms of words, or even of leavetaking. That was why Charlie had distorted my life, or, to be fair, why I had distorted my life for Charlie. I now looked back on him with impatience, uneasiness, something like despair. It is nearly always a fatal mistake to go against one's nature, however unsatisfactory that nature proves to be. One must be authentic if one is to be anything at all.

In the end my dilemma was solved by a call from Pearl Chesney. It was in the nature of a farewell, she said: she did hope to see me at Julia's, where Maureen was arranging a little tea party, on the following day, but she wanted to wish me luck, because, apparently, I had always been so kind. My heart ached: why is the affection of people like Pearl so shaming? Because it reminds us how straightforward affection can, and should, be? I promised that I should be there to see her off, and on my way home from the office I bought a pretty blouse that I thought might suit her, and the paper and the satin ribbon with which to wrap it. For it would be a melancholy day for her when she left London, and Julia, whom she had allowed herself to think the tiniest bit selfish, for an unknown flat in a dormitory suburb, with all the small routines that women on their own devise for themselves to fill the day, poor substitutes for the company she had once so enjoyed.

I was right; her eyes were humid, her darkly rouged cheeks slightly smudged. I put my little parcel in her basket and said, 'Open it later, Pearl. It comes with my love.' 'Oh, do sit down,' said Julia. 'Why all the fuss? She's not leaving the country. I can't believe', she went on, 'that Pearl would ever desert me. She'll be back here in no time, won't you, darling?' And she even got up and extended her hand to Pearl, who was still seated and who had to scramble awkwardly to her feet. It was as if Julia were taking a curtain call with her accompanist, summoned gracefully from her obscure position behind the piano. But there was something wrong with Julia, or so it seemed to me. Her voice seemed to have dropped half an octave, to become the bass voice of old women, and the features were slightly drawn.

There was a glass of whisky at her elbow, but it was untouched. It was entirely possible that she found Pearl's departure a strain, was reminded of how long they had known each other. If she felt sorrow it expressed itself, characteristically, as an almost malevolent divination of one's thoughts.

'You're looking very pleased with yourself. Anyone would think you'd found a man.'

I felt myself blushing. Contrary to expectations Dr Carter had not telephoned and I had begun to reproach myself for aberrant fantasies. And yet I had been almost sure . . . I was just beginning to consider my own foolishness when Julia took it into her head to torment me.

'Good heavens,' she said, raising her glasses like binoculars and surveying me through them. 'Wonders will never cease. Well, who is he? What's he like? Have you been to bed with him yet?'

I felt horror, as she supposed I would, at the idea of one elderly woman interrogating another in this manner.

'Behave yourself, Julia,' I said, but I could feel the blush gathering again. 'Don't you want to hear about my job?'

'Not in the least,' she replied. 'This is far more exciting than any job. Maureen, are we going to have tea or not?'

'I've brought a cake, Maureen,' I said desperately. Maureen now had my full attention. 'I'd love to drink Pearl's health in a cup of tea, and then I must fly.'

'Why?' said Julia. 'Is he coming to dinner?'

'Yes,' I burst out. 'Yes, he is.' It was the worst thing I could possibly have done. In my boiling discomfort I resolved to go straight home, ring Carter, and invite him to dinner. I was not happy about this; it was all wrong. But I had to escape Julia, to defeat Julia, even if I defeated myself in the process. That, of course, is exactly what I did, although I did not yet know it. She never forgave me for that incident, which I soon forgot, particularly as Dr Carter appeared to appreciate my call and did in fact drop in for a drink that very evening. But that I should have found companionship, of a kind which she insisted was obscene, grotesque, forbidden, while she remained alone she was never to forget. It was as if from that moment on she decided to take me seriously, at no cost to herself. The cost, she determined, would be all mine.

14

The bright days of spring gave way to a spell of unsettled
weather, dark skies, and rain chuckling in the gutters. I was
quite glad to get home after my stint in the office: undemanding
as my work was, it gave me a feeling that I had done something
unselfish, which was a great relief to me, although no doubt
based on illusion. I found the illusion necessary because I now
longed to perceive myself as a person of worth. I wanted to
be found likeable, even eligible. I was in no doubt that this
had something to do with the mirage of Dr Carter and his
presence in my life, even if that presence was in fact more of an
absence, for Dr Carter remained unbiddable, unpredictable. His
rare visits to my flat (and I had hoped for more) had not been all
that I had wished, had not revealed him as the ideal companion
with whom I might at last enjoy a serene friendship. He was too
rude, too fearless, too inattentive, when not in his surgery, for a
person of my anxious temperament to find entirely beguiling.
Old as I was, I was not defunct, and still hoped, as women
will, to be gathered in by someone responsible, given leave
to practise those comfortable talents which are so meaningless
when there is no one to benefit by them.

What he did, and this may have been beneficial, was to
shock me into speaking my mind occasionally, so that without
knowing each other at all well we soon became intimates of a
sort. I wondered if his solitary life, without a companion, had

fostered his eccentricity, or whether he was actually as impossible as his wife had obviously found him. He had a way of mocking my attentiveness which warned me, in a no doubt salutary manner, not to sink back into old and hopeful ways. I was not to be a wife again, it seemed. And yet, once I had got over my deference towards him, and experienced and expressed a certain amount of annoyance and disappointment, he was, I could see, pleased with me; he laughed and applauded, became appreciative, and relatively content. Yet I suspected that having found me so malleable he was inclined to keep his distance, and that if he were to start again it would be with a woman more noble and demanding than I could ever be.

Perhaps he was defending himself, as he had had to defend himself from so many predatory women. He was an attractive man, without the slightest vanity, which made him a rarity. Brisk and immaculate, he had that medical aura that commands respect; his attention, though initially hard to arouse, was, on occasion, swift and total. I say 'on occasion' for he was aloof and not expansive. After he had paid his initial compliment, as he had done to me at Caroline's party, he retired into himself, as if there were no further need for him to waste his time. His busy, active life supplied him with all his requirements, although in his own reclusive way I think he appreciated my company. To my disappointment, he was rather like a brother, whom I need not try to please. He himself, I think, whatever his own personal arrangements, preferred to think of me as someone whom he had always known but with whom he had recently resumed acquaintance.

He criticized me a lot, as a brother might, or perhaps as a boy might. He criticized my attempts to please him, mocked my domestic fussiness, but accepted its effects without a murmur, and with a hint of pleasure. Sometimes he gazed at me with an eye from which all speculation was absent. 'You're an attractive woman,' he said again, at our second meeting, when I had persuaded him to come for a drink. 'Why did you never marry again?' 'Perhaps I am not as attractive as all that,' I said sadly. 'Or perhaps I lack some basic instinct. I never thought that I could make that sort of decision, the decision that some women make so successfully. I always waited to be found, to be discovered. That seemed to be the honourable way of going about it. And now I see that it is quite wrong.' I was brave enough to speak my mind to him on these matters; he had that effect on me. I was genuinely interested to know what he thought. But he said nothing, merely nodded imperceptibly, as if I were confirming his diagnosis.

Although it was of some value to me to examine my own feelings in this way I found the process disturbing. No aspect of my history failed to disappoint me, or perhaps I was at an age at which it is more logical to look back than to look forward. And yet without Dr Carter I doubt whether I should have dragged these matters to the surface. I should have been sad but settled, whereas with him I was unsettled and not always sad. I was not at all sure that I wanted to marry again, but, like the girl I had been, I longed once more to be appropriated. Dr Carter's resolute failure to perform this service was, in a sense, a disappointment. However, I was still in two minds as to whether he might eventually condescend in my direction, which kept me active and alert, put off the prospect of old age until such time as I might finally renounce everything and succumb, and gave me, on waking, a sense of expectation which I found agreeable. I dressed as if I might meet him unexpectedly round every corner. I shopped carefully and more lavishly than usual. I always had the makings of a good meal in the house, in case he should invite himself. In fact he very seldom did, although he liked to turn up unannounced, sometimes on a Sunday afternoon, when I could think of nothing nicer than settling down with the papers. He was always unpredictable. I think his fear of intimacy kept him out of my flat. Anything of a domestic nature, such as I loved, found him at his most impenetrable.

He liked me, but had spent a lifetime trying to avoid what I represented. Whereas it cost him nothing to appear fraternal, a truth I was eventually obliged to admit. If forced into a confession he would have said that he admired me, yet I was never allowed to expend any care on him. He even disliked my unguarded look of pleasure when I opened the door to him. None the less he kept in touch, may even have thought of me as a special kind of friend, if only that were not to involve him in an expenditure of attention. Of emotion there was little trace. Emotion and its quagmires he could do without. Thus there came to be a ban on my own emotion, so that we conversed in the unguarded tones of the nursery, rude and honest in one way, quite dishonest in another. 'I'm tired,' I could say, or, 'I'm hungry,' he could say. But never 'I want', or 'I long for', or 'I am sick at heart'.

I got used to it, of course. One pays the price quite happily for an attachment. At least, women of my kind do. And I have to confess to a certain pride in it. I walked to work more briskly, greeted acquaintances with enthusiasm, was able to disregard the bad weather, which, had I been in a normal state, would have oppressed me. Whatever his shortcomings he was a factor in my life. He telephoned frequently, much to my surprise, although he never had much to say, and appeared to be talking to his nurse or receptionist at the same time. It was as if he were not averse to advertising my existence in the presence of another. It was acknowledgment of a sort. I found this alternately exhilarating and very worrying, as I was unable to determine my place in his list of priorities. What if the nurse or receptionist were my rival, and I were to be in ignorance of the fact? But in the end I shrugged and put up with it. Given the terms we were on I could always ask him. But I never did. I liked the illusion of belonging too much. That had always been my problem, and now it seemed too late to expect any improvement.

When the telephone rang, one warm wet morning, I assumed that it was Alan Carter, and prepared myself, with pleasure, for his usual barking and apparently absent-minded queries. I was in an agreeably confident mood, and it occurred to me that I might allow myself the indulgence of feeling a little more for him than I had thought acceptable. I was tired of taking my cue from him, indeed from anyone, and for a brief and beautiful moment had felt on the verge of a miraculous new life, in which others would take their cue from me. This illusion or delusion had kept me happy for most of the morning and was still with me when I picked up the telephone and expected to hear Alan Carter's voice. Instead there was a clearing of the throat, as if the speaker were shifting a massive obstruction, and then a query in a soft and excessively polite voice: 'Mrs Langdon? Mrs Fay Langdon?'

'This is Fay Langdon,' I said.

'My name is Clive Smallwood,' the voice went on. 'You don't know me. But I believe you know Miss Luckham?'

'Miss Luckham? No, I don't think I do. You'll have to excuse me, Mr Smallwood. I can't help you.'

'Miss Maureen Luckham? I believe you know her from Onslow Square.'

'Oh, *Maureen.* I didn't know her other name. Do forgive me.'

There was another clearing of the throat.

'Maureen and I were wondering if we might take you out to lunch. Today, if possible.'

'That's very nice of you, Mr Smallwood, but I don't quite see why you should want to do that.'

'You see, Mrs Langdon, Maureen and I have just become engaged. She has done me the honour of consenting to be my wife. And you were the first person she wanted to know.'

I was not surprised to hear this last remark, although Clive Smallwood's news had so stupefied me that I had to sit down, feeling suddenly faint.

'You met at the church, I imagine,' I said to him.

'At St Luke's, yes. We both hope to continue our church work.'

'Tell me,' I said. 'Why didn't Maureen telephone me herself?'

'I'm sure you appreciate her situation, Mrs Langdon. She has very little privacy at Onslow Square.'

'Has she told Mrs Morton?' I said sharply. 'Does Julia know?'

'I believe Maureen thought you should be the first to hear our news,' he said, in his soft, placatory, slightly furry voice. 'And we should like it very much if you would celebrate with us over lunch. Are you by any chance free today?'

168

'You must be my guests,' I heard myself say. 'Where would you like to go? I'm afraid I have to be at my office at one-thirty, so it will have to be early, if that is not too difficult for you. Or your work,' I added, not knowing what he did.

'I have no appointments today,' he said, in an entirely reasonable manner. 'We are going to buy the ring this afternoon.'

'What is your work?' I asked, rather as if I were Maureen's parent, trying to make sure that Clive Smallwood could maintain her in the manner to which Onslow Square had accustomed her. My single most insistent thought was of Julia. What would happen to Julia?

'I am a chiropodist,' he replied, in his milk drinker's voice. 'But my main interest is in the ministry. We both want to dedicate our lives in some way. In the meantime I do what I can to make people comfortable. I must give you my card when we meet. Would Peter Jones be all right? I know Maureen is fond of the place. She often treats herself to morning coffee in the restaurant.'

The idea of Maureen's lonely indulgence softened for a moment my reaction to Clive Smallwood's news. I was not noble enough to feel gratified at the prospect of Maureen's happiness, although I did experience a certain awe at the workings of fate. That Maureen, who only existed for me as a sort of fixture, an adjunct to Julia's own reduced life, should stealthily and in secret have embarked on this great adventure and have brought it to fruition was to me chastening. It was as though she had revealed herself to be made of some superior material, superior, that is, to my own lamentably tentative self. I felt for her a certain respect, although my liking for her did not increase. Above all I felt terror for Julia at the prospect of this defection. My only hope was that they might regard it as their Christian duty to tend Julia; in that case there might even be said to be an advantage in their being two instead of one. Maybe Clive Smallwood could move into Onslow Square. The flat was large; there was no reason why room could not be found for him. It would certainly be distasteful for Julia to have Maureen's marital life going on under her roof, but the alternative was too dreadful to contemplate. I did not think that Maureen, with years of devotion to her credit, would abandon Julia; what I did see was that Julia's life would not benefit from the change in Maureen's fortunes. I felt a pang of pity for Julia, a genuinely unusual woman, now at the mercy of someone who was not in any way her equal. It was Maureen who now had power over Julia, and something told me that she would not be altogether displeased by such a turn of events. I recognized in Maureen, and had done for a long time, something unabashedly female, something combative; for all her humility Maureen was a triumphalist. She would use her engagement, her marriage, to gain advantage for herself, and would have no hesitation in doing so. Julia would be vanquished by Maureen's continuous pantomime of satisfaction. There is a murky area in women which deepens once old alliances are invaded by a man. My impression was that Maureen would show no indulgence, unless recalled to a consideration of her heavenly duty. Even this would not be entirely satisfactory. Once women learn not to trust each other there is no going back.

And yet who could wish for Maureen to continue her life as before, alone and possibly shamed by her thoughts and her longings? She would no doubt attribute to God's mercy (and so should I) this late marriage of hers. It may even be that any marriage is a mercy and a blessing for two people desirous of being together; perhaps even my own marriage had been like that, at the beginning, whatever it had come to at the end. For a mature woman, such as Maureen was, in years at least, marriage is a right to claim the indulgence of others, to dress up, to expect presents, and for someone as lonely and deprived as I knew Maureen to be, it was a miraculous passport to things undreamt of. I was surprised by my own wistfulness, even pain, the wistfulness and pain of all unmarried women at a wedding, however unlikely. I was even reminded of my age, my occasional creakiness, a troublesome back tooth that I must see to. Nothing, I felt, could compensate me for my sudden feeling of loss. The steps that took me to my mirror were hesitant, as if I should not know the person I saw there, as if the face might be very old or very young, certainly undefended, in need of protection. It was with an effort that I dressed myself as becomingly as I could, for it no longer seemed to matter. For the next hour or two I was to be merely the witness of Maureen's good fortune. I was astonished at my own sadness. It was a sadness devoid of envy, or, if envy there was, it was only momentary. What I felt was my own vulnerability, which had done me such disservice in the past. My longing had no object, but seemed simply always to have been there, and now that there was no real reason to express it, to have become stronger than it had ever been before.

Such cosmic feelings as I experienced vanished once Clive Smallwood and Maureen presented themselves to my gaze. They had reached the restaurant before me and were seated expectantly. Maureen wore her pink track suit and Clive Smallwood a beige anorak over a green pullover; he had a plump womanish chest which looked as though it should not have been exposed in so confident a manner. One short arm was laid proprietorially over the back of Maureen's chair. Otherwise he was not unappealing, soft and sympathetic of feature, with a mildness of expression that betokened good temper. Within the barricade of his arm Maureen sat, waiting for me to kiss her, which I did after some initial hesitation. There was no mistaking her happiness; her face was beatific. It was also undeniably smug, as if her attractions could now be taken for granted, as if the world could only nod in recognition. I felt my usual mixture of pity and irritation, particularly as I had to sit through a lot of by-play when I handed them the menu. 'You choose, darling.' 'No, darling, you. Would you like the roast lamb? Don't forget that you'll be late home tonight. I think the lamb's the best idea, don't you, Fay?' 'You see how she orders me around,' said Clive Smallwood, removing his arm and taking Maureen's hand. He was rewarded with a playful punch on the shoulder. I sat there like a stone.

There was to me something eerie about Maureen's contentment and the innocence with which she displayed its less ingratiating characteristics. When she addressed her roast lamb it was clear to me that more than one appetite was in play. She contemplated the meat with almost unseemly enthusiasm. Clive Smallwood, having dispatched his food with the minimum of fuss, but also with a voracity equal to Maureen's own, replaced his arm on the back of her chair and watched her paternally. Little moans of appreciation escaped her as she rearranged the food on her plate with a predatory though dainty fork. Miming fear of our parental sternness she ordered chocolate mousse to follow; the corners of her mouth gleamed brown until she was obliged, with a sigh, to relinquish half of it, its richness proving too much for her. It disturbed me to see her adopting such manners, as if she were manifesting an essentially private enjoyment in a public place. To Clive Smallwood the whole performance was engrossing. He seemed to me a nice man, in disposition not too far removed from Doggie, slumbrous. I ordered coffee and signalled discreetly for the bill. But first there was work to be done.

'Maureen,' I said, as I had to. 'Have you thought of Julia?'

'Well, naturally I have,' she replied. 'I've prayed for her every night.'

'That's all very well,' I said. 'But have you told her?'

'We thought it might be better coming from you,' said Clive Smallwood, imprisoning Maureen's hand once more. 'Since you're such an old friend.'

'I'm afraid not,' I said. 'This is entirely your affair, Maureen. You must tell her as soon as possible.' In retrospect I see that these were the last sensible words I was ever to utter. 'None of this is my business, you know. Of course, I wish you both well. But you must do the right thing. You must both go back to Onslow Square this afternoon – no later – and tell Julia. Where will you be living, by the way?'

'Wherever the church sends us,' said Mr Smallwood. 'We hope to do mission work, you see.'

'I can't help feeling', I said, 'that you owe something to Julia. I think you should have prepared her in some way. She'll want to know how much she can rely on seeing you. As you know, she's old and rather helpless.'

'She has Mrs Wheeler,' said Maureen. 'Mrs Wheeler comes every day.'

'But not at weekends,' I reminded her. From a practical point of view I did not see that Maureen performed functions which Mrs Wheeler might not be prevailed upon to perform, for an extra consideration, but Mrs Wheeler, who had Mr Wheeler, and Michelle Wheeler, to look after, also had a cast-iron excuse to absent herself. And Mrs Wheeler did not amuse Julia, who considered her barely fit to talk to. 'You might change my bed,' was the extent of Julia's conversation with Mrs Wheeler. 'You might take these things to the cleaners when you go.'

'Mrs Wheeler is devoted to Julia,' said Maureen righteously. There was nothing to be done with Maureen now, that much was clear. She had renounced all ties with her previous life, and was basking in the glory of the present moment; she had been meek and now she was inheriting the earth. I watched her trying to tug a recalcitrant raincoat over her pink sleeves and wondered how soon she planned to leave.

'Remember what I said, Maureen,' I warned her. 'Go straight back to Onslow Square.'

'Shall I tell Julia you'll be round later?' she asked, complacently now, it seemed to me.

'Certainly not,' I said. 'She can telephone me when she wants to see me. I have my own life, you know. I work in the afternoons.'

'I think that's wonderful of you, Fay. To get out and about, I mean. So many people of your age just sit back and do nothing, don't they?'

I could see that she disliked me, and as if she realized this herself she instantly laid a damp-feeling cheek against mine. Clive Smallwood held out his hand, and we parted, in the teeming rain. I invented an errand in the opposite direction so as not to have to walk with them. I was as horrified as if Maureen had confessed to a crime, which, in a sense, of course, was exactly what she had done.

And yet she deserved her right to happiness, none more so, perhaps. No one could fault her for seeking her own life after all those years of voluntary subjugation. I felt dread for Julia, for and of her. What duties would come my way, just as I had put forth timid feelers to a life of my own? I had reached an age at which old ties, old loyalties made themselves felt, casting new acquaintances into shadow. A feeling of oppression persisted all through the afternoon, although I was busy and not too dismayed to feel some pride at my new competence. What right had this woman to lay such obligations upon me? All my adult life, it seemed, I had had to defer to Julia. I could do this for as long as she appeared to me monstrous, ridiculous. If she were to inspire pity in me I was lost. Only a telephone call from Alan Carter, telling me that he might look in on his way out to dine, saved me that afternoon. He was my alibi, though he did not know it. I refused to examine the extent of his ignorance. I refused, for my own sake, to believe that it was indifference.

'You seem unusually preoccupied,' he said. It was not an invitation to me to sink down and tell him my troubles. I had learnt that much by now. Nevertheless it seemed to me that he was the only other person I knew.

'An old friend,' I said. 'Elderly. Suddenly left on her own.'

'Like you, you mean?' It was his way of reminding me of my position. I said no more. It struck me that he was rather cruel. Or that he was defending himself, as he often felt called upon to do.

'What a rude man you are,' I said. 'You are exactly the same age as I am. And, as you once acknowledged, less attractive.'

He leaned back with a complacent smile. 'That's better,' he said. 'We might go out on Sunday. I thought of Highgate Cemetery.'

'An appropriate choice,' I said. 'Considering our decrepitude. You could come to lunch first, if you are not too feeble.'

We parted in our usual condition of armed truce. I was more than ever inclined to put up with him when I considered the alternative. Many women do this, unfortunately. I do not admire them for it, but I understand them thoroughly. I myself would once have despised such a tactic, but that was a long time ago, almost out of reach. Life had taught me to seek protection, however nugatory. I was, after all, a woman of my time, of my age. I was not strong enough, certainly not grand enough, to do as I pleased. Doing as I pleased had come to mean supplying myself with simple comforts, warmth, sleep, a certain amount of adornment. Heroines are not made of women like myself.

Next morning, of course, the telephone rang at nine o'clock. 'Now look here,' said Julia, in her new bass voice. 'There are things to be discussed. You might come round for a minute or two. Maureen has some astounding news.'

So Maureen had not told Julia of our meeting. This indicated that she was as frightened as I was. Heroines are not made out of people like Maureen either, I reflected. But as she was basking in glory anyway she would no doubt not recognize her own weakness. It occurred to me to wonder about her future success in the mission field, if she was to be so fearful of reaching her goal. But then she would have Clive Smallwood to exonerate her, and exonerate her he would, for no one could doubt that he loved her. She was no heroine but she was a fortunate woman.

Julia was seventy-four at the time. She had not grown old as a woman of Caroline's generation would grow old. She was immobile, and bitter. As I was leaving my flat my sofa spread out its arms to me, begging me to stay. Julia, on the other hand, was bolt upright ('Posture, Wilberforce, posture!') and dressed in dark blue linen. I saw that she was wearing both her pearls and her amethyst brooch. I was unprepared, however, for the look of frigid disgust on her face, the pinched nostrils, the set lips. Although it was only eleven o'clock there was a glass of whisky at her elbow, and a crimson imprint on the glass.

'Well,' she said, in a manner of greeting. 'Wonders will never cease. First you find a man and now Maureen does. Maureen, you might make some coffee.'

'She says she's getting married,' Julia announced, when Maureen was out of the room. 'You might get her a little present from me, the next time you're in Peter Jones. A little tablecloth or something.' Her hand was steady as she picked up her glass and drank from it.

'Congratulations, Maureen,' I said, in a moderate tone of voice, when she came back with the tray. 'When is it to be?'

'She says next month,' said Julia, who behaved as if Maureen were deaf or in some way absent. 'I've told her she can go as soon as she likes. She's no good to me here.'

'But Julia, I can stay for another fortnight,' protested Maureen. 'Until you get fixed up.'

'Fixed up?' echoed Julia, her eyelids in full play. 'Fixed up? What on earth do you mean?'

'Well, until you get a housekeeper, or something.'

'Why on earth should I want a housekeeper? I eat practically nothing. I'm waiting to die anyway. Life hasn't been the same since Mummy went, and Charlie, of course.'

'You can't live here alone, Julia,' I said.

'Why not? I suppose you want me to go into a home. Well, I might. Mummy was terribly happy in that place of hers. You might make a few enquiries, Fay.'

'Do you remember the name of the place, Julia?'

'No. There might be some correspondence in Charlie's desk. He dealt with that sort of thing. I dare say there's a waiting list. I shall probably die before they get to me.'

I opened the flap of the desk on to a maelstrom of papers, most of them bills. Some of these, I could see, were unpaid. Surely there was no shortage of money? Or did Julia simply not concern herself with such matters, half expecting Charlie to settle her affairs from beyond the grave? Someone had been through these papers, or rather had muddled them up, for Charlie would never have left them in such a state. 'Maureen,' I called. 'Have you been trying to sort out these papers?' 'Oh, she had a look,' said Julia, who had decided to behave as if Maureen were no longer there. 'I doubt if she made any difference. You might go through them for me when you have a minute. If your job doesn't keep you too occupied.'

This last was said not with deference, but, on the contrary, with a great deal of contempt. Women who worked, Julia implied, were not very important in the scheme of things, were part of a faceless army rather than unique individuals like herself.

In this she made no distinction between Maureen and myself, remaining indifferent to what we did, however well-meaning it was. I imagine that Maureen's honorarium had dried up with Charlie's death, for it was highly unlikely that Julia would continue to pay it, if indeed she had ever known about it. Maureen's anxious and ineffectual hovering would not have seemed to her to be worth anything in cash terms; in any case it was construed as devotion to her own person, and perhaps it was. As for myself, it was only fitting that I should work; what else was I good for? Since Julia had no perception of my true nature or feelings, nor – as I fervently hoped – of my life as a whole, she considered me to be uninteresting, and, more than uninteresting, inferior. Her estimates and values were all class-based. Occasionally a woman of exceptional beauty or accomplishment might be allowed to slip through the net, for Julia was generous in this way. Exceptional women aroused her interest and her calculations; husbands and lovers were assessed, much in the same way as clothes and jewellery, all seen as attributes of some kind of victory, which was in essence the victory of women over men. The strange thing about Julia was her indulgence towards a certain type of woman, although there was nothing dubious about this taste; rather, she regarded women as the normal sex, and men as aberrations or nuisances, at whom she would flap a tolerant hand, when not expecting them to subsidize her entire existence.

There was another element in Julia's decision to lump Maureen and myself together. She had perceived, wrongly, that we were both sexually active, and found this especially difficult to tolerate. She had regarded Maureen as sex-starved and ridiculous until Maureen had produced Clive Smallwood; since then the fervour in Maureen's gaze, her self-satisfied little pirouettes, and her occasional humming of an unidentifiable but possibly holy tune, had turned Julia icy with distaste. Certainly not with jealousy: rather with a bitter disgust. My situation was rather different. I was suspected of enjoying an illicit relationship, which was in fact not the case. But in suspecting me Julia was coming dangerously near the truth, for the illicit relationship I was supposed to be enjoying was not in the present but in the past. What she suspected now was what she had disdained to suspect some time ago. I doubt whether the idea that anything was afoot had ever occurred to her at the time when it was relevant and indeed justified. By some curious and infallible psychological mechanism she had misplaced it, but had now retrieved it to use against me in my innocent, my more than innocent friendship with Alan Carter.

The factor that had ruined my life, or the latter part of it, was the fear that Julia knew about my relationship with her husband and was biding her time until she decided to use her knowledge against me. Looking back now I think it unlikely that she knew anything at all, for to her I was too uninteresting to be eligible. Beautiful women do have a confidence that occasionally blinds them to the truth. I truly believe that Julia remained in total ignorance of Charlie's diversions, but, by the same token, she sensed in my present demeanour a liveliness, an alertness that could only signal some kind of sexual interest, and this she could not forgive. Her resentment she construed as disgust: the pinched nostrils, the set lips signified a physical revulsion, a recoiling from the evidence. That there were no grounds for her suspicions made no difference: a judgment had been passed, and the judgment was unfavourable. It was also, in some remarkable fashion, not far from the truth, the metaphorical truth of our respective lives. There was an essential sterility about Julia, who accepted love but could not bestow it. I make no excuses for myself. All I can say is that I have been ready to love and have been led into error for that very reason. I could not forgive myself, and indeed have never done so. Those who survive an adulterous love affair are retrospectively amazed at the flimsiness of the structure that supported it. In time they see that it cannot be granted the status of a love affair at all, that it was in fact a simulacrum, sometimes negligent, sometimes hasty, usually hidden. This was what had occupied my thoughts since Charlie's death. I liked him less in death than I had done in life.

His legacy to me was Julia, who obligingly lay like a dead

weight on my conscience. With Maureen's defection there was no one else left, although to her credit Julia now disliked me so actively that she would rather have suffered than have invoked my help. She made no appeal to me on that morning, the morning of the papers in the desk, nor would she. She would simply be there, alone, or with Mrs Wheeler, with whom she did not exchange more than a few phrases. She would continue to be immaculate and complaining, but too proud to accept favours, which made it astonishingly difficult to offer any. In my desperation that morning I promised myself that I would find the address of that home or contact her brother or do something, anything that would free me from the burden of Julia. Without her I might be able to look forward to a life of my own. With her there was no hope at all.

15

I aspired to normality. It seemed to me that it was all that I had ever aspired to; as others covet excitement and strangeness I hankered after a bourgeois calm. Each time I looked out of my window and saw a man departing for work, with his briefcase and his newspaper, I was alerted once again to the charms of a regular existence. I would even try to picture his homecoming at the end of the day, and his wife's welcome, and the meal they would eat: this picture would make me thrill with longing. I wished benevolent order on all those whom I encountered, but I also wished to partake of that order myself. In short I was tired of my solitary existence and longed to share my life again. I recognized my mood as dangerous, for I was no longer objective and amused; a melancholy had fallen on me and also a feeling of menace. My nights became troubled. I told myself that I was a foolish woman, beyond the age of love and romance; I even told myself that I was not in love, which was true. And yet the lure of an orderly life persisted, and with it this acute awareness of unease, almost of distress.

What I longed for was a man who was kind and who had only traditional or orthodox intentions. No such man had presented himself; the species may in fact be rather rare. I thought with surprise of my husband, Owen, who had been such a man and to whom, for that very reason, I had given my first loyalty. My marriage began to take on a dignity of which

I had not been conscious at the time. Owen had left no trace in my life. I hardly ever thought of him, and yet now, with this strange mood upon me, I was proud of him and grateful to him for the years we had spent together. If I had not wholly enjoyed those years then that was because I was aware that we were mismatched. Now I was not so sure. Owen had not been an articulate man, and moreover he disliked overt feeling, as if it might reveal dangerous depths, depths which decent men kept hidden. These were the depths which I had hoped to reach, and had failed to take the measure of his reserve. Now I blamed myself for not having sufficiently valued his simplicity of intention in marrying me. His wish that we should be married had always been marvellous to me, and in this curious late summer of mine I began to see how in this way he had proved himself superior to any other man I had ever known.

But Owen – with whom I had had very few real conversations – was gone, and I began to see that I had disappointed him. Or maybe I simply longed for a communion that would reassure me and would lift me from this painful restlessness, as if I must search for a haven before night fell. I see now that what I was experiencing was the panic of approaching old age, but at the time I merely thought that I would willingly sacrifice the rest of my life if only I might not be condemned to spend it alone. I had not done well on my own, and I did not feel worthy. I felt humble, apologetic, occasionally bitter. Nevertheless, I longed for some kind of gift, some dispensation of fortune for which I would gladly pay, however high the cost. I wanted one more summer, and would have been content to die at the end of it, before the dark days came, if I could live those few months as a normal person, with a husband whom I should see off to work in the mornings and welcome home at the end of the day with a loving smile. I wanted to employ those faculties which had once been mine, to fill my shopping basket with good things, to be on an equal footing with all the wives I met, and to welcome my friends before it was all too late, before I became a sad old woman in a solitary flat, with no one to love me and with too much time in which to dwell on my lack of company.

In practical terms this meant Dr Carter, whose desire to marry again was in inverse proportion to my own. Where I yearned, Dr Carter fled. Dr Carter had a pleasant time being rude and elegant and sought after; if he valued me at all it was for my convenience, not for my suitability. With me Dr Carter was always assured of a certain level of hospitality. I would adapt myself endlessly to his moods, never quite knowing whether he would choose to be forthcoming or withdrawn, never making him aware of any sadness I might have felt, always agreeable, non-committal, only angry when he wanted me to be angry, utterly reasonable. My anger made him laugh, reassured him in his dry cold decision to remain uninvolved. Although I knew that I could never love so unloving a man I also knew that he was drawn to me, and that if either of us ever decided to abandon our established positions and behave naturally we might arrive at an understanding that would surprise us both.

There was a great deal of anxiety in my attitude to Dr Carter. I wanted him to love me in order that I might consider whether or not I might allow myself to love him. This was the luxury I craved. At the same time I had to live with the disappointment that none of this was happening. For every moment of intimacy I would have to pay with an increased feeling of the distance between us; for every outing to Highgate Cemetery or the Soane Museum – his excursions were always inexpensive and involved a healthy mileage – I would have to face an abruptness for which I was no longer prepared. He would not always visit me when I invited him, yet delighted in calling unannounced. This was so disruptive to one of my settled nature that I became almost frightened of him, hating the tension that he maintained between us and resenting him for the freedom he so obviously enjoyed. For a time I was unwilling to go out in the evenings in case I missed a chance of seeing him. Fortunately, common sense asserted itself and I vowed that I should never wait for anyone again. Yet when I walked out on these lovely summer evenings I was filled with melancholy that I was walking alone, and I wondered wistfully if the telephone were ringing in my empty flat or whether a disappointed visitor were walking away from my door. The feeling was so unpleasant, so redolent of waste, that I would telephone him the following morning and invite him to dinner. He did not always come, but the contact made me feel more normal.

I was aware that my preoccupations were becoming too unbalanced to appeal to Dr Carter, who only valued me as someone independent, comfortably off, and quite attractive for my age. In other words he thought I was as selfish as he was, whereas in fact I was more selfish, since I wanted from him what he was not prepared – was perhaps unable – to give. He was fond of me, would have been shocked if I had told him that I did not want to see him again, and yet he was armoured against me. I was part of his bachelor life, and he thought that enough, whereas I regarded his bachelor status as temporary and suspected that if he were to renounce it and marry again I should have no part in that existence, for he would not be married to me. Someone bolder would have claimed him, and he would have succumbed, like any other man, for men can be quite cheap in this respect. All this I saw quite clearly. I saw that we might keep up this guarded and amusing friendship until something irreparable were said or done, and I had to strive mightily to suppress those words which would have told him of the rage and sorrow in my heart and of how he had caused them. And yet, on another level, he intrigued me, as I intrigued him. I told myself that I had only known him for a few months and that he was cautious by nature, but I knew that we had already reached a point at which we had ceased to be acquaintances. I told myself that my melancholy mood was unjustified; however, I could not shake it off. The children going to school, the old men walking their dogs, the ladies with their shopping baskets all seemed to me to be citizens of a world from which I was excluded. I tried, without complete success, to present a smiling face and an equable temperament to those with whom I came into contact. I still dressed carefully, still stepped out cheerfully into the sunny mornings. And yet I felt as if my days were numbered.

I understand it all now, of course. My days were in fact numbered by the fear that descended on me from time to time. This fear had to do with Julia's loneliness and my curious obligation to her, as if I depended on her favour, as if she might recall me at any time. Part of the reason why I left the flat so early in the morning and returned so late at night was a desire not to hear the telephone and Julia's demand – or was it a command? – that I should call on her as soon as possible. In this context alone Alan Carter would have seemed desirable, yet I was not unscrupulous enough to shelter behind his non-existent invitations. I went, haplessly, to Onslow Square when my conscience made my life sufficiently uncomfortable for me to seek the one thing that would momentarily cancel my account, yet this never entirely worked, for I was always castigated for not having come earlier, on the day before, for example, which, she implied, would have been more convenient. In reality her dissatisfaction sprang from the fact that I reminded her of the existence of a world in which she was completely forgotten. On these occasions it seemed to me that Julia would live for ever, for there was no appreciable alteration in her appearance, apart from a thinning of the features. The mask of her face was still impassive; above her high forehead the defiantly bronzed hair was carefully coiffed, yet I noticed that the rings were loose on her now slightly bent fingers, and one day I was disproportionately shocked to find her wearing only one earring. It was the first sign that her control was not what it once had been. 'Why, Julia,' I said. 'You've lost an earring.' 'I dropped it somewhere,' she replied indifferently. Later that morning I saw a gleam beside her narrow left foot. 'There it is!' I said. 'Beside your foot. Don't tread on it.' But as I bent down to pick it up the slow foot brushed over it and crushed it. This incident disturbed me. Julia said nothing, pretended not to notice. Mrs Wheeler, arriving with a tray of coffee, pursed her lips and nodded meaningfully in my direction behind Julia's rigid back.

These visits gave her little pleasure; what gave her pleasure was the discomfort they caused me. 'How's that man of yours?'

she would say. 'What's he like in bed?' Apart from the peculiar distress this question caused me I sensed in her attitude a loathing which could only be appeased by unseemly detail. It became a torment for me, and some form of perverse satisfaction for Julia to note the blush stealing over my face. The blush was for my inadequacy, my incompetence as a woman, unable as I was to deal with this question, either to confess the truth or to laugh at it. I had never encountered real malice in a woman before, and I was completely at a loss as to how to deal with it. If I hoped to inveigle Julia into some form of indulgence I paid dearly for my simple-mindedness in supposing that such a thing existed. 'He's very nice,' I would say, smiling brightly and willing my burning cheeks to subside. 'But you mustn't suppose that I know him all that well. It's only been a few months since I met him.' 'You must be very slow,' she would say. 'It wouldn't have taken me that long. I suppose that's the difference between us.' 'Quite,' I would reply. 'And now behave yourself. Have you heard from Maureen?' But this was another delicate matter, for Maureen had not invited Julia to her wedding. Her excuse was that Julia could not have made the journey to Devon, but I rather think she might have done, in a hired car. I might even have taken her myself. Julia had been shocked, as I had been on her behalf. When the ruined slice of wedding cake arrived she threw it in the waste-paper basket with a hand that trembled slightly and asked me to pour her a drink.

I think that her sadness was as great as my own, but that every vestige of human charity had deserted her. She still gained a certain pleasure from being rude to me, and my feeling was that I could hardly deny her this pleasure. For what did it matter? She had become so painful and burdensome a subject in my mind that I underwent actual encounters with her as a form of martyrdom. What did it matter if she were ruder one day than on another? The glorious sun shone outside the windows and I could eventually escape into it, leaving the brooding unforgiving presence until the next test of my faith. If my attendance were a form of expiation then it did not work for either of us. She could have tolerated complaints, grumbles, laments. What she could not tolerate was the small last hope she detected in my heart.

I believe that our meetings were damaging to both of us, for if they lacerated me they left Julia unappeased. She wanted scandal, and if possible defeat; she wanted me to provide her with an enthralling serial story in which I would appear in my worst light. 'What's his name?' she asked me repeatedly. When I could no longer withhold it I felt vanquished. 'Oh, Alan Carter. Yes, I remember. His wife ran off. Must be something wrong with him. Actually, I could do with another doctor – old Bannister's hopeless. You might ask him to call round.' I noted that she did not ask me to bring him round. The worst realization was that Julia would have amused Alan enormously. They would have got on like a house on fire. 'I'll mention it,' I said, as carefully as possible. 'But I believe he's very busy.' 'Then you'll just have to use your influence, won't you?' Her smile as she said this was the smile on the face of the tiger.

Thus frightened and humiliated I took no pleasure in the beautiful days, which became quieter when the schools broke up and families began to depart on holiday. My street took on a suburban calm, and I longed to preserve it, to enjoy it at leisure, in innocence, when my mood should change, if it ever did. 'Will you go away?' I asked Alan Carter timidly. 'I've got a house on the Isle of Wight,' he replied. 'We might run down there for a few days.' This was so major a development that all fear temporarily left me. So great was my shock of pleasure that I almost wished to be left alone to savour it. He was drinking a glass of white wine in my sitting-room at the time, on his way to a dinner somewhere. He liked to start the evening in this way, liked both my eager welcome and the safety of his early departure. I think he feared the complicity that the late hours bring. He was superstitious enough to believe that the later he stayed the more deeply committed he would become. Maybe this was true. Maybe he even regretted his invitation to me as soon as he had offered it. To me it hardly mattered at the time. My reaction of joy was of course excessive, for I knew him too well to suppose that he intended any meaning to be read into what would at most be one of his fraternal interludes. But to me it meant a treat, an excuse to dress in pretty summer clothes, to be accompanied, to have a definite answer when people asked me whether I were going away; to me the invitation was a promise of the normality for which I longed. 'When shall we go?' I asked. He said he thought the beginning of September would do well enough. There was a faint grumpiness in his tone as if my sudden radiance were displeasing to him. This did not escape me, but it could not entirely dim my pleasure. I poured him another glass of wine, and said, casually, 'You must leave all the housekeeping to me. Why don't you come to dinner next week? We can get it all settled then. Nothing more to discuss – we can just get in the car and go.' Even this was too much, but I no longer cared. Suddenly I could not go on as I was, eking out my careful existence, pretending that all was well, looking after the flat I did not much like, stepping out in the mornings with a smile on my face. I wanted my life back again, or as much of it as was left to me; I was tired of moderation and good manners. Even the promise of a few days in the company of a man almost too recalcitrant to be tolerated fired me up and the face I turned to him must have been different, for he bent and kissed it, then hurriedly, and without looking back in my direction, took his leave. We arranged that he should come to dinner on the following Thursday.

The intervening week was indescribably pleasant to me. We were not too busy in the office as so many people were away, and there was time to drink a cup of tea with Mrs Harding and to leave a little early. I surveyed the food in the shops with the eye of a connoisseur, planning our dinner, which I wanted to be light and simple, and at the same time turning an indulgent eye on my domestic fantasies. I had reached an age at which the fantasies alone were almost enough sustenance, yet here I was, in my early sixties, making arrangements for an intimate dinner with an attractive man of my own age, as I had not done for many years. A vegetable terrine, I thought, followed by a dish of baked chicken and rice, with a fruit salad to follow. My step was light, my energy renewed. Mrs Harding told me how well I looked.

Julia was ostensibly forgotten, although the slight febrility of my behaviour may have had something to do with the fact that while I had put her out of my mind she refused to be entirely absent. In unguarded moments her sceptical smile would materialize in the air in front of me, and I could feel her waiting, biding her time. I told myself that I should see her as soon as the dinner party was behind me; in fact, I told Julia this, gabbling my assurances in my desire not to have to talk to her at all, making otiose promises in exchange for my temporary freedom. I was just putting the finishing touches to the terrine on the Thursday morning when the telephone rang. 'Now look here,' said Julia, her voice low and cold, less the voice of an old woman than of an old man. 'Mrs Wheeler hasn't turned up. Says she's not well, not that I believe her. Swore she's coming in tomorrow. But I need someone today. There's no food in the house – not that I eat anything – and I haven't had my bath.' For one of Mrs Wheeler's indispensable functions was to be present when Julia took her bath, for with her weak hands and feet she was in danger of falling. I contemplated my own hands, which were sticky with aspic, and said, 'I'm sorry, Julia, I can't manage today. Can't it wait until tomorrow?' 'I had a bad night,' the voice went on. 'I feel so stale and uncomfortable. If you could just come round for an hour this afternoon I think I might have a bath and go straight to bed. I couldn't eat much. Perhaps you could bring some fruit or something.'

I put the telephone down very quietly, washed my hands with excessive care, refrigerated the terrine. I sliced the fruit for the fruit salad and put some in a plastic tub for Julia. I put two fresh rolls in a napkin and cut a wedge from the fine Stilton I had bought for Alan Carter. I was quite calm, but some of my early sadness had returned; my effervescent mood had disappeared, and had given way to a certain heaviness. I could still manage it, I thought. If I dressed first, asked Mrs Harding if I might leave early, went round to Onslow Square and then came home and

188

completed my preparations I could still manage. I should have time in hand. And if we had to eat at half-past eight or nine there was nothing unusual in that. I dressed slowly in a blue silk blouse and a blue and black print skirt, noted that the sky was clouding over, looked at my puzzled face in the mirror. Then, taking my basket, I left the house almost eagerly, anxious now to get the whole day over so that I could be alone again with no one, man or woman, to torment me.

It was very close, sunless, with a promise of a storm. 'Why, Fay, how nice you look,' said Mrs Harding. 'I hope Doggie is not going to spoil that pretty skirt.' I smiled sadly, my party mood gone. I got through the afternoon as though I had nothing better to do, as indeed was the case; my only desire was to help the people on the other end of the telephone, who were so much easier to help simply because they were so safely distant. At four-thirty I locked up, took my basket, and left. I calculated that if I got to Onslow Square just after five, or as soon after five as I could make it, I could leave by six or six-thirty at the latest and my evening would not suffer. Alan was coming at seven-thirty. Nothing need be lost.

I found Julia sitting in the drawing-room. She was dressed, and yet she looked dishevelled. 'You're very festive,' she said. 'What's it all for?' I went through to the kitchen to unload my basket and to make her a cup of tea. 'Alan Carter is coming to dinner,' I said. 'Which is why I can't stay. As soon as this tea is made I'm going to run your bath.' I vanished into the bedroom, where I was obliged to make the bed. I had the beginning of a slight headache; the oppressive weather, no doubt, and the anxiety, an anxiety I had no desire to prolong. I ran the bath, and took two aspirin tablets from a bottle on Julia's night table. A sort of hopelessness came over me. I contemplated racing back to the flat to cook the chicken. And the rice, always a delicate matter. And I had not yet laid the table. 'Come on, Julia,' I called. 'It's all ready for you.' 'Coming to dinner, is he?' she said, making her way slowly into the bedroom. She undressed equally slowly, revealing the lingerie of a *cocotte* on limbs which were beginning to look wasted. The whiteness of her body shocked me: I did not think I should be witnessing it. I lowered her into the sweet-smelling water of the bath, and turned my back. By this time I was trembling, although I did not quite know why. 'This man,' said Julia, behind me. 'Are you going to marry him?' 'Of course not,' I said, as lightly as possible. 'Come on, Julia, let me help you out.' 'But you're having an affair with him, aren't you?' She stood up unsteadily, and water slopped against the side of the bath, splashing a little onto the floor and onto my skirt. 'I am not having an affair with him,' I said with loathing. 'But you will, won't you?' 'There's no question of that. We might go away for a few days, that's all.'

I think that those few words were my greatest mistake. Julia laid a heavy wet arm round my neck, disarranging my hair in the process. 'Going away?' she said. 'Well done.' She pretended to fall, or maybe she did fall, I no longer know, and in her effort to hold on to me tore the stitches from the shoulder of my blouse. I could feel the slow uncoiling of my hair as it fell down my back. Her body, a dead weight, supported itself on my shoulders as I staggered back; she had renounced all responsibility for her movements, either that or she was more incapacitated than I knew. Horrified, I managed to get her into the bedroom. She drifted slowly to her dressing-table, contemplated her face, turning it this way and that. Her eye, when it met mine in the mirror, was ancient and amused. I suppose I did look amusing, with my hair flopping down my back and my wet ruined blouse. My one thought was to get home and repair the damage. Rain spattered like bullets against the window. Julia rubbed cream into her face, with a caressing gesture. 'Charlie loved to see me do this,' she said. 'He adored me. "You are the woman of my life," he said. "There will be no other." Has anyone ever said that to you?' Without looking back I ran out of the flat.

Rain was falling quite heavily, heavily enough to banish all taxis from sight and to jam up the rest of the traffic. I ran, as well as I could, all the way to Drayton Gardens. I must have looked insane. Inside the flat I found my hands trembling so much that I struck match after match without being able to light the oven. Miraculously, I managed to get the rice, the herbs and the stock into a baking dish. While the chicken was simmering in the rest of the stock I laid the table, then ran back into the kitchen to put the dish in the oven. Once everything was assembled I might just have time for a bath. I took out the wine, unmoulded the terrine, filled a jug with mineral water, and then the bell rang. I actually hesitated before opening the door, half hoping that anyone there would go away, even if it were Alan Carter himself. I was aware of my ripped blouse drying unevenly on me. 'Good evening, Madam,' said the two pale young people on my doorstep. 'Are you interested in learning more about the Bible?' At that moment the telephone rang. Shutting the door on the two young people I ran to the sitting-room to answer it. 'Hello, Fay,' said Pearl Chesney. 'I hope I'm not disturbing you?' Through the window I could see Alan Carter coming along at a steady jogger's pace. I promised to ring Pearl Chesney later, ran to the kitchen to turn down the oven. Turning, my skirt caught the corner of the terrine which I had put too near the edge of the kitchen table. The dish fell and smashed on the floor, sending a spray of carrot mousse over my shoes.

'What on earth is the matter with you?' asked Alan Carter, following me into the kitchen. He sounded annoyed rather than concerned. He was one of those men who hated to have his evenings ruined, one of the characteristics of an unmarried man, I suppose, or perhaps he saw too many distraught women all day to have any patience with them after working hours. For himself, he liked regularity, order, distance.

'Everything's gone wrong,' I said helplessly, beginning to weep.

'I can see that,' he replied, with a note of distaste. 'If you'll change your clothes I'll take you out to dinner.'

'I don't think I can,' I said, sitting down and wiping my eyes on a tea towel.

He poured himself a glass of wine. 'I didn't realize you were so moody,' he said.

'Of course you didn't,' I burst out. 'Oh, it's not your fault. You like an orderly life. So do I. I am a very orderly person. But things go wrong, even in an orderly life. You never seemed to realize that. You never asked me what I liked, what I wanted.'

'Why should I?' he said, annoyed. 'It's not up to me to put your affairs in order.'

'Why not?' I said slowly. 'Why not? Why shouldn't you ask me what I wanted? Because you don't want me to want anything?'

'There's no need to be hysterical,' he said. 'As for what you want that's neither here nor there. You invited me to dinner. I offered to take you out, as the dinner seems to be on the floor.'

'I have a rather bad headache,' I said. 'If you don't mind I'd rather go to bed.'

'That seems to me the best idea,' he said. 'Goodnight. Ring me in the morning and tell me how you are. We might be able to get together another time.'

Slowly, with the sound of an abruptly closing door echoing in my ears, I cleared up, threw the food away, took off my ruined clothes and put them in the linen basket. I should never wear them again. I lay in bed with burning eyes until the light faded and finally died. It was all quite trivial, I told myself. A ruined dish, a ruined evening. At my age one should dismiss such things as unimportant. But it had been important, crucial, in fact. I had shown Alan Carter an unpleasant side of myself, a hapless deranged side; he had seen me with my hair lying on my shoulders and my blouse ripped and my eyes red: we should not recover from this. I had probably lost him, that fastidious and so-successful unmarried man, in the way that women lose to men when they are not very vigilant. I had asked, in the worst possible way, for his succour, for his support, for his indulgence. Really, I had been asking for his love, and he knew it. This was a terrible problem for him, for he was not prepared to give it. Whatever his desires or his intentions they did not include a madwoman with a disorderly appearance. In his mind I was to remain stately and pleasant, a possibility, no more than that. Whatever I brooded upon was to be my own responsibility, not his. I was a widow and he was a divorcee; there was to be no question of marriage. I saw that now, too late.

I saw also that it was not entirely his fault. One does not give men sufficient credit for their hurt feelings. I had disappointed him. A more skilful woman would have avoided this. But I had always been impatient, susceptible. I wanted happiness. I wanted a full life. This one is not always able to procure for oneself. I wanted his co-operation, and this I seemed to have forfeited. I would have given anything to turn back the clock, to shut the door on the ruined kitchen, and to present myself, smiling, and saying, 'Sit down. I shan't be a minute. I'm just going to change. It's only an omelette, I'm afraid. We've been busy today. Why don't you pour yourself a glass of wine and relax until I call you?' All this should have been possible. But I had not been able to manage it.

Behind my own ruin lay Julia. I knew this, had known it even before the fiasco had enacted itself. It was as if she had willed it. Ridiculous though this may sound I knew it to be true. Whether out of past resentment or present frustration she had brought about my defeat. It was important to me to believe that she had brought it about because of my chance – so slender! – of happiness. This was not revenge. Julia's revenge would have been more terrible, more immediate. She could have tormented me so much more successfully had she intended to, could have deployed her remarkable resources to humiliate and ostracize me. She was not a good judge of character, that was all. She could only see herself. Had she been a subtler woman I really think she would have seen to it that I came to grief, in a way I dared not even imagine.

These were the thoughts of the middle of the night. In the morning, still with an aching head, I realized that it was all exaggerated. Probably all that she had ever known, ever seen, was a speculative glance from Charlie in my direction. That was enough for her. And maybe this had all taken place a long time ago, before I was ever aware of it. Maybe it all went back as far as that holiday in Nice, when Charlie and I had sat in a café, waiting for Julia to finish her interminable toilette, harmlessly reading the papers. What stimulated that ancient grudge was the prospect of my going away with Alan Carter, with whom she thought I might be happy, as indeed I had. I should never see her again, although I might not supply her with what she wanted to hear, an amusing story of how I had spoilt my last chance. I was not able to do this. Therefore I must abandon her, as I had always wanted to do. Strangely, I found this idea very difficult.

The weather was cool, grey, a disappointment after the radiant days that had gone before. I remembered standing in the rain outside the house in Gertrude Street after the burning days that had preceded Owen's death. This was dead reckoning. I sat in the flat with my hands in my lap, knowing that I should not be going on holiday that summer. My holiday was over. I rang the surgery and got through to Alan straight away. 'I'm so sorry about last night,' I said lightly, for lightness was all. 'I get these awful headaches from time to time. Will you let me give you dinner again, next week, perhaps?' 'I'm rather busy,' was his reply. 'I'm glad you're better.' (But I had not said so.) 'I'll give you a ring.' I put the telephone down very carefully, knowing that I should have to wait a long time before I heard from him again.

After this I was very calm. At the end of the morning, as I was about to go to the office, I remembered Pearl Chesney and called her back. She seemed delighted to hear my voice. It appeared that she was coming to town the following day. 'It's very nice here, of course, and lovely to be so near Colin and the boys, but I do miss my London!' I invited her to come and have coffee with me. 'And you'll be seeing Julia, I suppose,' I said. 'Oh, yes, dear. I do miss her. Funny isn't it? Here I am, with a life of my own at last, and yet I think of her all the time.'

'Well,' I said slowly. 'I suppose she is a memorable woman.'

'That's it, dear. Memorable. You always did have a way with words. We did have some laughs, didn't we?'

I put on a cardigan to go to the office. After all, I was

an elderly woman and it was incumbent upon me to look after myself. I think that day marked the beginning of my real old age, although all things considered it has not been too bad. I sat in the office, taking comfort from my pale blue cardigan, with Doggie by my side, reasoning with myself. I was free now, free of encumbrances, free of hope, that greatest of all encumbrances. The idea was not particularly terrible. I was surprised at how little I felt. It was not until I was preparing to lock up and go home, when a shaft of late sun pierced the heavy cloud, that I felt a little pain. I thought of a house on the Isle of Wight that I should never see. 'No, I shan't be going away,' I said to Mrs Harding. 'I can carry on here, if you feel you can trust me.'

'Then I can tell my sister that I shall be coming to her,' she replied. 'What a treasure you are, Fay. Have a good weekend.'

Old times, sad times. I feel better about them now than I did then. Then I felt like a girl, bewildered, although I was of an age to know better. This girlishness of mine, persisting in spite of the evidence of my body, had proved my enemy to the end. For it was the end of something, and I knew it. No more excitement, no more expectation, no more power. The old are disempowered. I caught sight of myself in a plate glass window as I walked slowly, more slowly than usual, towards Drayton Gardens. I reminded myself of someone, but someone I had not seen for a long time. It was not until I was in the flat and smoothing my hair in the glass that I recognized myself. I looked like my mother.

16

Pearl sat opposite me in the other chair, the chair that was meant to be occupied by a companion, the chair that I had placed by the hearth in a facsimile of domestic contentment. And yet I was glad of her company. I had become humble and quiet since what I thought of as the débâcle, and desirous of simple affirmations of goodwill. The smallest cliché pleased me, for I saw it as a counter in a game of conversations which admitted of no ambiguity. Conscientiously I played this game as if I were a beginner, a novice, as indeed I was, for I had graduated in an academy where words were used as a disguise and where the whole object was to divine the unspoken intention. It was an utter relief for me to observe to a neighbour that the nights were drawing in or that it was cold enough for a touch of frost and to have these observations accepted and confirmed.

Pearl was of inestimable comfort to me since she thought and spoke in such terms but did so as if they were new minted: it was a measure of her peculiar innocence that she believed eagerly and passionately in those statements that obviate the need for originality of thought. 'Dear old London,' she said, as she sank down into the other chair. 'Although I understand that women are not too safe on the streets now. And the transport doesn't get any better, does it? I waited twenty minutes for a bus. I could have taken the underground, but

I'm a bit nervous. You read such terrible things, don't you? All these young unemployed people with nothing to do. I wonder they don't bring back National Service.' She accepted a cup of coffee from me, her colour high, her trusting eyes bright with the anticipation of a day in town. Exile had not diminished her enthusiasm, although I sensed that she was much lonelier than she had thought possible. Her humility and her loyalty forbade her from ever mentioning this in other than well-worn phrases, with humorous references to getting old and to her salad days being long past. The truth was that she had nothing to do. The little flat, the little bit of shopping were not enough to keep her occupied. Her son was at the mercy of his wife, and her grandsons came only on alternate weekends, with a lot of dirty washing and the occasional girlfriend. Without her telling me I knew that Pearl was endeavouring to make herself useful to this family of hers, and that she paid for the Sunday visits with a multiplicity of small services, mostly of a stay-at-home nature. Part of her enthusiasm, as she took a shortbread biscuit, was due to the fact that she was once again enjoying a life of her own. She had escaped, she had been welcomed, and was now being entertained. She was such a decent woman that these factors were sufficient to make her happy; she did not look beyond them.

I too was glad that she was there. One returns to the company of women when any blow falls, when the lump in the breast or the unexplained smear of blood are discovered, when the threats which are peculiar to a woman's life come uncomfortably close. Then, only one's own kind will do. After that one turns with weary tolerance to the problems of men, and the problems that men cause, as if they are unimportant, as perhaps they are. Perhaps one needs a viewpoint of such terminal exactitude in order to get it all right in the first place. This, however, is rarely available. Before me Pearl, her pebble-dash coat open on to a dress printed with red and purple flowers, breathed the satisfaction of one who has come through. She had the innocence of a nun, or of someone who no longer has any truck with men, who finds men to be irrelevant, unless they happen to be sons. I remembered how she had always been a little uneasy in Charlie's presence, as if he were an intruder, a foreigner of some sort whose language she did not speak. Her loving attitude to women was that of a girl, before the unity with her friends is destroyed by love, marriage, and other defections.

I had prepared a simple lunch of cold curried chicken and the fruit salad from the previous evening which was still intact. My pleasure in doing this was amply rewarded by Pearl's delight. As if by mutual consent we kept off the subject of Julia until the table was cleared and she was back in her chair with a cigarette and another cup of coffee. This seemed to us the behaviour appropriate to the occasion, although we were both anxious to get down to the matter in hand. Finally, with a look at the clock, Pearl said, 'I mustn't monopolize you, Fay. I'm sure you're busy. Just put me out when you want to and I'll make my way over to Julia's. You've seen her recently, have you?'

'I saw her the other day,' I said. 'And frankly I'm very worried. She can't go on living there alone, Pearl. She's never done a thing for herself, and by now she's probably quite incapacitated, although one never knows, with Julia, how much she wants to do, as opposed to how much she can do.'

'I'll never forgive Maureen,' said Pearl. 'Sneaking off like that without preparing her, and not even asking her to the wedding.'

I must have looked surprised, for she explained, 'I telephone her every weekend, you know. On a Sunday evening. I think that's when she feels it most.'

'What are we to do?' I asked. 'She can't stay there on her own. I've even wondered whether she has enough money.'

Pearl lowered her voice, as if Julia might overhear us. 'I've thought about that,' she said. 'I doubt if Charlie left much. He was pretty extravagant, I understand. There were other women, you know. Don't ask me how I know this. I don't even know if it's true. But years ago, before I met you, Fay, I heard him on the telephone, and I had my suspicions. Later he became more careful.'

She paused delicately, and I looked out of the window. Finally I said, 'Has she no one left? What about that brother of hers? The one she dotes on. Although I've never seen him there.'

'Well, that's it,' she said excitedly. 'They've fallen out. The old lady left him all her money, even though he never deserved it. He was never any good, you know. He lives abroad somewhere. Spain, I think it is.'

I imagined this character as seedy, hearty, with ruined teeth and an expensive watch. His drink would be gin and tonic, and it would always be to hand. After an undistinguished and possibly fraudulent career in the motor trade his mother's money must have seemed like a gift from the gods, for although Julia appeared to dote on him he was not similarly devoted to her, or so it seemed. Maybe she bored him. She had once shown me a photograph of a handsome enough young man in an open-necked shirt; the photograph, which had been taken some time ago, was faded, but one could see that the teeth were bad even then. He was part of Julia's personal mythology, the young man of infinite promise but with certain forgivable weaknesses who had, in some unspecified fashion, let himself down. I had known, in looking at the photograph, that he had probably cost them a great deal, not only in anxiety but in terms of hard cash, and I had wondered whether Julia's marriage to Charlie was entirely disinterested. For at the beginning, when I first knew them, Charlie had been, or had appeared to be, a man of substance.

I had written off Gerald, as the brother was called, although in the early days of our acquaintanceship his name was frequently invoked as the acme of masculine perfection. Julia too had her weaknesses, although not many were apparent. She had loved Gerald, rather more, it had seemed to me, than a sister need love a brother. She was one of those women who make an enchanted garden of their childhood memories and frequently parade them for the benefit of those who rarely give their childhoods a second thought. Her eyes would stray to the photograph, and one would hear, with a certain amount of impatience, the familiar words, 'Did I ever tell you about the time when Gerald and I . . .' got lost, or nearly drowned, or ate all the cake at someone's birthday party, reminiscences which were to me frankly embarrassing but which caused an unfamiliar look of tenderness to cross her face. She and her mother had, on many occasions, lamented his lack of good fortune, and had assumed jealousy of his looks and charm to be the reason why others inexplicably failed to help him on his way. He did not get on well with Charlie, I remembered, which was why he was such an infrequent visitor. 'I'm afraid there's a bit of jealousy there too,' Julia had once said with her appalling and unconscious honesty. 'You mean that Gerald is jealous of Charlie's success?' I had once asked. 'I mean', she had replied, 'that he's jealous of Charlie for being married to me.' I had blushed at the implications of this, but she seemed to think the situation entirely understandable.

The clue to Julia's wintry heart, therefore, must be in her childhood, when the sexes divide, but before they decide to interact. Two children, admired for their beauty and their boldness, petted by a weak and possibly foolish mother, and encouraged by their mutual recklessness, had had a love for each other that no other love could efface. At least this may have been true of Julia, though not necessarily so of Gerald. I did not understand this myself, for I had always thought adult emotions more interesting than the childish variety. Although my own childhood had been a contented one I now felt no nostalgia for it, no wish to return to days of infancy. But Julia's bitterness, so frequently directed against present circumstances, must have been occasioned by the knowledge that childhood was past, and that she was no longer one half of an indulged pair. Gerald must have been the only man to whom she felt equal, for to all other men – and women too – she felt superior. All this, of course, was supposition on my part: I had no means of confirming it. Yet as I thought about it the final piece of her enigmatic personality seemed to fall into place.

'Pearl,' I said. 'Is there no way of bringing them together again? Could she not go out there and live with him?'

'Well, he'd be the problem, wouldn't he? Would he want her? He's got his own life, and a bit of money at last. He lives with a friend, I understand, another man.'

He would, I could see that. Our voices were now low, conspiratorial, although there was no one else in the flat. Yet there was a new purpose in my mind. If there had been happiness at the beginning, might there not be a chance of the same happiness at the end? I saw this Gerald as essentially dubious, or perhaps not so much dubious as unreliable, with a heartlessness about him that only one other person could match. I saw the two of them in the sun, endlessly reminiscing about their childhood, while the companion made himself useful with the drinks. With money there would also be servants, which meant that she could live her life as she had always intended to live it. And age and infirmity are always easier to bear when the sun shines every day and life seems like an endless holiday. I looked again out of the window. The day was grey, chill, with an air of sullenness about it, as if it would never end, never change.

'How do we get in touch with him?' I asked.

Pearl was shocked. 'You're not thinking of going straight to him, are you? Behind Julia's back? Anyway, I haven't got his number. I had it when he was living in Baron's Court, but he's been away for four or five years now, maybe longer. Julia knows where he is, of course. We could put it to her, I suppose. But it's not really any of our business, is it?'

'Pearl,' I said. 'She can't live alone. You know what she's like. She only eats if someone else puts the food in front of her. Maureen's gone. Mrs Wheeler, unless I'm very much mistaken, won't come back. I don't know when Julia last paid her. That leaves me. I can't look after her, Pearl. There's no reason why I shouldn't, but I'm not going to do it. I'm tired of Julia. I don't enjoy her company and she doesn't enjoy mine. Within a few weeks – what am I saying? Within a few days – we should hate each other. And the idea of two old women quarrelling sickens me. I want a bit of peace. After all, I'm alone too, you know.

And I'm getting used to it, or I will soon.' I turned my head at this, to hide the moisture in my eyes. 'She had better go to Spain,' I said, dabbing at the tears that would not stay in place.

'Well, of course, dear. If you think it best.'

Pearl was uneasy. I was ruining her day. She gathered up her bag and her scarf and made preparations to leave.

'I'll join you later,' I said. 'You go round and have a nice chat with Julia, make a cup of tea, if there is any. She'll be delighted to see you. I'll come round after work and put the idea of Spain into her head. I take full responsibility,' I added. 'If it doesn't work out she can always come back. But at least Gerald will have the name of that place her mother was in. Why didn't I think of that before? She seems not to mind the idea of going there. But she must be looked after. Someone must look after Julia.'

I saw her off, and walked to the office, deep in tangled thought. Getting it right was what mattered, I saw that now. Once I had got it right I should go away myself. For some reason I felt broken-hearted. Julia's plight had brought me face to face with my own: I too should grow old, and there was no brother, however problematic, to care for me, or to pay others to care for me. The events of the previous evening had made it quite clear that no one would rescue me from what suddenly seemed a frightening solitude. The presence of a man at one's side – or not even at one's side, but in the wings somewhere – reassures one that life is a normal, manageable business: his disappearance signals the beginning of the dark days, days when one doubts one's own durability. And however reassuring the company of other women one longs to break out of the prison of female preoccupations in order to get back to the business in hand, the continuity of life itself. I have been in the company of women who greet one with delight but who, after fifteen or twenty minutes, become restless, not because one's company is unsatisfactory but because it is beside the point. Such patent inattention was never within my grasp, and now it never would be. Waiting to be chosen, I had incurred my own disgrace. There was no alibi for me. I must go on as best

I could, into that old age that already had me by the arm. All that I could do for myself lay in the direction of lightening the burden. And if I could at the same time lighten Julia's burden I should feel cautiously relieved. It was not that I could bring about a happy ending. There was no question of that now, for either of us. My efforts would be motivated by a desire for tidiness, reduction of pain. They might be – probably would be – misguided, but there was no indication that they were utterly wrong. With myself as prime mover in this affair I felt extremely vulnerable. Glancing above me at the curdled sky I invoked help, but none came.

After my work was done, and the office locked up, I set out for Onslow Square with my usual mixture of exasperation and dread, grateful only that I should not be alone to enjoy Julia's company. No Mrs Wheeler answered the door. It was Pearl who let me in, her features bunched into a grimmer expression than had been there earlier in the day. Mrs Wheeler's absence was already noticeable, in the film of dust that covered the many small tables, the sour smell that came from the unchanged water in which Julia's favourite yellow lilies were obviously dying, and the discarded pages of *The Times* which eddied round the legs of her chair. A glance into the bedroom revealed, as I had expected, that the bed had not been made. I thought I saw signs of neglect in Julia herself, but a closer look told me that I had been imagining a decay of which there was no trace, unless it was in the heightened colours of the face, brilliantly applied on to a waxen ground. How long was it since she had left the flat? Her movements were somehow not on record; she was always immobile when one saw her, so that one assumed that she had been in her chair since the beginning of time, awaiting one's arrival, as a potentate awaits emissaries. Although her appearance was now frail she must have been immensely strong to withstand a regime which consisted mainly of privation, for, as she was so fond of saying, she ate practically nothing and never, or rarely, breathed fresh air.

On this afternoon, which I already thought of as the final afternoon, she was well put together, if not as immaculate as usual: the hectic face on the thin neck rose too sharply out of the collar of a silk blouse, and the shoulders in the tweed jacket were a little hunched. She looked like Miss Havisham in *Great Expectations*. The gaunt frail hands were clasped round a cup of tea. Pearl had already been busy in the kitchen, but her frightened expression told me that she had not expected to find the mess that Mrs Wheeler had left. I could imagine it: the sticky plates bearing ancient crusts of toast, the dishcloth soaking in brown scummy water. The drawing-room windows badly needed cleaning; a brighter day would have sent shafts of dust motes onto the carpet. Pearl was not the only one who was frightened. Something told me that Julia herself was frightened, but was too proud to show her fear, certainly to one such as myself.

'Julia,' I said, accepting a cup of tea. 'Do you ever hear from your brother? Where is he now?'

'No, I haven't heard for a little while,' she said, but tenderness struggled with grief and broke out in a reminiscent smile. 'Oh, I'm sure he's all right. At least, he couldn't wait to take himself off.'

'Where is he?' I repeated.

'He lives in Spain,' she said. 'In Mijas. We went there once on holiday, when we were little. He must have remembered it. It was quite unspoilt in those days. We had such a lovely holiday – but of course that was a long time ago.'

'Why don't you go and visit him?' I asked.

'Because he doesn't want me to,' she said.

'But Julia, how do you know that if you haven't spoken to him?'

'He could have invited me, couldn't he?' Fierce hurt was in her voice, as if this were the only subject that had preoccupied her in the past weeks or months or even years. Rage made her voice uneven, but it was the rage of childhood, hot and tearful and mixed with disappointment.

'You could always invite yourself,' I said gently. 'People do, you know. They say that they'll be passing through and that they'd love to look in. It's done all the time.'

'I could never contemplate such a thing,' she said, with a return of something of her old grandeur.

'But don't you want to see him again?' I asked.

With those words an incredible thing happened: tears came into her eyes, into those adamantine eyes whose gaze fell so pitilessly on others. Without waiting for her reply I took from Pearl's outstretched hand the piece of paper on which I read a long telephone number: this could only be Spain. I dialled it and waited; after a few seconds a languid voice answered, so like Julia's own that I nearly gasped with surprise. 'Do forgive me,' I said. 'You sound so like Julia. I'm with her now. I think she'd like to speak to you.' I handed over the receiver and retired into the background with Pearl. I just heard Julia say, 'Gerald?' with a girlish intonation of eagerness, saw her tilt her head provocatively, and then I vanished into the kitchen to do the washing up. It seemed indelicate to stay.

When I went back, ten minutes later, Julia and Pearl were already at the whisky, shakily congratulating each other.

'Such exciting news, Fay, dear,' said Pearl. 'Julia's going to Spain.'

'Excellent,' I said, picking up and sorting out the pages of *The Times*. 'When are you going?'

'You're very anxious to get rid of me,' said Julia, in her normal tones, and then I knew it would be all right.

Once we had settled on a date, and Pearl had promised to stay with her while she made her preparations, and I had arranged a car to take us to the airport, there was a general air of relief, even of tearfulness. We were all aware that this was a leave-taking. Julia would walk out of the flat with a magnificent disregard for what she left behind. Quite clearly I should have to deal with whatever business remained undone, but it seemed a small price to pay. There was, after all, no reason for her to stay. Far from leaving home, she was going home, back to childhood, back to her first affection.

'He was always the one I loved the best,' she said, with the honesty that never failed to shock me. She left one in no doubt that she recognized the implications of what she had said, or

205

even that she had acted upon them once, long ago, when such games seemed innocent. 'Where the apple reddens never pry, Lest we lose our Edens, Eve and I.' I thought those words so sad when I first read them, as if a woman's love were hedged about with danger and with sorrow. And the words were a warning to the unwary, for nothing is straightforward in this life, however ardently one desires it, the one true outcome. On this day of days, with both of our futures decided, I felt a grief that was not merely personalized but general, and an unwilling solidarity with all female destinies. Cast aside now, no longer suitable as partners, we could only rely on alliances forged long ago. The old law, the commandment to go forth and multiply, was still the best, the only one that could stand the test of time. But for those who had not obeyed the commandment, or had mismanaged it, there was little on offer. One could seek solutions, but the solutions were not always forthcoming, or available. One should not lose heart, though this was difficult. One should – one must – remember that it was difficult for everybody. Inroads were constantly being made, the will under permanent threat from the mortal body.

I thought of Alan Carter, who could have preserved me from this knowledge and who had not done so. From neglect, from refusal, from lack of imagination: it no longer mattered. One could not love such a man, and therefore further meetings, if there were to be any, would be inconsequential, insignificant. One longed for, fought for, significance, and a certain respect. Only the fortunate do not feel the lack of such commodities. Walking home, under the still churlish sky, which was already darkening into winter, I thought indifferently of the empty kitchen that awaited me. There was nothing to eat, and I lacked the heart to buy food and to cook it only for myself.

On an impulse I turned and went back to Onslow Square. 'I'm taking you both out to dinner,' I announced. Both looked at me in astonishment, but I was not in a mood to brook refusal. 'Where would you like to go?' I asked. 'The Savoy Grill used to be quite good,' said Julia, who rallied first. 'Or the Caprice.' Pearl was already in her coat: the prospect of further hospitality lightened her heavy features, drawn by the afternoon's events and the fatality that hung over them. 'We'll find something nearby,' I said firmly. 'Then we'll put Pearl into a taxi. She can take a taxi home. Yes you can,' I said, in the face of her as yet unuttered protests. 'The Savoy Grill will have to wait, I'm afraid. This will just be the three of us. Nothing to dress up for.'

'True,' said Julia. 'Pointless to go to such places without a man.' She looked agitated at the idea of venturing out, but disappeared into the bedroom and reappeared ten minutes later wearing an entirely new and rather too heightened make-up. 'After all, we are only three old women.' Swiftly she stuffed cigarettes and a lighter into her bag.

'Even old women have to eat,' I said, turning out lights.

'Oh, leave them on,' Julia said, with a magnificent gesture. 'I'm done with turning out lights. I'm finished with all that. *And* with Maureen. *And* with Mrs Wheeler. Not that she'll ever come back.'

'And with me?' I asked. 'Are you finished with me?'

We were standing at the front door, almost anxious for her reply.

'You're not a bad little thing,' she said, carelessly, but with Julia nothing was unplanned. 'Silly, like all women. But I doubt if there was ever any harm in you.'

So ended my thraldom. This partial reconciliation, if that was what it was, eased some of my pain. We had a surprisingly agreeable evening. We found an Italian restaurant, or rather we went in search of one of which I had already heard. Julia, between us, each of us gripping an arm, made unsteady progress, but it was progress of a sort and we were disproportionately delighted with her. We drank a lot, and our faces flushed, no doubt unbecomingly. There comes a time when one lets go, or gives in, and we had reached that time. We drank wine like old lags and ate ice cream like girls. Assuaged, eyes bright, lipstick smudged, we sat back and nodded at each other in recognition. Around us young couples went through their courting rituals. We recognized those too. With a sympathetic yet satirical eye we watched them, undeterred by good manners. It was they who became self-conscious, I noted.

'Such a funny way they do their hair now,' said Pearl. 'All that frizz.'

'No style at all,' agreed Julia, although I thought the girls looked very pretty. The young men seemed to me cool, cruel, talkative, although I knew that they were uncertain as to how the evening would end, whether the old rules still applied. For us there was no longer any uncertainty. Waiters looked alarmed as we staggered to our feet, then respectful when they saw the size of the exorbitant tip. The night air hit us like a blow in the face. Pearl laughed weakly. I was quite glad I was near home. Of the three of us Julia was easily the one most in command. 'Rather an amusing evening,' she said, surprised to have enjoyed herself so much.

We saw her back to Onslow Square, and then I put Pearl into a taxi. Suddenly I was on the pavement, alone, in a deserted street. A full moon shone fitfully through shifting cloud. The next moon would be the hunter's moon, the golden moon, the most beautiful of the year. And after that? Better not to think. I walked very slowly back to Drayton Gardens, past the silent garage and the locked-up hairdresser's. I was no longer dismayed. A sadness had settled on me, but it was devoid of fear. I made a note to myself not to drink too much too often, but I was not uncomfortable. In the flat I drank glass after glass of water, then prepared for bed. I told myself that there was nothing to prevent me from inviting Alan Carter to dinner. If Julia had reminded me, that afternoon, of Miss Havisham, from whose fate I had rescued her, then I should have a sporting shot at being Estella. I should invite Alan Carter to dinner, and then I should break his heart.

For I had not yet said what I might have said. I had not yet mocked his coldness, his so carefully devised opacity. I had it in my power to leave him shaken, shocked. Whether I did this or not I still had it in my power to do so. This knowledge cheered me, added a little decisiveness to my thoughts. Waking in the night and stumbling into the kitchen for yet another glass of water, I knew that when the time came, if it ever came, I should say none of these things. Yet there remained with me the enticing knowledge that I might say them if I wished, and that he, all unsuspecting, would never know just how tenuous was his self-esteem, which to him had always been more important than my own. Maybe this weakness was already known to him. The difficulty of his position would be enhanced by the fact that I now knew it too.

On the following day, although I felt slightly hollow, and had to do battle with a considerable headache, I noted that a certain anxiety had left me, and with it many ghosts, past and present. I no longer thought of myself and my own life as once I had. What had happened to me had at last become irrelevant. I looked around me with a clearer eye, no longer wistful and appeasing, but, rather, inclined to have expectations, even demands. I had at last caught up with my real age, and although I was fully prepared to play the part of an old lady I felt younger in my own mind. There were to be no more indulgences; what strength I had – and I still had quite a lot – must be conserved to protect me against whatever illness might come to put an end to all speculation. I knew at last that the inevitable would happen to me, and that neither love nor friendship would be my protection. Naturally I should, given the chance, have wished for a hand to hold mine at the end, but it seemed that this was not to be. I hoped that I should have the courage to be exacting, querulous, formidable when the time came. Somehow I did not have the patience for good behaviour any more, and I felt all the better for having lost it.

Pearl had moved into Julia's flat and was almost as happy as she had been in those early days, when the two of them conspired to make Julia an unforgettable stage presence. We kept in touch: an unexpected mood of comradeship had descended on the three of us, and even Julia would telephone me at the end of the day to tell me what she had decided to pack. This preoccupation, and the ministrations of her former dresser, restored something of the authority of her younger days, and she no longer felt the need to snub and belittle, as disappointment and frustration had inclined her to do. After her long claustration she woke to a new effectiveness and was determined to give a final performance. Her voice even held a note of hope. I thought that praiseworthy, for I did not know what sort of a welcome awaited her in Spain. It might be that she would be forced to return to Onslow Square, yet she behaved as if she were never coming back, and I had the conviction that I should never see her again. This conviction was strong, so that all her preparations, of which I was kept informed, had an air of finality. I did not know what would happen to the flat, nor did it much bother me not to know, for I felt that Julia had the matter in hand. If it suited her to give one final performance then I should respect her wishes. Others could deal with the details. I did not know who these others might be, but the shades of managers and agents seemed to be summoned up simply by virtue of her determination to be gone. I busied myself with tickets and timetables and recounted the information in those nightly telephone calls which had now become standard practice. I even arranged a wheelchair, for I thought she might be overcome with weakness when the moment came. Even if the chair were not needed it seemed to me that Julia might accept it as a prop, and one that would enable her to make an unusual exit.

Her plane was to leave at midday. The weather was cold but clear, with a hint of sun behind the ever present cloud. When I got to Onslow Square I found Julia looking exceedingly pale and exceedingly chic, in a light grey suit, with a fur coat over her arm. Mountains of luggage were stacked in the hall, which now looked frankly neglected. In the drawing-room the light struck dully on the acid yellow and white, colours which were in any event intolerable under an English sky. Pearl had made coffee, which we drank, thoughtfully, unable to think of much to say. I did not ask Julia for her last instructions, for I did not intend to carry them out, whatever they were. I viewed the prospect of newspapers and letters piling up with absolute equanimity. I washed up the cups and put them away, aware of dust even in the kitchen. 'Keep your keys,' I said involuntarily. 'In case you need to collect anything.'

I had ordered a car and Julia was sufficiently mistress of herself and the occasion to charm and dazzle the driver into carrying all the suitcases down. A flicker of excitement had brought a little colour into her pale cheeks. I thought it would be fitting if we could recapture something of the spirit that had visited us in the restaurant, but that was not to be. Our journey to Heathrow was passed in silence, although Julia was able to express sympathy with the driver over his various complaints: in the end theirs was the only conversation. Pearl was badly affected, I could see. For her the adventure was over. I was quite calm, but preferred to keep my thoughts to myself. I gazed out of the window at the hideous landscape, and began to plan a trip myself. Fiesole, I thought, or Istanbul. There would be no one to see me off, but I should have to get used to that, used to wandering around with a guidebook, or sitting alone in a café: a mute life, no longer subject to modification.

At the airport dread descended on us. Pearl and I struggled with the luggage while Julia tried to maintain a regal presence. I could see how hard she struggled, and I willed her to succeed. We had to say goodbye before we were ready to do so, for the attendant was already present with the wheelchair. This may have been providential; the strain was beginning to tell on us. 'Goodbye,' I cried, although the crowd was so dense and the noise so distracting that I doubted whether she could hear me. Pearl was already in tears, while I was nearly incapacitated by a mixture of anxiety and relief. 'Goodbye!' I shouted, behind the backs of people pushing trolleys. 'Goodbye, Julia. Good luck.' As if in answer her hand was briefly raised. She did not look back.

I took Pearl back to the café, sat her down, and let her cry. 'It's for the best,' I said, and then I remembered that that was what people said to grieving relatives after a death in the family. 'It had to happen this way,' I amended. 'Just think! In three hours' time Julia will be in the sun.' Nevertheless we felt diminished, and we clung together as we made our way to the taxi rank. I brought her back with me and made a strong pot of tea: neither of us felt like eating. We spent the afternoon together, as if we were recovering from a deep shock. Fortunately it was the day I did not go to the office. 'Do you think she'll telephone when she arrives?' asked Pearl anxiously. 'I'm sure she will,' I assured her. 'Then I'd better get home and wait for her call,' she said. 'To tell you the truth, Fay, I'm rather tired. I'm quite looking forward to being in my little flat again.'

As I was. Julia had done this for us, she had reconciled us with the inevitable. The evening darkened outside the windows as I thankfully drew the curtains and put on the lights. I promised myself little treats – television, an early night. These were now to be my lot. But, for the moment at least, I was thankful, thankful to grow old unobserved. Tomorrow I might feel differently. But then tomorrow is always another day.

17

She never came back. Whether this was from pride, as I suspected, or because she had been made genuinely welcome we never discovered. All the news we had of her was contained in the messages on two postcards, which we examined with a care which would not have disgraced a couple of palaeographers. Pearl's card said, 'Arrived safely. Weather marvellous. Love, Julia.' Mine, which was more mysterious but more affecting, stated, 'Should auld acquaintance . . . Regards, Julia.' There was no address. Thus she had effectively put herself out of reach.

For a little while this was a torment. The ghost of Julia, whom nothing escaped except the correct interpretation of what she saw, looked on sardonically as I, a plump spry figure, pretended to myself that all was well. In some secret depth, the depth to which I consigned unbidden truths, I knew that she was merely tolerated by her brother and his friend, that she was having to adapt herself to their grudging and ambivalent company, that the green paradise of childhood loves was effectively cancelled, and that there were no happy endings. At least, I thought, as if to reassure or comfort myself, she will have servants and the warmth of the sun. And then I shrugged at my continuing and guilty concern. Julia was no worse off than the rest of us. I thought of my old people on the telephone to me at the office, unable to get out, to shop or feed themselves, sometimes suffering from painful conditions, and dependent on the likes of Mrs Harding and myself for a little cheer. I thought of Pearl, sad-eyed and trusting, marooned in her tiny flat in a suburb which held no charm for her, brooding on her memories in which her grandchildren expressed no interest. Last of all I thought of myself, growing old alone, with all hope gone.

Gradually things returned to normal. Pearl's anxious telephone calls became less frequent, although I could rely on her wistful voice on Sunday evenings, at the time when she used to talk to Julia. She wanted to chat, to discuss the week's news, to exchange a favoured set of platitudes for the ones I would dutifully counter in return. I associate these calls with a particular melancholy, with the aching vacuum of a late Sunday afternoon, with fading light and infrequent footfalls on the pavement outside my window, with clouds of ennui rolling up from South Kensington or down from Earls Court, and with my regularly reinforced suspicion that I must get away or fall into a trap from which there will be no release.

I dread the weekends. I dread the pretence that drives me to the shops on a Saturday morning, and the shame of buying a solitary chop and a few vegetables, which I cook for my lunch. I feel the burden then. I dread the calm of Saturday afternoons, punctuated only by the distant roar from the football terraces. Something stops me from going out, as if I might be in danger of missing a visitor, though no one comes. I sit by the window, with my hands in my lap, looking out and waiting. Old habits are not easily discarded and sometimes leave an unconscious trace. I watch the light fade with a sort of anguish, an anguish which is not entirely temporal. I perceive the symbolism of the end of the day. I usually sleep badly on a Saturday night and am always awake to hear the thud of the newspapers on the doormat. I try to take things slowly, but am always ahead of myself, and frequently sit down to lunch – an omelette – at midday.

Then there opens before me the prospect of a visit to the Victoria and Albert Museum, which has come to signify all the elaborate disaffection of a Sunday afternoon in South Kensington. It is not a benighted spot. On the contrary, it is fairly prosperous. But on a Sunday it looks undignified, with a flotilla of ice-cream vans outside the Science Museum and papers blowing round the ankles of people descending the steps to the warm iron breath of the underground. Behind the window of the Polish teashop ancient faces break into vivid conversation, elaborate compliments, fervent expressions of welcome. I hurry home, away from this touching cordiality, and while I am drinking my own cup of tea I think of all that was begun and not finished, the excursions to Highgate Cemetery, and everything that should have followed but did not in fact take place.

I sometimes see Dr Carter. I see him at Caroline's dinner parties, where he is still produced as a partner for me, and where we converse with almost natural goodwill. Or I pass him in the street, where we both raise our hands in greeting, pleased to see each other and pleased to be committed to no more than passing courtesies. I never broke his heart. I never made an opportunity to do so. I knew that any invitation I proffered would be fraught with embarrassment on both sides, so I simply did not invite him. I told myself that when my feelings had settled down I should invite him again, because at my age one does not easily forgo a friendship. But my feelings never did seem to settle down. Does one become more easily moved in the latter part of one's life? If so, I am glad that I never had children, for I think I should have ended up weeping for them all the time. So I keep myself to myself when this dangerous mood is on me, for another aspect of old age is loss of dignity, and I still have enough pride to see to it that mine remains intact, at least as far as the outside world is concerned.

During the week, of course, I am fine. I have my work, my little routines and pleasures, my easy life. I keep well, and am lucky enough not to require the services of a doctor, which reminds me that I must find a new one. Perhaps Dr Carter will notice that I have removed my name from his books and set on foot some sort of enquiry. On the other hand he may understand, as he understood everything that was not said between us. He is still unmarried, as I am, and losing his looks, but I still find him attractive, as perhaps do other women. During the week, when I am doing really well, I look forward quite actively to the day of our next meeting, for he still holds the key to any future I might have. I never thought this of any man before, and it seems exceedingly unfair to the memory of my husband, with whom I was, briefly, so much in love. It may seem ridiculous for a woman of my advanced years to think of the future, but I imagine that one always does and always will, and even in one's last days one will be wondering what is to come.

That is why I rarely look back. Those old songs that I used to sing, when I was innocent of their longing, do not haunt me. If I were to succumb to them again the pain would be immeasurable. They would remind me of the durability, the hopelessness of desire, as if underneath all experience lurks the child's bewilderment. Why do you not love me? say the songs. And if I love you, why do I still yearn for something beyond? These songs seem to me profound because they underline a rather sophisticated acknowledgment, namely that the act of love is finite and that what is being voiced is not only the disappointment of this but one's exacerbated need for perma- nent transformation, exacerbated, that is, by the act of love itself. 'Only Make-Believe', runs the song. And 'You Are My Heart's Delight'. And 'I'll Be Loving You Always'. But though the words are affirmative the melodies are in a minor key, and sadder than they know. I could not sing them now. I know too much of this cruel world to sing them with the touching faith of yesterday, when, in my very far-off girlhood, I thought that such moods were simply the prelude to experience and not the result of experience gained. When young one can still aspire to sublimity. Old age knows that this is, and probably always was, in devastatingly short supply.

But when I keep away from the old songs and my own disappointments I really think I manage rather well. The years have passed, and they have been, on the whole, satisfactory. Everything fades a little. I am out and active every day. I give help where and when I can. My dear friend Millie, now a widow like myself, occasionally comes to stay when up in town for shopping. Some parts of the past have not quite lost their sweetness, or so I think when we both rejoice in each other's company. Looking at her is like looking at a mirror image of myself. We always hearten each other, indulge in little extravagances, laugh at our vanity. For it survives! In these moments I see Julia's eyelids descending in amusement, not altogether good-natured, as she contemplates this spectacle. At least I think that is what I see. Sometimes I see a cranky old woman in a wheelchair, planted out of sight beneath a palm tree. And this despite her death, which I read about in last Monday's *Times*. So irrelevant did her death seem that I almost looked forward to discussing it with her, felt something like a quickening of interest. 'What was it like?' I should have asked. The eyelids would have come down again as she considered. 'Not all that bad,' I can hear her say, in her most famously throw-away tone. 'You might give it a try one of these days.'

FOR THE BEST IN PAPERBACKS, LOOK FOR THE

In every corner of the world, on every subject under the sun, Penguin represents quality and variety – the very best in publishing today.

For complete information about books available from Penguin – including Puffins, Penguin Classics and Arkana – and how to order them, write to us at the appropriate address below. Please note that for copyright reasons the selection of books varies from country to country.

In the United Kingdom: Please write to *Dept E.P., Penguin Books Ltd, Harmondsworth, Middlesex, UB7 0DA.*

If you have any difficulty in obtaining a title, please send your order with the correct money, plus ten per cent for postage and packaging, to *PO Box No 11, West Drayton, Middlesex*

In the United States: Please write to *Dept BA, Penguin, 299 Murray Hill Parkway, East Rutherford, New Jersey 07073*

In Canada: Please write to *Penguin Books Canada Ltd, 2801 John Street, Markham, Ontario L3R 1B4*

In Australia: Please write to the *Marketing Department, Penguin Books Australia Ltd, P.O. Box 257, Ringwood, Victoria 3134*

In New Zealand: Please write to the *Marketing Department, Penguin Books (NZ) Ltd, Private Bag, Takapuna, Auckland 9*

In India: Please write to *Penguin Overseas Ltd, 706 Eros Apartments, 56 Nehru Place, New Delhi, 110019*

In the Netherlands: Please write to *Penguin Books Netherlands B.V., Postbus 195, NL–1380AD Weesp*

In West Germany: Please write to *Penguin Books Ltd, Friedrichstrasse 10–12, D-6000 Frankfurt/Main 1*

In Spain: Please write to *Alhambra Longman S.A., Fernandez de la Hoz 9, E–28010 Madrid*

In Italy: Please write to *Penguin Italia s.r.l., Via Como 4, I-20096 Pioltello (Milano)*

In France: Please write to *Penguin Books Ltd, 39 Rue de Montmorency, F-75003 Paris*

In Japan: Please write to *Longman Penguin Japan Co Ltd, Yamaguchi Building, 2–12–9 Kanda Jimbocho, Chiyoda-Ku, Tokyo 101*